Armageddon Core

Ultra Meridian Series: Book 3

Theo Mann

Invisible Publishing Company

Ultra Meridian Series

Contents

Chapter 1

S herrif Mace Davenport jerked the Drifter *Dryad Circe* back and forth to dodge Howitzer fire smashing the ship from behind. More shots glanced off the wings, but in a moment, the bombardment stopped.

"The Daggers are pulling back to rejoin the Reserve Wing," Beauty reported from the tactical cradle behind Davenport.

"You better run!" Emmett yelled to no one in particular. He sat in the command cradle between Davenport and Beauty even though Emmett wasn't working the controls. He just sat there enjoying the ride.

Davenport took advantage of the lull to check the area around the Drifter. "Is anyone else coming out to stop us?"

"There's nothing between us and Ultra Meridian," Beauty replied. "Are you sure you want to go back there?"

"Do we have any other options?"

Beauty didn't answer right away. Davenport heard the creature tapping at the tactical controls and waited for Beauty to say something.

That silence drew out longer and longer. Neither Beauty nor Emmett said anything. That answered Davenport's question.

He gunned the engines, but he was in no big hurry to go back to Ultra Meridian. He would love to go back to the outpost and resume his duties as sheriff. He'd like nothing better than to return to the old life that had been stolen from him.

He didn't want to go back at all if he only had to leave Ultra Meridian again. The Confederate Corps Reserve Wing would never let him vanish into obscurity after everything that happened. He would be stupid to think that.

He entered the atmosphere and took a tour around the dusty landscape he knew so well. The Ultra Meridian jail had been restored. The plane surrounding the building and the sandy hills looked exactly the way he remembered them. Nothing had changed except for Davenport himself.

The planet didn't give Davenport the same feeling of comfort, serenity, and welcome that it used to. He faced too many dangers here and nearly lost his life too many times to ever feel totally safe here again.

"It looks all clear," Beauty remarked.

"At least the Reserve Wing isn't here," Emmett added.

Davenport flew another lap around the jail. His friends were right. The *Dryad Circe's* sensors would have flagged any Reserve Wing ships in the atmosphere or on the ground. None of the resident criminal organizations came near the outpost, either. They kept to their own territory.

"Aren't you going to land?" Emmett asked.

Davenport shrugged. "I suppose I better."

He wheeled the *Dryad Circe* and started to descend toward the jail. This was the view every other ship got when they came to land here. They had to get his stamp before crossing to Sacron Enigma. They didn't know what to expect from him then and now the shoe was on the other foot.

He fought down rising tension and lowered the landing gear to set down outside the jail. At least he would be able to go inside and start getting to know his new jail.... until the next disaster struck......as it was bound to do......sooner or later.

He took his eyes off the building and glanced down at the controls when a laser flashed out of nowhere. It smashed the ship from port and knocked the *Dryad Circe* reeling.

"Hey!" Davenport yelled. "What the....?"

Beauty squealed in alarm as another barrage pounded the cockpit. The glass smashed in Davenport's face and he flinched away to protect his eyes. He had all he could do just to hold the ship level.

More lasers erupted from somewhere. Davenport didn't have time to see where they came from. He fought the helm trying to steady the ship, but the next shot splintered the tail off.

The *Dryad Circe* wobbled dangerously and dipped toward the ground before Davenport wrestled the Drifter under control.

"You said there was no one around!" he hollered over his shoulder.

"There wasn't!" Beauty screeched. "The hills are loaded with minerals. They block scans...."

Another jet of lasers zinged past the cockpit. Davenport veered in time to avoid getting his face shot off, but the last beam severed the ship's nose.

"We gotta get out of here!" Emmett yelled.

"Like where?" Davenport countered.

Another smash struck the port wing and ripped it off. The wing tilted away from the fuselage and a second blast detonated the engine ten feet from the cockpit. The explosion smacked the ship hard to starboard and the *Dryad Circe* flew straight into another laser's path.

"Return fire!" Davenport roared.

"I'm trying!" Beauty shrieked. "I can't locate the...."

"They're in the hills!" Emmett pointed across the plane to the low peaks surrounding Ultra Meridian. "They're shooting from there."

Beauty fired in the direction Emmett indicated. Davenport tried to position the ship for the best advantage, but the Drifter wouldn't cooperate with one wing missing.

Beauty unloaded the Howitzers only to get hit on the starboard side. "Another bunch is firing from the south!" Emmett called. "No, wait! They're in the east. They're all around us!"

A cruel bang struck the ship's underside and the shot ricocheted into the starboard wing. It erupted in flames and then the starboard engine blasted the hull.

The *Dryad Circe* cartwheeled sideways, turned a somersault, and slammed down hard on the ground. Davenport's head snapped downward on his neck and he hung there limp and battered in his harness.

"Is everyone all right?" Emmett murmured.

Beauty whimpered. Davenport didn't want to be all right. This was one hell of a way to come back to Ultra Meridian. What was he thinking? Oh, yeah. He remembered now. He didn't have a choice.

Everywhere and everyone else in the Confederacy had been trying to kill him. Why did he think Ultra Meridian would be any different? It wouldn't. Nothing would ever be different. He could look forward to a lot more years of this—probably for the rest of his life.

Everyone and everywhere would keep trying to kill him until, one of these days, someone succeeded. That was the sum total of the miserable life he had to look forward to.

Another crash jostled the wrecked ship. Davenport made the mistake of looking up. The view through the shattered cockpit window didn't cheer him up any.

Just then, Dice stormed out of the back and tried unsuccessfully to force his way into the cockpit that was way too small for him. "What the holy hell is going on?"

"We crashed," Emmett replied.

"Tell me something I don't know. *Why* did we crash?"

"Because someone was shooting at us."

Dice opened his mouth, but another spray of lasers cut him off. They pounded the ship from three sides. They came so thick and fast that Davenport wasn't sure anymore where they were coming from.

"Like now!" Emmett screamed and started fumbling to get out of his cradle.

Davenport clawed at his harness. Lasers pounded the cockpit and caved in the hull above him. Another strike smashed the glass the rest of the way in and it scattered on his head and shoulders.

He couldn't stop now, but the next hit compressed the bulkhead behind him. The metal hull plates dented inward so he couldn't escape.

Dice came charging back and slammed into the cockpit entrance, but his big shoulders stopped him in his tracks. "Come on, Davenport!"

"I'm ......"

Beauty slithered under the ship's crumpling sides and seized Davenport's jacket. Beauty gave a ferocious tug and dragged Davenport out of his seat.

They both hit the floor and scrambled out of sight. Another blast hammered the roof and the whole cockpit folded in on itself. Beauty screamed again and retreated from the danger. He blocked Davenport from the only path to safety—if there was a path to safety.

Davenport prepared himself to force Beauty through the tiny gap still remaining when Dice dove into the hole. He grabbed Beauty's wrist and hauled Beauty through in a second.

Dice flung Beauty aside and, before Davenport could move, Dice lunged for him. Another devastating crash flattened the ship just as Dice slid Davenport out of the cockpit and flung him down the gangway toward the rear.

Dice vaulted to his feet. His weight banged through the ship on his way to the weapons locker. "Come on! We have to arm up and get out there before they destroy this crate!"

Davenport, Emmett, and Beauty dragged themselves to their feet. There was no time to lick their wounds. More blasts and explosions went off all over the place. More hull sections bent inward making the interior smaller and smaller.

Davenport pulled up behind Dice. Dice ripped open the weapons locker....and all four men froze staring into it. It was empty.

"What the holy hell?" Emmett whispered. "How can a Reserve Wing fighter craft not be carrying any weapons?"

Davenport smacked Dice's shoulder. "The jail! Come on! Quick!"

He darted to the loading hatch and cracked it. The ramp slammed open on the dusty plane outside.

A blast of pelting wind and stinging sand hit him in the face. He couldn't even enjoy the smell of being back at Ultra Meridian. He dreamed of this moment for weeks. Now all he wanted to do was leave.

Dice roared in fury, but another concussion of laser fire startled all four men into a run. The shots dogged Davenport's footsteps across the plane. As soon as he left the *Dryad Circe,* another sizzling jet of lasers pounded the ship to smithereens. It went up in a massive explosion behind Davenport's back. That was the end of that ship.

The four friends set off at a sprint through the wind. Beauty sprang along on his hands and feet and overtook the others. Emmett fell behind and Davenport slowed to make sure Emmett made it.

Lasers rained all around them. One smashed the sand next to Dice's foot and spat dust in his eyes. He bellowed again and nearly steamrolled Davenport trying to get away from the assault.

Davenport, Dice, and Emmett tightened closer together. Beauty pulled way out in front and almost got plastered by another laser exploding right in front of him.

The blast bowled him sideways. Davenport dashed over and started to pick him up while Dice and Emmett made the last desperate run for the Ultra Meridian jail.

Davenport tugged Beauty forward only to run into another geyser of sand and dirt shooting all around him. He tried to push toward the jail, but he couldn't get through all the concussions rocking the landscape.

"This way!" Beauty snatched Davenport's sleeve and tried to pull him back toward the wrecked *Dryad Circe.*

Davenport didn't know what Beauty wanted to do, but they couldn't get to the jail this way. Dice and Emmett were already inside.

Another cruel strike cracked in front of Davenport and he staggered backward. He stumbled after Beauty heading toward the wreck.

Whoever was shooting at them adjusted their aim and started bombing the plane around Davenport and Beauty again. The pair wouldn't get to the wreck alive.... or anywhere else for that matter.

Without warning, Beauty spun around and slammed into Davenport running the opposite way. "NOW!!"

Beauty took off at impossible speed making for the jail. Davenport understood in a heartbeat and bolted after him.

That one instant when they both changed direction bought them enough time to get ahead of the bombardment. Davenport couldn't keep up with Beauty's speed, but he ran fast enough to make it to the jail in one piece.

Chapter 2

Davenport staggered into the jail panting hard. The Reserve Wing had set up the new building exactly like the old one. The sheriff's desk occupied the center of the main room with one barred cell to one side. It was a scene out of Davenport's forgotten past.

Dice and Emmett stood in front of the weapons locker. "We can't get it open."

Davenport went over to them and studied the electronic code pad above the door handle. "It never had a lock when I was posted here."

"What are you going to do?" Emmett asked. "You know the Reserve Wing didn't actually program this lock to release for you—not after you went on the run and become an outlaw. You're hunted in every corner of the galaxy. They wouldn't want you accessing these weapons."

Dice slammed Davenport hard on the shoulder. "Just like the rest of us. You're in good company, pal."

"I'm honored," Davenport sneered over his shoulder. "I've finally achieved my life's ambition."

Beauty eased back over to the door and peered out at the sky. "Whoever they are, they aren't targeting the jail. I wonder why not."

"They must not want the Reserve Wing coming after them," Emmett guessed.

"Aren't you going to at least try to open it?" Dice rumbled in Davenport's ear.

Davenport didn't give himself a moment to hesitate. "What do I have to lose, right?" He stuck out his hand and pressed it against the pad.

The pad flashed green and the lock clicked. "No way!" Dice growled. "They're screwing with you."

"Who cares?" Davenport pulled open the locker and started taking down every weapon on the racks.

He passed three XQ65s to Dice and took two for himself along with plenty of ammunition cylinders and new sidearms. He armed Emmett, too, but Beauty wouldn't come near the locker.

"Why are they leaving you on the books as sheriff of this dive?" Dice asked.

"Probably because they haven't hired a replacement yet. The Confederate Corps has to list someone as manning this outpost even if I'm not here in person. I'm a name in an entry. That's all." He swiveled around the desk to Beauty's side and looked out. "Beauty's right. The bombardment has stopped."

"Now what do we do?" Emmett asked. "We can't stay in here for the rest of our lives."

Dice laughed out loud. The sound carried across the landscape. The mountains themselves seemed to be listening. "You'd like that, wouldn't you? Then you wouldn't have to scratch your varnish."

"Varnish!" Emmett countered. "What are you talking about?"

"Anyway, there's no food in here," Beauty muttered. "We would have to leave sometime."

Davenport beamed down at the creature. He was really starting to like this alien. Davenport pulled from his pocket one of the many peach ChunkyTenders that Beauty had given Davenport when the Mad Men captured and imprisoned him.

Davenport handed it over and Beauty cracked one of his crazy grins in return. He took it and gazed down at the wrapper in beatific rapture.

"Oh, will you look at this!" Dice snarled. "Davenport and Beauty are best friends now."

"That doesn't get us out of here," Emmett interrupted. "What are we doing here anyway?"

"Last I checked," Dice replied, "we were here trying to find the third component."

"I say we contact the Armageddon Core," Davenport suggested. "If Friend doesn't already know where the third component is, she'll have some idea about where we can go to look for it."

"How can you be sure it's even on this planet?" Dice countered. "Your informant said it was on the *Blood Calliope* and that turned out to be wrong. It could be floating around in space for all we know."

"Then it would definitely be safe from Admiral Joyce," Emmett replied.

"It has to be here," Davenport went on. "We picked up traces of radioactivity on the *Blood Calliope*. That means the third component was on the ship when it crashed.

Someone lifted the component after that....and whoever did it wasn't Admiral Joyce because he's still looking for it."

"How the hell do we find the Armageddon Core without a ship?" Dice countered. "We could be trooping around this wretched planet for the rest of our lives and never find them."

"I know where their headquarters are," Davenport replied. "We've been there before, remember?"

"You have no guarantee they'll be there waiting to welcome you with open arms," Dice countered. "You're the Sheriff of Ultra Meridian, remember? Everybody hates you."

Davenport laughed. "How could I forget?"

"I don't mind going back to the Armageddon Core," Emmett remarked. "If Fiddler is still alive, she'll go back to them, too. We can meet up with her there."

"You're a sentimental old fool, man," Dice growled. "There's more to life than Fiddler."

Emmett glared at him. "Do you have any family?"

Dice looked away scowling and didn't answer.

Davenport went to a different cabinet and ransacked the supplies. He pulled out a pair of goggles and a mask for himself and another set for Emmett. Davenport studied Dice and Beauty on the side. "I don't think I have anything that will fit you two."

"To hell with it," Dice rumbled. "I ain't wearing that shit anyhow."

"You'll be sorry," Davenport warned. "You won't be able to see anything out there."

"I'll take my chances." Dice hefted his XQ and locked the ammo cylinder into place. "I don't need to see to be able to hit them."

Emmett laughed.

"What about you, Beauty?" Davenport asked. "How will you protect your eyes and lungs from the sand?"

"I'll be fine."

Davenport didn't argue. Beauty sounded pretty certain of that. Davenport learned a long time ago not to ask too many questions on how Beauty did anything.

As far as Dice was concerned, Davenport made a mental note to stay behind Dice or to the side of anything he might be shooting at.

Davenport strapped his goggles over his eyes, pulled on his mask, and looked outside again. The laser bombardment had completely stopped.

"What are they doing?" Emmett muttered.

"They're still out there," Beauty replied. "They're waiting for us."

"Can you see who they are or *where* they are?"

"They're all over there." Beauty swept his bony finger in a wide arc from the east, to the south, and around to the west. He covered almost the entire circle of the horizon.

"How the hell are we supposed to get through, then?" Emmett asked.

Davenport pointed to a spot directly to the west. "The Armageddon Core's cave is that way. Get to the hills. Whoever attacked us won't be able to ambush us there."

"Keep telling yourself that, porkchop," Dice boomed. "You'll notice that they already did ambush us."

"Let me put it this way. They won't be able to ambush us *as well* there. Now come on. We aren't getting it done in here."

Davenport pushed forward to the threshold, got his XQ into position, and took off running onto the plane.

Emmett and Beauty rushed out behind him. Dice came last and the friends pivoted their weapons in all directions searching for their hidden attackers.

Nothing happened for a second. The laser bombardment didn't restart. None of the deadly blasts landed nearby to threaten the party.

Davenport approached the western hills. Was he really going to get away as easily as that? He didn't want to believe it. He *didn't* believe it.

He swiveled sideways to make sure the rest of the mountains were peaceful, too. They were. There was no one there.

He made one the last sprint for safety....and gulped when a bunch of masked figures emerged from the hills right in front of him. They blocked his path and they raised their laser rifles to cut him to shreds.

That wasn't the scariest part, though. At his first sight of them, he recognized parts of their alien bodies not concealed by their masks and clothes. Each one had a long, extended proboscis covered by a specially constructed piece of the mask.

Their clothes covered all of their skin, but Davenport didn't need to see that to recognize them.

Four legs attached to each hip joint. The aliens ran by rotating their hips in a windmill pattern. Each leg touched the ground and then spun upward toward the back while the others dropped down into position from the front.

The aliens ran seamlessly with no break in tread and they covered the ground impossibly fast. Their masks concealed their eyes so Davenport couldn't make eye contact with them—not that he wanted to.

Davenport froze for a second watching them come. He became aware of Dice, Emmett, and Beauty standing still, too. They were all too stunned to shoot.

The oncoming aliens' shoulders operated in a similar way to their hips. Their arms could move in a full circle spinning their guns behind them, to both sides, and even into the air without interruption.

The frontrunners fired lasers at the four friends and one of the beams pinged off Davenport's XQ. That sound snapped him out of his trance and he returned fire, but more of the same aliens came out of nowhere to surround Davenport's group.

He laid down a barrage of shots to drive them back, but they quickly outnumbered the four men. Davenport backed away to consolidate his position. He ran into Dice and glanced over his shoulder.

Davenport's stomach tightened all over again when he spotted more aliens charging across the plane. They came from the south and the east to cut off any retreat.

"To the jail!" he roared. "Fall back to the jail!"

Davenport, Dice, and Emmett crowded together in a defensive knot. They fired outward blasting as many of the aliens as they could, but it would never be enough against so many.

Beauty huddled in the center. He was totally unarmed. Davenport really had to stop trusting Beauty so much.

Without warning, Beauty darted out of their huddle, skipped across the gap between their party and the aliens, and grabbed two laser rifles from fallen attackers.

Beauty retreated back to Davenport's side, but the aliens cut him off. They pinned him down with heavy fire.

He cowered there for a second and Davenport prepared himself to storm out there to defend Beauty. Lightning quick, Beauty turned both rifles on the aliens and returned fire just as fast. He dropped four of the enemy and raced back into position.

"Fall back!" Davenport bellowed. "Go!"

Dice faced backward toward the east so he went first. Davenport and Emmett glued their bodies to Dice's sides. Davenport didn't want to take his eyes off the enemy to see where Dice was going.

Davenport took another step backward every time his friends retreated. They inched one painstaking step at a time back onto the plane. The jail seemed so far away.

The aliens closed in from the south and east. They kept up a steady rain of lasers, but they didn't stop the four men from getting to the jail.

Davenport realized too late that the aliens must be trying to drive the party back to the building, but he couldn't figure out why they would want to do that. Davenport stopped walking, but it was too late. Dice grabbed him and yanked him over the threshold.

All the shooting died as Emmett and Beauty ducked inside. A single glance through the open door showed Davenport all those aliens surrounding the Ultra Meridian jail.

He took one more step backward toward his desk. He caught a fleeting glimpse of something whizzing through the air. A rocket soared through the door into the jail and then a deafening bang knocked him out cold.

Chapter 3

Davenport dragged himself upright and blinked the glue out of his eyes. He looked around and saw Dice asleep against a nearby wall. Emmett and Beauty huddled nearby.

Davenport's face didn't feel right. He pressed his wrist to his nose, but it wasn't bleeding anymore. Something dry and crusty stuck to his upper lip so his nose must have been bleeding before he woke up.

He scooted over to his friends, but he didn't say anything. He didn't have to.

The three of them cowered in the corner of a room full of the same aliens who attacked Davenport's party at the jail.... except that the aliens didn't have their masks on anymore.

Their large, soft, cow-like eyes blinked too slowly and their proboscises undulated when they moved or talked. Their scaly skin had a dark, swampy look and a second, transparent eyelid kept flicking over their eyes at random times. These aliens didn't belong in the desert.

Davenport wedged himself between Emmett's shoulder and Dice's giant frame. "You boys all right?"

"Perfect," Dice growled.

Davenport left it at that. None of them was all right or perfect and they wouldn't be. This was the most danger that Davenport could remember being in for a long time. Not even almost getting killed several times came close to this.

Almost as soon as he got into a sitting position, the aliens in the room pretended to notice the four men hunkered in the corner. The aliens strode over and stood over their prisoners.

"We are Typhon Elexor," one of them announced in a deep, rumbling voice.

Davenport nodded and started to stand up. "I'm Sheriff Davenport. I'm the Sheriff of......"

The alien clubbed him to the ground hard. Davenport collapsed between Dice's feet. "Bad idea," Dice muttered.

Davenport dragged himself up cradling his splitting head. Dice had his eyes open now, but he hadn't moved.

"You attacked our wind mines!" the first alien roared. "You killed our men and destroyed our windmills. Admit it!"

Davenport's head shot up and his jaw dropped. "What?"

The alien lunged at him so fast that Davenport didn't get a chance to react. The creature dove for Davenport, seized him by the throat, and smashed his head back against the wall. "Three days ago! You flew into our territory and fired on our windmills. You destroyed four of them. Two days ago, you came in the night and left our guards dead. Now you will die."

"We.... didn't...." Davenport choked. He fought to breathe against the alien's murderous grip.

The creature hurled Davenport down even harder and straightened up. "Who are you working for? Who paid you to sabotage our wind mines?"

Davenport gagged and coughed trying to get his voice working. He tried to retreat from these aliens, but the wall blocked him from going anywhere. "We.... just landed here.... You saw us.... You destroyed our ship......You must have recognized..... it wasn't the same ship that attacked the wind mines."

The alien straightened up and glared down its proboscis at Davenport. It was a very tall male—almost as tall as Dice. The creature's eyes didn't look capable of glaring at anyone, but Davenport couldn't mistake the hatred radiating at him from the whole alien group.

"The attackers crashed their ship in the canyon," the big alien boomed. "You could have gone and used a second vessel to pretend to land here."

"No...." Davenport scrambled for some way to explain himself. "We were....in Reserve Wing custody until today. You can check with Stalwart *Rambler*. We stole that Drifter from the Reserve Wing."

"Don't tell him that!" Emmett hissed. "He could be working for the Reserve Wing."

"Typhon Elexor hates the Reserve Wing as much as we do." Davenport turned upward to face the alien, but Davenport didn't try to stand up again. He picked up his star from the front of his jacket and held it out for the alien to see. "I'm the Sheriff of Ultra Meridian. I've been on this planet for seven years. I've never interfered with Typhon Elexor business before and I never will. I never touched your wind mines or your guards. This is the first time I've ever set foot in your territory. I swear it."

The alien scowled down at him in silence and didn't speak. Davenport held his breath waiting for some reaction.

When it came, the alien kicked out hard and nailed Davenport in the chest. He smashed Davenport back into the wall and walked away. All the other aliens left with him. They stalked out of the room and left the four prisoners sitting there alone.

Davenport crumpled to the floor with an agonized groan. Now he knew what being the Sheriff of Ultra Meridian was worth—like he didn't already know.

He survived this long at Ultra Meridian by keeping his nose out of Typhon Elexor's business. No one could live long making as enemy of these creatures.

Dice grabbed him, hauled him up, and jostled Davenport back into a sitting position. "Nice try, pal. Keep your star to yourself next time."

"He listened," Beauty remarked. "We would be dead now if he didn't believe you."

"Who in the holy hell would have the balls to attack the Vultus Wind Mines?" Emmett whispered. "Someone has a serious death wish if they went that far."

Davenport frowned trying to clear his head. "Huh."

"What?" Dice asked.

"I was just thinking...."

"Well, don't, okay?" Dice snapped. "Don't think. You'll only get us all killed that way."

"No, listen. When the Mad Men caught me and took me back to Admiral Joyce, they kept demanding to know where the Ithium cartridge was."

"We already know all that," Emmett countered. "Everyone is after the Ithium."

"Just listen to me for a second. I told them I didn't have it. I told them I left it on the *Artemis Rex*, but they didn't believe me."

"You didn't tell them that," Beauty interjected. "You told them you hid the Ithium at the...."

Beauty fell silent and his eyes widened to two saucers of amazement.

"First I told them that I left the Ithium on the *Artemis Rex*—which was the truth. They didn't believe me and they threw me back in that hold. Then you came to see me and you told me to sit tight while you sabotaged their ship."

"Is this going somewhere?" Emmett asked. "Does any of this get us out of here?"

"After Beauty visited me, the Mad Men came back. They questioned me again about where the Ithium was and I told them I hid it at the Vultus Wind Mines. I knew hearing that would freak them out and I was right. They didn't want to go after it anymore. They wanted the Ithium, but they didn't dare to enter Typhon Elexor territory."

"What the hell did you tell them a lie for?" Dice countered. "They could have brought you here themselves and then where would you be?"

"I knew they wouldn't. They were scared shitless of Typhon Elexor."

"I'm not surprised." Emmett glanced toward the door where the aliens left the room. "Everyone is scared shitless of them."

"I'm not," Dice boomed.

"Will you listen to me?" Davenport murmured. "Someone who heard me must have come here to find the Ithium. Someone on the Mad Men's ship must have survived the *Rambler*, attacked the windmills, and then killed a bunch of guards. That's the only way they could have gotten access to the minefield to search the place."

"Who would do that?" Emmett asked.

"One of the Mad Men." Davenport turned to Beauty. "Was there anyone on the ship who wasn't in the Rambler's prison hold when Dice attacked?"

Beauty shook his head. "No one. No one survived."

"This is really weird," Emmett muttered. "If you and the Mad Men are the only people who know you said that...."

"The Ithium isn't here, grandpa," Dice barked. "The Ithium is lightyears away in Sacron Enigma where we left...."

"Shhh!" Davenport interrupted. "They're coming back."

The friends fell silent as the same aliens reentered the room. They didn't try to talk to Davenport and his crew this time. The aliens grabbed the four men, stood them up, and marched them away.

Davenport tried to study his surroundings on his way outside. He and his crewmates were probably the first people to ever see Typhon Elexor territory in person.... which meant these criminal aliens planned to kill the party as soon as they found out who hired Davenport to sabotage the mines.

Davenport agreed with Emmett. He found it hard to believe anyone would be deluded enough to mess with Typhon Elexor, but obviously someone was.

The room in which the four men had been held opened onto a long gallery. One whole broken wall gave a view across a massive square carved into the bedrock.

Hundreds of aliens from the same species played around down there, mingled on more tiered galleries rising in stories around the square, and passed the party on their way down the passage.

The very top of this underground structure rose to the planet's surface. The giant edifice had been carved into the rock and plunged at least twenty stories underground.

A galvanic field coil protected the courtyard against wind and sand entering from above. The sunshine gave the building a tropical atmosphere where people could go about their business in relative comfort.

None of these aliens carried weapons. Not even the aliens escorting Davenport's crew bothered to threaten the prisoners.

The aliens' confidence told Davenport loud and clear that he would never get out of here alive. Typhon Elexor would find out he was telling the truth about not disrupting the mines. Then they would kill him and his friends anyway.

Their escort guided the four friends down the gallery, turned a corner, followed the adjacent gallery, and entered a large room at the end. Dozens more aliens crowded inside.

They all stood. None sat or relaxed at all. They gazed in rapt attention at another alien at the far end. He paced up and down in front of the crowd reciting something in another language.

He wore long, decorated robes and a bizarre headdress that distinguished him from every other member of his kind. His voice rose and fell in a sing-song melody that harmonized with itself.

"What are they doing?" Emmett hissed in Davenport's ear.

"He's reciting their history. Typhon Elexor is the surviving remnant of the Namiall race. Their shaman predicted a cataclysmic geological disaster on their home planet. Only a handful believed him and they escaped on the *Typhon Elexor*. The ship crashed here and the planet blew up. No one else survived and the survivors have been living here ever since."

"How do you know so much about them if you've never been here before?"

Davenport had to smile to himself. "You learn a few things when you've been working at Ultra Meridian as long as I have."

"Does this get us out of there?" Dice fired back.

His voice echoed through the room and interrupted the recitation. The shaman paused and a bunch of people turned to glare at the visitors.

The shaman didn't resume. He swept his robes to the side and Davenport's escort shoved the prisoners forward. The aliens jostled Davenport and his friends into the space the shaman had been using. Now everyone in the room stared at the four intruders instead.

Davenport expected another confrontation with the same tall guy as before, but the creature yanked Davenport backward to face the crowd. The guards stayed behind the four prisoners so Davenport couldn't even see them from here.

The aliens in front of him all looked identical. He couldn't tell the males from the females until one stepped forward and stood right in front of Davenport.

The voice coming out from under the proboscis was unmistakably female. "Do you know who I am?"

"No," Davenport replied.

"My name is Kiriala and that...." She nodded past Davenport's shoulder toward the aliens standing behind him. She could only be talking about the big guy who attacked Davenport earlier. "That is my mate, Yovis, and we all know who you are. You are the scum who attacked our wind mines."

"No!" Davenport murmured. "I was just explaining to your man that we never set foot in your territory before you captured us. We were in Reserve Wing custody until earlier today. We would never dare to go to the...."

Someone punched Davenport hard in the back of the head and he buckled to the floor. Yovis must have done it. He was standing closest to Davenport and Davenport didn't see who else who would have done it.

Davenport heard Dice and Emmett talking fast while strong hands hauled Davenport to his feet.

"We didn't damage your mines!" Dice bellowed. "We have no idea who did it! Davenport has been using his position as Sheriff of Ultra Meridian to protect Typhon Elexor for years."

Davenport struggled to see straight. His eyes didn't want to track right. His head wobbled on his neck and he was having difficulty staying upright. He felt Dice holding him up while Davenport's senses kicked back into gear.

When they did, he came face to face with Kiriala studying him. Her eyes darted down to his star. "You are the Sheriff of Ultra Meridian?"

"Yeah," he gasped. "I was."

"You *were*?"

"The Reserve Wing...." His vision swam again and he started to fall over, but Dice supported him.

"The Reserve Wing attacked the jail and blew it up," Dice finished. "They drove Davenport out. He's been gone right up until today. He couldn't have attacked your mines. You can check with the Reserve Wing....and the Sheriff's Service. They'll have records of his movements...."

"We don't deal with them." Kiriala waved her hand and the guards moved in from behind. The original males that held the four men in that room grabbed the friends and kicked them down on the floor.

Seven of them pounced on Dice. They kicked out his knees and grappled him to the ground. He started to lose his temper until the aliens pointed laser rifles in the prisoners' faces. Beauty squeaked in terror.

"Your story is flimsy at best," Kiriala growled. "Even if you are telling the truth, we can't allow you to live. No one can survive once they come inside our stronghold."

She waved to her people and all their rifles hummed as they cycled up to fire. Davenport braced himself for the end.

A screeching alarm startled everyone into turning around. Kiriala walked away and Yovis glared back and forth between Davenport and whatever she was doing outside Davenport's line of sight.

Yovis jammed his rifle barrel hard into Davenport's cheek. Yovis was just itching to carry out this execution and Davenport never doubted for an instant that Yovis would do it.

Kiriala came strolling back and waved to her people. "You're in luck, Sheriff. Someone richer and more influential than we are wants you and is willing to pay for you."

She signaled her people for the second time. The males hauled Davenport and his friends off the floor, shook them, and all the aliens lowered their weapons.

"I don't like this," Dice murmured in Davenport's ear.

"What are you going to do with us?" Davenport asked.

"Never mind," Kiriala replied. "You'll be just as dead either way."

She swiped one of her arms at Yovis who shoved Davenport forward. The Namiall marched the prisoners back onto the gallery. Davenport didn't like this, either, but anything was better than getting shot in the head.

The rest of Typhon Elexor kept going about their business like Davenport's visit was just par for the course. None of the surrounding aliens even looked at the prisoners.

Yovis steered Davenport back around the corner, back to the same room where Davenport had regained consciousness. He couldn't hope he would go there, not after Kiriala's warning.

Yovis stopped the party at a different door next to the original room. He opened it and motioned Davenport and his friends inside.

This room wasn't much bigger than a closet, but Davenport didn't see anything dangerous in there. Anything would be better as long as it meant getting away from these murderous aliens.

He stepped inside and Dice, Emmett, and Beauty joined him. There was barely enough space for all of them to stand up together. Yovis shut the door and silence fell over the four friends.

"Do you still have any ChunkyTenders?" Beauty whispered to Davenport.

"You're thinking about food now?" Emmett rasped. "You're crazy!"

Davenport patted his pockets and located another ChunkyTender. "It might be kinda squashed, but it should taste the same."

He handed it over and Beauty tore open the wrapper, but at that moment, the room in which they stood blasted upward with incredible force. It rocketed away picking up momentum by the second.

The G force buckled Emmett's knees. He would have fallen if the other three bodies hadn't clamped him in place.

"What the hell!" Dice roared.

"We're launching!" Davenport yelled over the noise. "They're sending us into orbit."

"Let me guess where we're going!" Emmett countered.

Davenport didn't want to guess where they were going and he didn't want to go back into orbit. All the enemies who wanted to catch him were in space. He would have thought until this morning that he would have been safer on the ground, but that was obviously a mistake.

The noise and pressure on the room's walls built to a howl and then, with a sudden woof, everything went silent.

Davenport strained his ears to listen. The silence plagued his nerves even more than the noise and danger.

Something clunked against the walls and then silence descended again. Davenport stiffened. Here it came.... whatever it was.

Scuffling noises drifted through the walls and then the wall in front of him unfolded. It slammed down on the floor and the four friends peered out. They were in the hold of a Reserve Wing Stalwart and a bunch of armed soldiers held the four men at gunpoint.

Davenport hardly noticed them. His eyes locked on a tall officer standing well back from the rest. The man smiled at Davenport in cold, malicious triumph. It was Admiral Killian Joyce.

Chapter 4

Someone bumped Davenport's shoulder, and before he could move, five more Reserve Wing soldiers shoved into the capsule that carried the four friends away from Ultra Meridian.

An officer shot his arm past Davenport's ear, pressed a syringe to Dice's neck, and injected him with something. Davenport struggled to do something, but it was too late.

Dice went limp and his massive weight collapsed. He toppled against Davenport and Emmett. They could only scramble out of the way as Dice hit the floor.

The soldiers surrounded Davenport, Emmett, and Beauty in guns. Rough hands seized Davenport and stopped him from getting near Dice.

"You bastards!" Davenport raved. "What did you do to him?"

Admiral Joyce strolled over. "Calm down, Sheriff. We couldn't have him going on another rampage, could we? Don't worry. The truth serum won't hurt him. It will just stop him from using his strength against us. You can't blame us for that, can you?"

"You son of a bitch!" Davenport tried to charge Joyce, but the soldiers held him back. "You won't get away with this! I already told you I don't know where the Ithium is!"

"Oh, I believe you. You would do anything to protect your friends, wouldn't you? You're such a Boy Scout, Sheriff."

Davenport fumed in rage. Damn it! How did he wind up back in this cocksucker's clutches so quickly?

He didn't have Marshall Lawrence Healey, the Wide Patrol, or the Chorion Team to help him out this time and now Dice was out of commission. Davenport had Emmett and Beauty. That was it.

The soldiers parted to let a medical team in and the medics loaded Dice onto a stretcher. Davenport tried one more time to break away, but he already saw that it was hopeless.

Dice sprawled on the floor and then flopped on the stretcher where the medical team put him. His head lolled and his half-glazed eyes didn't register anyone around him. "Davenport……" he slurred.

"Dice!" Davenport yelled, but Dice didn't respond.

Admiral Joyce sauntered over to the stretcher and pretended to inspect Dice's giant, inert frame. "You see, Sheriff, if you left the Ithium on the *Artemis Rex* the way you say, one of your friends must have moved it. Either they hid it on HTWV-983 or one of them took it off the planet. Now I have no choice but to go through them one after the other to find out which one of them took it."

He meandered over to Emmett and then halted ominously in front of Beauty. Davenport fought harder than ever to get over there. He didn't want Joyce even looking at Beauty.

"You piece of shit!" Davenport hissed. "You won't get away with this."

"Do you honestly think a lowlife sheriff like you can stop me?" Admiral Joyce sighed with feigned resignation. "I have the whole Reserve Wing at my disposal—the whole Confederacy. I can use any resource to retrieve the Ithium. You have nothing. You have a handful of criminals and wayward aliens. You can't stop me."

Joyce came toward Davenport until the two men confronted each other face to face. Joyce's presence infuriated Davenport. He would rather kill Joyce than look at him.

"You're too noble for your own good, Sheriff. You should have stayed a criminal. Then you wouldn't be in this situation."

"I will never stop fighting you!" Davenport snarled. "Never!"

"Of course you will. All your friends are gone. These pathetic creatures can't do anything for you. As soon as they help me find the Ithium, I'll be done with all of you. You'll go somewhere you won't bother anyone again and I'll go back to whatever I was doing before you decided to get in my way."

He waved to his men, but they didn't take Dice or the others away like Davenport expected. They didn't take everyone back to the medical lab the way they did before. In fact, they never left the hold.

Joyce went over to Dice who lay in a stupor on the stretcher. The admiral knelt down next to Dice and leaned over him. "Where's the Ithium?" Joyce asked.

Dice groaned, tried to raise one mighty arm, and let it flop to the floor. "Planet…."

"Do you mean HTWV-983?" Joyce's voice strained with suppressed excitement.

"Planet...... HTWV-983...." Dice moved his big head back and forth like he was either asleep or drunk.

"Where on HTWV-983 did you put it?" Joyce demanded. "Tell me where you put the Ithium."

"Fiddler......"

Joyce spun around and glared at Davenport. "What is Fiddler?"

"She's my daughter, you son of a bitch!" Emmett spat. "If you harm a hair on her head...."

"She's one of our crew," Davenport interrupted. "We lost her on the planet. We haven't seen her since."

He hoped to High Heaven that Joyce would forget all about Fiddler and he was right. Joyce bent over Dice and raised his voice. "Where on HTWV-983 did you hide the Ithium?"

"Swamp......tree......."

"This is hopeless! The Ithium could be anywhere." Joyce shot to his feet and stormed over to the soldiers. "Throw them in the hold. We'll take him to HTWV-983 and he can find it for us."

The guards started hauling the prisoners away and Emmett went nuts. "You bastard, Joyce!" he roared. "If you mess with my daughter, I'll hunt you down and cut your balls off! I'll kill you with my bare hands!"

Davenport struggled, too. He tried to fight his way back to Dice, but one of the guards clubbed him across the cheek.

Davenport hit the floor and came to a second later being dragged into the prison hold. Were the four friends back on the *Rambler* where they started? Were they being taken back to the same hold they fought so long and hard to escape from?

The guards hurled him into a cell and he bounced off the wall. His head exploded in stars and his legs refused to support him.

He crumpled onto the hard stone floor and huddled there in a ball waiting for the next disaster to strike.

Emmett came over to him. "Are you okay?"

Davenport tried to speak, but the connection between his brain and his mouth wouldn't link up. He gasped in pain every time he moved his head.

Emmett dragged him over to a wall and propped him against it. Davenport cradled his head on his arms for a second while he waited for the world to stop spinning.

"We have to get out of here!" Emmett kept muttering. "I have to find Fiddler. She could be in danger."

"We're the ones in danger, pal," Davenport growled.

"But he's after her! He's trying to find her."

"He doesn't give a shit about her. He doesn't even care that she exists. As long as she doesn't have the Ithium, she'll be fine."

"But if she hid it......"

Davenport forced himself to look up. He could no longer deny that, yes, he was back in the same prison hold on the *Rambler*. All the fighting, all the danger, all the effort to get off this ship had come to nothing.

Now he had lost most of the people who ever tried to help him. He had lost Fiddler and Lyons and now he'd lost Dice, too.

Dice's stretcher lay across the cell with him lying utterly senseless on it. He was still breathing, but he no longer flopped and lolled around. His giant arms splayed across the floor on either side of his big, motionless body. He had his eyes closed.

Emmett paced up and down the cell. Davenport had never seen Emmett this agitated.

Davenport thought fast. So Fiddler hid the Ithium on HTWV-983. She hid it somewhere only she and Dice knew about. Davenport knew she was smart, but he must have vastly underestimated her.

A rush of affection filled his heart for all his friends. They had risked everything to help him. They had shared his dangers and he ached at the thought that they might still be in danger.

He was the one who put them in this danger. He was the one who started all of this. He never should have let them come with him or risk themselves for him and his mission.

Davenport extended his hand toward Emmett. "Hey, man. Come here. Sit down here."

Emmett refused even to look at him for a minute. Emmett kept glaring through the bars at the hold outside, but there was nothing to see. Joyce had locked them up in one of the holds with no other prisoners in it. Davenport, Emmett, and Dice were the only people here.

Davenport jerked his head sideways and suffered another stabbing pain behind his eyes. He squinted through it and looked all around him just to make sure. "Where the hell is Beauty?"

Emmett finally turned around. "Huh?"

"Beauty. Where is he?"

Emmett blinked at Davenport, then at Dice, and finally at the surrounding. "I…. uh…. I don't know."

Davenport rested his head against the wall. Beauty had a way of slipping through the cracks at just the right time. Davenport waved to Emmett again. "Come here, man."

Emmett walked over to him, but he still wouldn't look at Davenport. "If anything happens to her…."

Davenport caught Emmett's sleeve and Emmett finally allowed Davenport to tow him down to the floor. Emmett sat down next to him and leaned back.

"We'll find her," Davenport told him. "If you're right, she'll go back to the Armageddon Core. Hell, she's probably with them now and we're stuck in here."

"She better not be on that stinkin' planet with a bunch of Cannibals," Emmett snarled.

"She's tough. She can handle herself."

Emmett gulped and his voice cracked. "She isn't, you know. She isn't as tough as everyone thinks."

Davenport patted his shoulder. "I know, man. She's your little girl and we'll do everything we can to find her and get her back. I promise you that."

They both fell silent. Davenport had no idea how he would fulfill that promise, but he had to make it. He had to do his best for these people and for the Confederacy.

He didn't see anything he could have done differently. He had to take the Ithium from the *Echo Omicron*. He had to go on the run to hide it from Joyce.

He didn't ask the *Echo Omicron* crew to come back for him. He didn't assign the Chorion Team to come with him. Ekol Thaine did that.

He tried to put the matter out of his mind, but it kept bothering him. Fiddler was only one of eleven people in danger because of Davenport. He felt just as responsible for each of them as he did for her.

Where was the Chorion Team now? Where was Lyons?

He couldn't help any of them. He couldn't even help himself.

Chapter 5

Davenport swam out of a fitful sleep, tried to adjust himself into a more comfortable position, and failed.

Emmett lay curled on his side on the floor at Davenport's side. Davenport slept sitting up. He didn't want to sleep at all, but exhaustion eventually got the better of him.

He tried again to shift his weight to the other side, but the hard floor made his bones ache. He should just bite the bullet and lie down like any sensible man would.

He didn't want to make himself comfortable here—not that he ever expected to be comfortable here or anywhere else. How much longer would Joyce leave Davenport and his friends to rot down here?

He already knew the answer to that. Joyce would leave Davenport and his friends to rot down here until the *Rambler* got to HTWV-983. Then the shit would really hit the fan—as if it hadn't already.

A low growl woke him from his thoughts. Dice started moving around on his stretcher and Davenport crawled over to him. "Hey!" Davenport whispered. "Buddy! Can you hear me?"

Dice groaned again and turned his head from one side to another. Then he cleared his throat and raised one arm.

He started to move his hand toward his face and seemed to forget mid-movement what he was trying to do. He put his arm down, compressed his lips, and twisted over on his side.

"Dice!" Davenport murmured. "How you doing?"

Dice grunted something and sniffed. "Leave me alone. I'm sleeping here."

"Do you remember how you got here?"

Dice stiffened with his eyes closed and then pried one of them open. Dice glared up at Davenport. "Davenport?"

"Yeah, buddy. It's me. How are you feeling?"

Dice shut his eyes and growled again. "I feel like shit."

"Sit up and talk to me."

Dice raised his great horned head, tried one more time to open his eyes, and collapsed. "I can't.... I can't get up."

"Try harder."

Davenport's heart skipped a beat watching Dice rally his strength, plant one hand on the floor, and shove himself up on one elbow.

He swayed there breathing hard while he dragged his bleary gaze around the cell. "What the hell happened? Why do I feel so drained?"

"They drugged you." Davenport tried to get hold of Dice's arms to haul him up, but Dice weighed too much.

Dice scowled at Emmett asleep across the cell. "Hold up a sec. Did I......I didn't! I couldn't have!" His head flopped and his chin hit his chest. "Shit! I told him where the Ithium is! Shoot me now, Davenport."

"Forget it. They dosed you with truth serum. You couldn't help it."

Dice covered his face. "I'm so sorry, man. I don't know what to do. I messed up. All this time.... All this work......"

"Knock it off." Davenport took hold of him again. "Come over here and sit with us. You've been unconscious for almost twenty-four hours."

Dice heaved himself upright, but it took all his strength just to push himself off the stretcher. Even then, he had to crawl over to the wall.

The noise and talking woke up Emmett and he moved out of the way to let Dice through.

Dice collapsed sitting between them. His head hit the wall and he shut his eyes. "I'm a tool, Davenport. Just leave me here."

"Will you shut up? No one blames you."

"I never should have let her talk me into it. I should have told her to hide it on her own. She told me it would be safer if fewer people knew where it was. I should have listened to her. I should have told her to leave me out of it. I shouldn't have run the risk that I might t ell."

"Dude!" Davenport countered. "This isn't your fault."

"I can't forgive myself." Dice's hand flew to his head and Davenport winced. Whatever was making Dice so weak must be taking him to the brink of emotional collapse, too. "This is all my fault."

"None of this is your fault," Davenport told him again. "It could have happened to anyone."

"How are we going to stop him from getting it?" Dice choked back emotion. "I can't do anything to stop him! I'm useless to you like this."

"Will you stop it? You're my friend. Do you honestly think I did all this so I could use your strength? Stop talking like that."

Dice looked up at him and their eyes met. Davenport risked a lot for Dice on more than one occasion. If Dice didn't understand by now why Davenport did it, then they were going to start having a serious problem.

"You're the man, Davenport," Dice muttered. "You should be a hell of a lot more than a sheriff."

"Well, I'm not more than a sheriff. Shit, I'm not even a sheriff anymore. Christ knows why I keep wearing this damn star. I should just sack it up and go back to Ekol like Joyce says. I was never cut out for a life on the right side of the law."

"Now you're just blowing shit out of your ass," Emmett interrupted. "There is no one better cut out than you for a life on the right side of the law."

"Just what I was about to say," Dice growled with some of his old bite.

Davenport didn't reply. He sat with his last two remaining friends. They understood. They knew who and what Davenport was. They knew well enough that they could remind him in his darkest hours.

"So what are we gonna do?" Dice finally asked. "How do we get out of here—or rather, how do *you* get out of here? You can't take me with you."

"I've made a decision," Davenport announced.

Dice groaned. "Please no."

Davenport chuckled. "I think we should give him the Ithium."

"What? No!" Emmett yelled. "What the hell have we been doing all this time to keep it away from him if we're just going to hand it to him on a silver platter?"

"Well, keeping it from him hasn't exactly worked out, has it? He's going to find it anyway. He'll kill us all if we stand in his way."

"So that's it?" Dice countered. "You're just going to stand aside and let him pull whatever plot he has in mind?"

"I didn't say that. I said we let him have it so the rest of us aren't directly in his firing line. Then we figure out a way to stop him another way."

"You heard what he said," Emmett argued. "He said he'll make us all go away as soon as he gets it. We'll be just as in his firing line once he gets it as we are now. We might as well keep going the way we are."

"Keep going until all of us are dead.... even Fiddler?" Davenport waited a second for his words to sink in. "Too many people have already gotten hurt in this mess. The boys might be dead already. I can't let anyone else get hurt."

Neither of the others answered for a minute. Davenport said the words that had been bothering him for the last twenty-four hours. He became more certain of them as the seconds ticked past.

"Look," he went on. "We're on our way to HTWV-983. Joyce is going to take you back to wherever Fiddler hid the Ithium. You won't be able to stop him, and if you try to fight him, he'll just drug you again until you show him."

Dice grunted again and didn't answer.

"He already said he would go through all of you one person at a time until he found out who took the Ithium. That means Emmett and Beauty are up next, followed by Fiddler, Lyons, and the boys. Just hand him the damn thing and be done with it. I couldn't live with myself if any of you got hurt again."

"I guess we could play it that way," Dice growled. "Anything would be better than taking another dose of this stuff. At least it's starting to wear off."

"It isn't," Emmett murmured.

"What do you mean?" Davenport asked.

"Truth serum has a half-life of fifteen minutes before it starts to wear off. Joyce already got the information he wanted from you and you can feel for yourself that the drug isn't making you want to spill all your secrets to us. Can't you?"

Dice frowned at Emmett and Davenport got a sick feeling in his stomach. "What are you saying?" He thought he already knew.

"Something in the drug made Dice weak. It isn't the same thing that makes people tell the truth. If someone gave you or me truth serum, we would be back to normal as soon as the drug wore off, but Dice isn't back to normal. If he's this weak this long after taking the drug, it might be permanent."

"No!" Dice yelled. "It can't be! It has to...."

"Easy." Davenport rested his hand on Dice's arm, but he already felt how weak Dice was. He couldn't even stand up.

"It can't be! I can't be like this! I can't!"

"It might not be permanent," Emmett went on, "but it sure is lasting a lot longer than what would happen to a human taking truth serum."

Dice collapsed against the wall whimpering in despair. "This can't be happening!"

"We'll fix it." Davenport squeezed his arm again, but he didn't have a clue *how* he would fix it. What if Emmett was right and Dice never regained his strength?

Davenport shuddered at the thought and he could only imagine how Dice felt about it. What would Davenport do without Dice's strength?

He just assured Dice that he wasn't friends with Dice for his strength.... but still. Dice wasn't Dice without his strength. Davenport didn't know how to understand this weak, pathetic, whimpering creature at his side.

Dice startled Davenport by jerking around. Dice drilled Davenport with a furious glare and snarled through locked teeth. "Kill me, Davenport. If I don't get better, you have to end it. I can't live like this."

"Take it easy, buddy." Davenport struggled to keep the tremor out of his voice. "We aren't there yet. We might still be able to fix this. You could be back to your old self. Just...."

Dice spun the other way and looked at the opposite wall. He kept his head turned and refused to look at Davenport or Emmett.

"Listen, pal," Davenport murmured in his ear. "Beauty is gone. He disappeared when Joyce threw us in this cell. He's at large somewhere on this ship."

Dice whipped around just as fast. "Seriously?"

"He isn't here." Davenport waved at the cell. "We don't know where he is. He can help us get out of here."

Some of the old fire returned to Dice's eyes. "Are you sure?"

"Don't give up yet. We'll get you out of here and we'll figure out a way to counter the serum's effects. You aren't finished yet."

Dice's features hardened. "Make me one promise, Davenport."

"Anything, man."

"When we catch Joyce, I want to be the one to twist his damn head off."

Davenport had to laugh in relief. "If you want to be the one to kill him, you'll have to fight me to get to him first."

"And me," Emmett cut in.

Dice scowled into Davenport's eyes for a minute and then cracked a big grin. "I'll wrestle you for him."

"It's a deal."

Davenport faced front and the three men relaxed in the silence against the wall. Davenport didn't have to figure anything out right now. He could just enjoy this moment of reprieve. It might be the last one he got for a while.

Chapter 6

A loud yell snapped Davenport wide awake. "On your feet! Get your hands above your heads and move over to the back wall."

He unstuck his eyelids and looked up at least twenty Reserve Wing soldiers holding him at gunpoint.

Davenport and Emmett scrambled to their feet. Davenport started to help Dice up, but the soldiers reacted too fast. They charged the bars and brandished their guns in Davenport's face. "Get your hands up! Put your hands behind your head before we open fire!"

Davenport's arms shot up and he laced his fingers behind his head. Dice tried to push himself onto his hands and knees and collapsed again. He slumped in a sitting position next to Davenport's ankle.

"Get on your feet!" the soldiers roared. "Get back against that wall—now!"

"I can't," Dice murmured in a choked undertone. "I can't stand up."

"You!" the soldiers yelled at Davenport and Emmett. "Get over there! Turn to the wall and keep your arms up."

Davenport hated moving away from Dice, but Dice nodded to him and Davenport backed off. He and Emmett turned to the back wall and the soldiers started unlocking the cell.

He stole a peek over his shoulder to see what they were doing. They hustled into the cell and injected Dice with another dose of truth serum. He tried to struggle, but he lacked the strength to stop them.

He folded onto the floor and another medical team loaded him back on the stretcher. The soldiers held Davenport and Emmett at gunpoint and marched them out of the hold following Dice's stretcher.

Davenport swallowed hard when he saw Dice in another stupor. Whatever the serum did to him would get so much worse, now that he'd had two doses instead of one.

Did Joyce really plan to keep dosing Dice until he couldn't raise a finger again? Davenport couldn't imagine a worse fate, especially for someone as strong and ferocious as Dice. It was a fate worse than death.

The soldiers steered Davenport and Emmett back upstairs to the cargo hold where Typhon Elexor's box first deposited them. They exited the *Rambler* into the dank, damp forests of HTWV-983.

The usual insects clicked in the high canopy. None of the Cannibals or Mexia's people were here anymore. The whole planet sounded deserted and as quiet as the grave.

Admiral Joyce strolled down the *Rambler's* ramp and cast a superior glance around at the surroundings. He sauntered over to Dice's stretcher. "This is the spot where the *Artemis Rex* spent the most time on this planet. Is this where Fiddler hid the Ithium?"

Dice raised one arm and pointed before his arm slapped back down on the moss. "Swamp...."

Joyce, Davenport, and Emmett all turned to look in the direction Dice pointed. One of the planet's thousands of swamps stretched into the distance. Faint light winked through the canopy and glistened on the water's unearthly surface. The whole place breathed with some hidden mysterious presence.

"She hid it in the swamp?" Joyce demanded. "Where?"

"Under tree.... roots......" Dice didn't look. He didn't seem capable of focusing his eyes on anything.

He wasn't having any trouble pointing, though. A massive tree lay on its side in the swamp. The roots stuck up above the water in a giant flat fan at least twenty feet tall.

"You—Davenport!" Joyce pointed at Davenport. "Go get the Ithium. He says it's under the tree roots."

One of the soldiers prodded Davenport in the spine. His curiosity got the better of him and he started toward the tree. If this worked, he could finally rid himself of that rotten Ithium once and for all. Maybe then he would be able to get the Sheriff's Service and a few others to help him stop Joyce's plot.

Davenport headed out to the water's edge. "Where is it?"

Joyce bent over Dice and then called, "He says it's between the roots and the trunk.... under the water."

Davenport examined the problem and finally climbed up on the roots. He used them as a ladder to clamber onto the tree trunk. From here, he could squat down and thrust his arm into the water.

He rummaged around in the mud. He adjusted his position to check closer to the roots and then farther away. Joyce kept muttering furiously in Dice's ear, but Davenport still didn't find anything.

Joyce finally shot to his feet and stormed over to the water's edge. "Come down from there—now!" He waved his arms around to motion Davenport back to solid ground.

Davenport climbed down and the guards grabbed him. They yanked him nearly off his feet and shoved him over to Emmett. Joyce ordered one of the soldiers to climb up and repeat the procedure, but without success.

Joyce barged back over to Dice and bellowed down into Dice's face. "It isn't there! The Ithium isn't there! You lied! Where did you put it?"

Dice pointed to the tree again and then collapsed, totally unconscious. Joyce whirled away and Davenport shuddered at the look on the admiral's face. Davenport had never seen Joyce this angry—ever.

He sliced his finger at Emmett. "Dose him!"

Davenport tried to jerk free from the soldiers holding him, but the medical team already stood right behind Emmett. They injected him with the serum and Emmett buckled onto his knees.

Joyce propped his hands on his knees and yelled in Emmett's dazed face. "Where is the Ithium?! Where did you put it?!"

"On the *Artemis Rex*......"

Joyce spun around so fast he almost fell over. He barged back to Dice and pointed down at him. "Kill him."

"NO!!" Davenport roared.

He didn't understand how he managed to free himself. The next thing he knew, he was sprinting across the clearing. One of the soldiers raised an XQ and aimed it at Dice's head.

Davenport skidded between them. "NO! You can't kill him! He told you where he hid it!"

The XQ barrel banged Davenport's eyebrow, but he ignored the weapon. He concentrated everything on Joyce.

"Where is the rest of your crew, Davenport?" Joyce thundered. "Where are they? I'll go through them one person after another, and if they don't talk, I'll kill each and every one of them in front of you! Now WHERE ARE THEY?"

"The boys...." Davenport stammered. "...they.... got away.... with Healey.... They went....to the Needle.... I don't know...."

"What about the others?!" Joyce roared. "Where is Fiddler?"

"I.... I don't know......The Mad Men.... took me away from......"

"WHO ELSE, DAVENPORT?!" Joyce bellowed. "WHO ELSE WAS WITH YOU?!"

"Uh.... Lyons......."

"WHERE?!" Joyce snatched the soldier's XQ and moved it aside so it pointed at Dice again.

"NO!!" Davenport dove in front of it and blocked Dice with his whole body. "I don't know where Fiddler or Lyons went! I'm telling you the truth! We don't know where the Ithium is!"

Joyce straightened up shaking with rage. His lips quivered and his nostrils flared white. He glared down at Davenport in such fury that Davenport felt certain Joyce would kill him now.

"We will track those boys to the Needle...." Joyce hissed through gritted teeth. "And then we will find this Fiddler and Lyons. If they won't cooperate, I swear to God I'll blow all their heads off.... starting with him." He pointed at Dice and stormed off to the ship.

Davenport collapsed on the ground. His whole body shook. Now what was he supposed to do?

The soldiers came over and yanked him away from Dice. Davenport didn't try to fight them when they dragged him back on board the ship.

Dice was so out of his mind on the drug he didn't even know Davenport was here or that he threw himself in front of a gun to save Dice's life. Dice might never regain consciousness. He might be like this for life.

The soldiers flung Davenport into the cell along with Emmett. Davenport stayed where he was waiting for them to bring Dice back, but they didn't.

Davenport eventually got so agitated from waiting that he paced up and down the cell. "What the hell is wrong?" he muttered. "Why don't they bring him back?"

Emmett didn't answer. He sat bowed and silent against the wall without speaking.

The agonizing minutes ticked by and the soldiers still didn't bring Dice back. The cell felt gut-wrenchingly empty without him. Davenport and Emmett were the last two left. How soon would the soldiers come and take Emmett away, too.

That thought snapped something in Davenport's mind. He sprang over to Emmett and bumped into the old man when he sat down.

"We gotta get outta here, Emmett," Davenport hissed. "We can't wait around for them to start killing people."

Emmett blinked down at the floor and didn't say anything. His total lack of response sent Davenport into a frenzy.

He shot to his feet and went back to pacing. "We have to find a way to contact Beauty. We have to find out where he is."

"It's too late, Davenport," Emmett murmured. "If Beauty is still on this ship, he won't stick his neck out for us."

"You're wrong, man. There has to be a way."

Emmett went silent again. Davenport's words fell into a vast well of silence and they didn't come back. They didn't make a dent in Emmett's despair.

Davenport turned his back on Emmett. He couldn't think about Emmett anymore. Emmett was gone. Davenport was already alone.

That left Davenport on his own to deal with this. He kept thinking about Dice. Someone had to get Dice out of here. Davenport made Dice a promise to help him beat this. That one promise kept Davenport going.

Chapter 7

Davenport woke up sore again. He hadn't been able to stay sitting up. He finally caved and lay down on the hard stone.

He dragged his aching body over to the wall and rested his forehead in his hand. He'd been racking his brain all night to find a way out of here, but he couldn't do that without some help from outside.

Where was Beauty? Why didn't he show himself? Did Beauty know how bad things were getting with Dice?

Emmett's words infected Davenport with doubts. What if Beauty fled to save himself? What if he abandoned the other three to their miserable fate?

Davenport still couldn't understand why Admiral Joyce didn't remember Beauty. Joyce hadn't said one word about drugging, questioning, and threatening Beauty.

What if Beauty was the one who took the Ithium from Fiddler's hiding place? What if Beauty had the Ithium on him right now?

Davenport chuckled thinking about that. He could take just one moment in this nightmare to appreciate the irony. That would be so rich if the Ithium was on the *Rambler*, right under Joyce's nose, this whole time.

Here was Joyce flying all over hell and gone searching for the Ithium. He wasted all this fuel and truth serum for something already on board his ship.

Davenport cut off his laughter soon enough. He didn't want to wake Emmett.

Davenport looked around the shadowy prison, but the view only depressed him. There was no way out of here—not until Joyce came to take him out again.

Even then, Davenport wouldn't be able to do anything as long as Joyce kept threatening the others. Joyce really had Davenport's number. He knew exactly which buttons to push to get Davenport to do whatever he wanted.

Davenport looked down at the floor. He should go back to sleep. Whatever happened, he would need rest to keep his strength up. He was the strongest member of their party now. It felt strange to find himself in that position after spending so long with Dice, Laub, and the other Chorions.

Soft whispering sounds set his nerves on edge. He discounted it at first and then he knew he wasn't hearing things.

He got stealthily to his feet and tiptoed to the bars. He peered up and down the aisle at the other cells. Did Joyce bring more prisoners down here? He'd been careful to keep Davenport and his friends isolated from everyone except the soldiers.

The whispering came from the very far end of the hold. Two doors occupied both ends where stairwells led to the upper decks.

Davenport didn't hear anyone come in or out. He only heard one voice and—yes! It was coming closer.

All at once, another whisper came from the shadows. "Back away from the bars, Davenport."

"Beauty!" Davenport whispered. "Where have you been?"

"Don't worry, Davenport. I've been working on a way to get us out of here."

"How? Do you know where Dice is? The admiral gave him another dose of truth serum. Dice is......he's really weak...."

"I know where he is. I'm keeping an eye on him. Don't worry. He'll be all right."

Davenport gulped to ease the tightness in his throat. He never dreamed that talking to a friendly voice on the outside would mean this much.

Beauty's words tore at Davenport's heart. *He'll be all right*. Davenport didn't want to believe that Dice would be all right. Davenport wanted to protect himself from the devastation of finding out that Dice would never recover.

He didn't want to believe it now. Beauty's promise made Davenport's heart ache.

"Move back, Davenport," Beauty whispered. "Move away from the bars."

Davenport took a step back without thinking first. "Why? What's going on?" He glanced up and down the hold again. "Where are you, Beauty?"

"I'm right here." The whisper came from right outside the bars, but Davenport couldn't see a thing. "The Reserve Wing keeps this hold under surveillance. If the security team sees you standing here talking to someone, they'll get suspicious. I have to stay against the bars so they don't see me."

"Okay, man. Just tell me what you want me to do. I'm.... I can't do anything in here, but I'll do what I can. We just have to get Dice off this Stalwart before Joyce does something really bad."

"I saw what you did for Dice on HTWV-983, Davenport," Beauty murmured in an even more meaningful undertone. "We will get him off this ship and we will bring him back to his full strength. I promise you that."

Davenport compressed his lips holding back emotion. He wanted to pour out his gratitude to Beauty, but he didn't trust himself to speak without breaking down completely.

"Listen carefully, Davenport. This is much more dangerous than the Mad Men's ship."

"I.... I know. Just tell me what to do."

"The hard part will be getting Dice off the ship. He can't walk. I don't even know if he'll regain consciousness in time. We have to find a way to move him. If it was just you, me, and Emmett, it would be easy."

Davenport nodded at nothing. Beauty might not even be able to see him, but Davenport hung on every word with everything he had. He craved every precious word of hope and promise.

"You'll know when the time comes, Davenport."

"How will I know?"

"Trust me."

That last whisper faded into silence and Davenport knew Beauty was gone. He wouldn't come back. Davenport wouldn't see him.... until he did.

Trust me. Davenport could live or die on those words. Beauty would get Davenport and Emmett out of here. Beauty might have started out hating Davenport's guts, but Beauty would never let Dice go down this way. Davenport kicked himself for doubting Beauty a few minutes ago.

Davenport scooted over to the wall and resumed his usual place. He couldn't sleep now if his life depended on it. Not even knowing sleep would help him escape could make him close his eyes.

Emmett woke up a few hours later—or at least he sat up. He leaned against the wall, shut his eyes, and started breathing heavily again.

"Beauty's here," Davenport whispered to him.

Emmett stopped breathing for a second, and when he restarted, he didn't go back to sleep. He kept his eyes shut, but he stayed tense. "Just tell me what to do."

"I will as soon as he tells me," Davenport murmured.

Emmett snorted, shifted away, and curled his knees to his chest. Davenport passed the time by mentally going over every inch of the *Rambler*. He'd seen more of the ship than he wanted to the last time he escaped from it. Dice must be on the medical deck.

Beauty was damn right about moving Dice. How in the hell were Davenport, Emmett, and Beauty supposed to move that giant body when Dice couldn't even walk? Davenport thanked the stars Beauty was the one thinking about these problems so Davenport didn't have to.

Davenport was all finished thinking for the rest of his life. He was all done making decisions and trying to save the rest of the world.

He smirked to himself again when he remembered. He'd just risked his ass trying to save Dice and he was about to do the same thing again. Hell, he would probably do it a whole lot more before he got to go on vacation from making decisions and risking his ass. His life was turning into very little else these days.

He only had to think about Fiddler, Lyons, Healey, and the Chorion Team to know he would do it in a heartbeat. He wouldn't dream of doing anything else.

Chapter 8

Davenport stiffened to high alert when the prison hold door boomed open. Only the soldiers would make that much noise.

He got to his feet and Emmett stood up, too. Whatever Beauty was going to do, he would do it now.

Emmett and Davenport approached the bars as the soldiers pulled up outside the cell. Half the group held the prisoners at gunpoint while some sweaty corporal unlocked the bars.

The soldiers and officers yelled at Emmett and Davenport. They threatened and bellowed, but the whole thing existed in another dimension of reality from Davenport. None of this meant anything.

Did these soldiers really think Emmett and Davenport planned to put up a fight? Fighting would only stop the pair from getting to Beauty's escape plan.

The soldiers yanked the two men out of the cell and propelled them up the stairs. They didn't go back to the medical deck or the cargo hold or outside. They kept climbing and Davenport hardened his nerve when the soldiers halted outside of Admiral Joyce's office.

Davenport had been here once before and he had no desire to repeat the experience, especially not without another sheriff, four deputies, a Confederate marshall, and the whole Chorion Team to help him out.

The soldiers flung back the door and nudged Emmett and Davenport inside.

Admiral Joyce exploded the instant he spotted Davenport. This jackass was really starting to lose his grip.

He propped his fists on the desk, leaned across it, and started blasting off in a thunderous tirade. "What the hell did you do with him, Davenport? I swear to Christ, when I find him, I'll make you watch me cut him to pieces. You put up a pretty good show on HTWV-983. Now I know you're full of shit. Now tell me where he is! Answer me or pay the price!"

"What are you talking about?" Davenport returned. "Where is who?"

"Don't give me that shit!" the admiral roared. "You stole him! You did something with him. Now tell me where he is. You can't get away with this."

"Who?" Davenport repeated more slowly in case the admiral didn't hear him the first time. "Who did I steal?"

"The Adik, of course! Who the hell else would I be talking about? You stole him from the medical deck. If he dies because my people couldn't give him proper care, I'll see you sent up to the Terminus Anathema on a murder charge! You think I don't have enough on your already, but you'll find out I can be very...."

Davenport blinked at him. "Dice is gone? Are you saying Dice is gone?"

"What the hell do I care what his name is? He was in intensive care and then he vanished. We've searched the whole Stalwart. What did you do with him? Do you realize you just issued that man a death sentence?"

Davenport shut his mouth with a click. "So he's a man now? You sure haven't been treating him like one."

The admiral reacted with lightning reflexes. He yanked a sidearm from his desk and aimed it at Emmett's face. "Start talking, Davenport. Tell me where the Adik is. You might not care if he lives or dies...."

"You foul piece of shit!" Davenport hissed. "Don't you even DARE to say that to me!"

Admiral Joyce cocked the sidearm and clenched his teeth. "Say goodbye to your friend, Davenport. Just remember I tried to do this the easy way and you wouldn't see reason."

Admiral Joyce sliced his eyes over to Emmett and his knuckles whitened to fire. Davenport opened his mouth to intervene. What could he say? He had no blinkin' clue where Dice was.

Did Beauty know Dice's condition was as grave as this? Would Beauty put Dice in danger to get him away from the Reserve Wing?

Davenport couldn't tell Joyce anything that would save Emmett's life in time. Joyce didn't look at Davenport again. Joyce didn't care anymore if Davenport offered any information about Dice's whereabouts.

Davenport had to act. He had to move in front of the gun or at least attack Joyce to stop the admiral from killing Emmett.

At that moment, a loud beep sounded on Admiral Joyce's desk. The admiral didn't move when another man's voice came through from out of sight. "We found him, Sir! We found the Adik."

"Where is he?" Joyce snapped.

"He's on the...." A stream of static interrupted. It went on and on and only cut out to let a snatch of words through. "Bringing him through now."

Joyce dropped his gun and punched something on his desk. "Repeat, Sergeant! Where is the Adik now?"

"We're just bringing him through to the...." More static cut off the rest.

Davenport's pulse quickened. This whole scenario was looking more and more like one of the Chorion Team's lunatic muddles. This couldn't be an accident. Davenport had seen too many crazy sabotage plans come to fruition to ever believe that again.

Joyce sidestepped around his desk, pointed in Davenport's face, and hissed through gritted teeth. "We aren't finished here. When I get back...."

The door burst open and a bunch of officers hustled in. "Sir! The Adik is...."

Joyce froze. "He isn't on the rampage again, is he?"

"No, Sir! He's.... he's disappeared again! I don't understand it, but...."

"HOW?!" Joyce roared. "You said you had him!"

"We did, Sir! We found him unconscious on his stretcher and we started to bring him back upstairs and then he just...."

The silence that ended this sentence sounded even more sinister than whatever the man had been about to say. Beauty. This one had Beauty written all over it.

Joyce sliced his forefinger from Davenport and Emmett on one side to the officers on the other. "Guard them! Make sure they're here when I come back."

"But, Sir...." someone stammered. "Don't you want us to keep searching for the Adik?"

Joyce opened his mouth and closed it a few more times. He struggled to answer, huffed, and stormed out of the office.

Davenport and Emmett exchanged glances. What should they do? Beauty still hadn't given them the word to do anything.

The officers and soldiers exchanged glances, too. Then they left to follow Admiral Joyce.

Davenport and Emmett looked at each other again. They were all alone in Joyce's office. Should they try to escape now? Were more soldiers standing outside?

Another signal came over Joyce's controls. Davenport hesitated and then dashed around the desk to take a look.

The screen showed a layout of the *Rambler's* many decks, corridors, and departments. A single Adik life sign blipped along a little-used corridor five decks down.

Dice was moving at a steady clip considering Beauty said that Dice couldn't walk. Someone must be moving him. He was in the engineering section. Davenport could see this, so why didn't the rest of the *Rambler* crew see it, too?

None of the security teams were anywhere near the engineering section. They were searching the cargo hold, the launch bays, and even the fuel system.

"What is it?" Emmett murmured.

"Dice.... he's not far away." Davenport fiddled with a few more readings. He could pick up every human life sign on the ship. The office was unguarded. "Come on. We're getting out of here."

He took a peek outside before he dared to show himself, but the corridor outside was empty.

"I don't know about this," Emmett breathed.

"Neither do I, but I trust Beauty. This could be our only chance to get out of here."

"If they catch us, they'll kill us."

"The way I see it, we have a choice between doing this and going back to the cells," Davenport replied. "I'm not doing that without at least trying. What do you say?"

Emmett's features hardened and he nodded. Davenport veered off to the stairs, jogged down to the engineering section, and headed in the direction he hoped he'd seen the Adik life sign. There could only be one Adik life sign on the whole ship.

The engineering section followed the same layout as the rest of the *Rambler*. A long corridor crossed the section from one stairwell to the other. Rooms and compartments opened on either side. Each one housed some component of the ship's engine systems, and by another one of Beauty's miracles, the section was totally deserted.

No crewmen worked down here. The engines hummed along perfectly, but no one attended them, checked them, or adjusted them the way they should.

The whole scene became more surreal the farther Davenport ventured down the corridor. This unearthly silence couldn't last. The soldiers would show up looking for Dice and then they would find Davenport and Emmett, too.

Davenport peeked into each room and compartment searching for Dice and Beauty. He finally found them near the far end.

Dice's stretcher lay on the floor in front of the diffraction oscillator. Beauty pranced around behind him messing with the oscillator. Beauty shot a crazy grin over his shoulder at Davenport and then went back to what he was doing.

Davenport cast a furtive glance down the corridor just to make sure it was still clear. Then he hustled over to Beauty. "What are you doing down here, Beauty? How do you plan to get Dice out through *here*? There's no way out."

Beauty gave Davenport another grin and this one dripped with menace. "Distract them, Davenport."

"Huh? What do you mean—distract them? Distract who from what?"

Emmett squatted down next to Dice. "He's waking up."

Davenport crouched down next to Dice, too. Davenport squeezed his arm. "Hey, buddy. How you doing?"

"Davenport......" Dice rasped. His big head rotated from one side to the other. He moved his eyes around, but he didn't focus on anything.

"Rest easy, big guy. Beauty's gonna get you out of here."

"Davenport.... I'm sorry.... I didn't mean to tell him......"

"Easy, pal. You didn't tell him anything."

Dice didn't respond. His head lolled the other way.

"They're coming, Davenport," Beauty called from over by the oscillator.

Those words set Davenport's hair on end. He looked around the room and saw, for the first time, that a bunch of larger XQs had been assembled in the corner.

Now he understood. He lunged for the weapons and grabbed two. Emmett had the same idea and both men planted themselves between Dice and the doorway.

Beauty cackled with glee behind their backs and Davenport's scalp prickled. Beauty must have planned this. He was going to spring his trap. He just needed Davenport and Emmett to occupy the soldiers while he did whatever he was going to do.

Davenport could do that. He leveled his XQ at the doorway and counted down the seconds before the whole situation blew up in his face.

He didn't care anymore how messy it got or how many explosions he had to survive. He was getting the hell out of here and taking Dice with him.

The righthand stairwell banged open and voices echoed down the corridor. "They're in the oscillator room! They can't get out! Make sure you don't hit the Adik."

Davenport thought he recognized Admiral Joyce's voice mixed up with the others, but he might have been wrong. His blood pounded in his ears. The soldiers were right. He and his friends were trapped in this room.

Then he remembered. The oscillator was one of the most sensitive and explosive devices on the whole Stalwart. The soldiers would be shooting at Davenport and Emmett with the oscillator right behind them.

Some of the soldiers' shots were bound to hit the oscillator and then....

Davenport didn't see how any of the four friends could survive that, but he was so far beyond caring that he didn't hesitate. He rotated his XQ to his shoulder and Emmett did the same. They both aimed for the doorway.

If the soldiers fired the first shots, Davenport and Emmett would have to take cover. That would give the soldiers a clear shot at the oscillator. Davenport couldn't let that happen.

He measured the distance by how loud their voices sounded. He held his breath, and the instant the first man rounded the corner, Davenport opened fire. Emmett joined in and they blasted three soldiers away right off.

Davenport kept up a steady hail of gunfire on the doorway. So much dust and exploding plaster clouded his view that he couldn't even see if anyone was there or if they were shooting back at him.

He got lost in the fog of his own mayhem until something bumped his foot. He didn't let up shooting when he glanced down.

A choke shell rolled across the floor. Time stood still as he looked down at it.

Beauty rocketed out of nowhere, collected Davenport and Emmett in one flying tackle and they slammed hard against the opposite wall just as the shell detonated.

The whole room rocked with a bone-shattering boom. Davenport ducked under his arms as another colossal smash jolted the floor under him.

He listened for more gunfire, but Beauty was already on his feet. "Get up! Quick!"

He dragged Davenport to his feet and shoved him away. Davenport couldn't see a damn thing with all the dust and smoke around. He heard soldiers yelling in the background, but he couldn't see them and no one seemed to be shooting at him anymore, thank God.

Beauty yanked Davenport's hand and disappeared into the fog. Davenport got hold of Emmett's sleeve. He didn't want to lose Emmett in this chaos.

They stumbled through wreckage and Davenport found Beauty crouching over Dice's stretcher. Beauty was murmuring in Dice's ear and Davenport couldn't understand him.

Beauty took a step back and the stretcher hovered off the ground. He started guiding it toward the oscillator......except that the oscillator wasn't there.

Davenport blinked the dust out of his eyes and found himself in the *Rambler's* cargo hold. Ten gleaming Dagger-class fighter craft lined the deck and Beauty pushed Dice's stretcher toward the nearest one.

Davenport looked around him in stunned, stupid shock. How did he get into the cargo hold?

A massive section of broken-off concrete, twisted metal bars, and rubble surrounded the four friends. Beauty had to clamber over boulders and gravel to get to the Daggers...but yes, he really was taking Dice on board one of them.

Shouts from above made Davenport look up. Soldiers peered down through a yawning breach in the hold's ceiling. They pointed and yelled to each other. That explosion must have dropped the four friends from the oscillator room to here.

Beauty stuck his head out of the Dagger. "Come on! They'll be here any second."

Davenport staggered over to the ship with Emmett at his side. "What the hell did he do?" Emmett muttered.

"It looks like he blew up the oscillator."

"If he did, the *Rambler* will overload and...." The two men halted and looked at each other. Then they both charged the Dagger.

Beauty was in the process of clamping Dice's stretcher to the bulkhead. Beauty waved Davenport to the cockpit. "You fly, Davenport. You're the best at it."

Davenport didn't argue. He had to get his friends off the *Rambler* before the Stalwart overloaded and blew them all into next week.

He scrambled to power up the engines. He checked the readings from the rest of the ship. Beauty was right. The soldiers streamed down the stairwells trying to intercept the fugitives...and they weren't coming alone. They brought Howitzers this time.

Davenport gulped and checked the rest of the hold for any way out. The giant hatch that should let these Daggers out remained firmly closed and locked. Maybe....

He signaled the bridge hardly daring to hope someone would respond.

"Go!" Beauty called from the back. "Dice is ready. Get out of here now!"

"How?" Davenport yelled. "I can't...."

The soldiers burst into the hold and let loose with their Howitzers. Shots pinged off the Dagger and Davenport reacted on pure instinct. He launched the ship, but he was still locked in here with all those guns aimed at him.

He opened up the Dagger's onboard guns and plastered the soldiers, but that didn't help him escape. "Do something!" Emmett screamed.

"Like what?" Davenport yelled back.

Another catastrophic explosion struck the *Rambler* and the hatch wheeled off into space. It didn't open. It just.... left. It split from the hull and tumbled away into nothing.

The hull depressurized instantly and the force ripped soldiers, Daggers, Howitzers, and everything else out into space. Davenport punched the engines and streaked away.

Chapter 9

Fiddler hunkered behind a rock and surveyed Ultra Meridian from her hiding place. This position sheltered her and Lyons from the wind and Fiddler raised her mask and propped it on top of her head. "Someone's been shooting around here. Look. Someone blew up the jail again."

Lyons lifted her mask, too. She squinted toward what was left of the building in the distance. "Who would attack the jail when there isn't even a sheriff around here anymore?"

Fiddler pointed to a pile of blackened metal across the plane. "See that? It's a Reserve Wing Nitrol. It crashed here recently. Where there's smoke, there's fire."

"Are you saying the Reserve Wing is here?" Lyons made a face. "You're imagining things."

Almost in answer to her words, three Stalwarts descended from the atmosphere to land on the plane. Fiddler and Lyons had to pull their masks down to protect their faces and lungs from dust and sand.

The Stalwarts touched down and dozens of officers streamed from their holds. They headed over to the jail and more Daggers descended to join them.

"What were you just saying about me imagining things?" Fiddler yelled to Lyons through their masks. "It looks like we're sharing the same delusion."

"What are they doing here?" Lyons asked, but that question answered itself just as fast.

Fiddler hunched lower behind her rock and tensed every nerve when a whole bunch of masked aliens streamed onto the plane. They came from the mountains surrounding Ultra Meridian and she saw at one glance that they belonged to Typhon Elexor.

"What the holy hell?" Lyons hissed.

Fiddler couldn't move or breathe. Her jaw dropped inside her mask watching Typhon Elexor approach the Reserve Wing officers. The two groups joined and talked together in full view.... except that no one was here.

Fiddler's pulse quickened. Was she really seeing Typhon Elexor working together with the Reserve Wing?

Typhon Elexor had a reputation as one of the most ruthless criminal syndicates in the Confederacy…. right behind Mount Refractory, Ekol Thaine, Calyx Elkanon, and a few others.

So Typhon Elexor and the Reserve Wing were taking advantage of Ultra Meridian being abandoned to meet in secret…. or what they thought was secret. They didn't know Fiddler and Lyons were watching them…. not that anyone would believe the two women if they told anyone.

The Reserve Wing was sworn to stop Typhon Elexor and bring the syndicate down. That was the Reserve Wing's stated mandate—to preserve law and order. What a joke.

"If the Reserve Wing is here," Lyons remarked, "they must still be looking for the third component."

"Which means we need to find it." Fiddler laid her hand on Lyons's arm and pulled her backward. "Come on. Let's go find the Armageddon Core. At least we can kick back with them for a while until we decide what to do."

The two women retreated. Fiddler was just about to duck behind the rock where she would lose sight of the gathering out there.

She froze when a bunch of crewmen rushed out of a nearby Stalwart and ran over to the assembled officers. They talked rapidly and then Fiddler's heart dropped when the Reserve Wing crews pointed toward Fiddler's and Lyons's hiding place.

"We have a problem, "Lyons whispered.

Fiddler braced herself for a fight and then her worst nightmare came true when Typhon Elexor broke away and set off coming straight for her position.

She spun away and grabbed Lyons, but Lyson was already bolting into the hills.

Fiddler plunged down an embankment, into one of the desert's many channels, and took off running for all she was worth. She should have headed for the Armageddon Core's hidden cave, but when she ran up another hill and looked back, that thought went out of her mind. She couldn't lead Typhon Elexor back to the Armageddon Core or Fiddler would put them in danger, too.

The Daggers launched for the plane and screamed after the two fleeing women. The Daggers angled into the canyons to run the two women down.

Armed Typhon Elexor attackers streamed across the plane and poured into the canyons. What looked like hundreds of them streamed from hidden spots all over the surrounding mountains to join the pursuit.

"What did we do?" Lyson yelled.

"We saw them! Run!"

Both women were already running as fast as they could. Lyons stumbled and Fiddler caught her before they both raced on.

Fiddler darted from one canyon to the next searching for somewhere to hide. Typhon Elexor didn't know this part of Ultra Meridian as well as they knew their own territory. They knew enough, though. The two women had to find somewhere to get under cover before Typhon Elexor caught up with them.

What if Typhon Elexor figured out that Fiddler and Lyons were the ones who attacked their wind mines? That would be terrible.

Fiddler couldn't let that happen, but she hadn't run more than a hundred yards before the Daggers streaked overhead. They unloaded their Howitzers into the hills trying to blast the women to death.

Fiddler cut hard to the right and almost ran into a blast pulverizing the hillside next to her. Dirt, rock, and ruptured sod spat in her eyes. She sprinted the other way, steamrolled Lyons, and almost fell under another bombardment striking the canyon floor.

Lyons collided with Fiddler from behind. At least a dozen Daggers howled overhead. They blasted the canyon to rubble chewing up the mountains on both sides.

Rocks pelted Fiddler's jacket and a large clod smashed her in the face. Her goggles shattered and she had to tear them off just to see where she was going.

The sight that met her eyes didn't cheer her up at all. Four Daggers zoomed past the two women. The ships unloaded into the hills up ahead and bombarded them with crushing power. Rock, dirt, and sand dislodged and cascaded into the canyon. The Daggers were trying to cut off Fiddler's route and they were succeeding.

She looked everywhere for any way out. More Daggers swiveled sideways and caved in side canyons the women might have been able to use to escape. Fiddler and Lyons were boxed in.

Fiddler's adrenaline kept her running right up to the end. She and Lyons halted in front of a giant heap of debris blocking their path. They couldn't climb out without the Daggers mowing them down.

Fiddler looked back in the direction from which she'd come. All thought that she could get out that way evaporated when she confronted dozens of Typhon Elexor fighters approaching from behind.

They leveled their weapons at her. They would kill her to stop her from telling anyone that they were working with the Reserve Wing.

Lyons backed into Fiddler and both women raised their weapons. These laser rifles wouldn't do any good against so many enemies. The Daggers could flatten the two women with a single well-placed shot.

Then Fiddler had another terrible thought. Why didn't the Daggers and Typhon Elexor kill the two women already? They must have orders to capture instead of kill.

If the Reserve Wing got hold of Fiddler, they might be able to get her to tell where she put the Ithium. She couldn't let that happen.

She pulled the rifle strap off her shoulder. She turned the gun so the muzzle pointed toward her head.

"What are you doing?" Lyons screeched.

Fiddler barely heard her. Fiddle couldn't let herself fall into Reserve Wing hands. She would end it right here.

She dropped on one knee and planted the rifle butt on the ground. She bowed her head over the barrel and grabbed the muzzle. She almost put it in her mouth when a rocket whistled out of the bare mountainside. It corkscrewed through the air and smashed one of the Daggers to smithereens.

The ship boomed in a ball of fire and all the other Daggers spun away to confront the mystery attacker.

Another rocket peeled out of a hillside on the canyon opposite edge. It came from directly behind the Daggers and it exploded another ship. The Daggers never saw either shot coming.

Fiddler launched to her feet, all thought of ending it gone out of her mind. She spun her rifle around and pinned the stock to her shoulder. "Come on!" she roared to Lyons and started marching toward Typhon Elexor.

The aliens tightened ranks before her. They aimed dozens of weapons at her and Lyons, but Fiddler didn't care about that.

More rockets whizzed back and forth above her head. They crisscrossed the sky blasting Daggers from all sides. The Daggers whirled this way and that, but they couldn't find whoever was shooting at them.

Typhon Elexor paid no attention to the Daggers meeting their end. The aliens focused all their firepower on the two women.

Lyons tried to hold Fiddler back, but Fiddler shook Lyons off. She clenched her fingers to fire when a deafening torrent of gunfire belched from out of sight.

It came from behind Typhon Elexor and a swatch of aliens toppled. Another belch of gunfire cut down half their number and the aliens whirled backward to face whoever was shooting at them.

A Skimmer dove through the crowd of survivors. Howitzers erupted from its flanks and carved a path to Fiddler and Lyons.

The Skimmer pivoted sideways and skidded next to Fiddler. "Get on!" Flack yelled.

Typhon Elexor raised their weapons again to gun her down, but at that moment, two more Howitzers unloaded from the hillsides surrounding the alien position.

Fiddler caught sight of two more tiny women dressed all in desert brown. They materialized on the hillsides above Typhon Elexor and fired their Howitzers down at the aliens.

Fiddler didn't wait to see any more. She scrambled onto the Skimmer behind Flack and motioned Lyons forward. "Come on!"

Lyons swung her leg over the seat behind Fiddler and Flack took off at eye-watering speed. She slalomed around the last remaining aliens and vanished into the winding canyons where no one would find her.

Chapter 10

Fiddler climbed off the Skimmer in the Armageddon Core's hidden cave. Lyons put her feet on the floor and collapsed in a breathless heap. "Let's not do that again, okay?"

"They won't stop looking for us," Fiddler replied. "We know their secret now."

Flack pulled off her goggles and mask. "What secret?"

"Typhon Elexor is working with the Reserve Wing," Fiddler replied. "That's why they came after us. That Stalwart must have picked us up when we were watching them have their little powwow."

"You aren't the only ones who know. Look."

The three women turned around to see Friend seated at her long desk. Dozens of computers blinked before her eyes. They fed her information all down the long table.

Fiddler walked up behind her and looked at what Friend was pointing at. One of the computers showed a video feed of Ultra Meridian. Friend was replaying the scene Fiddler and Lyons just witnessed.

Typhon Elexor came out of the hills to hobnob with the Reserve Wing. So now Friend had ironclad proof. Fiddler and Lyons were witnesses and now Friend had caught the conspirators on camera.

"We have to find the third component," Lyons remarked from behind Fiddler's back. "Do you know what happened to it after the *Blood Calliope* crashed here?"

Friend started to turn around to answer when more Skimmers whizzed into the cave. They were all brand new, state of the art, and heavily armed with Howitzers on their side fenders. The Armageddon Core started unloading their rocket launchers and XQs

"Where did you get those?" Fiddler asked. "We didn't have any Skimmers when I left."

"These?" Frost pretended to kick her Skimmer. "Someone must have left them lying around. We found them so we took them."

Fiddler furrowed her brow. "By 'lying around', do you mean some Reserve Wing officers parked them at Ultra Meridian and came back to find them gone?"

Frost, Flack, and fizzle shared a laugh. "It might have been something like that, but they should know better than to leave stuff lying around at Ultra Meridian."

"Davenport always kept this Skimmer parked behind the jail," Fiddler remarked. "You never tried to steal that."

"That's Davenport. He's different."

"Why is he different?" Lyons asked.

"Because he's the sheriff." Flack went over to one of the supply shelves and took down a boxed PureLife meal. She held it out to Lyons. "Are you hungry? Take this."

Lyons blinked at it and then her eyes shot upward to meet the much smaller woman's bright brown eyes. "Are you serious? You're.... just giving it to me?"

"Sure. You're our guest." Flack shoved it into Lyons's hands.

Fiddler had to smile at Lyons's reaction. Lyons probably hadn't had a PureLife meal in a long, long time—if ever.

Lyons went over to a crate against the wall, sat down, and just gazed at the box for a long time. She didn't move. She just admired the box.

When she finally tore open the wrapper, the magnificent smell of succulent pork cutlet, roasted vegetables, and cherry pie willed the cave.

Lyons pulled a fork out of the box, stuck it into a pile of mashed potatoes, and put it in her mouth. Her eyes drifted half-closed and she moaned in ecstasy. "Oh. My. God."

Fiddler and her friends laughed at her, but Lyons was already digging into the rest of the meal.

"Don't tell me you need a PureLife meal, too, Fiddler," Frost remarked.

"Naw. I don't need it. Save it for the diplomats."

The women laughed again and they turned to each other. "So what are you doing here?" Fizzle asked.

"We came back to find the third component. Can you help us, Friend? What can you tell us about the *Blood Calliope*? The third component came to Ultra Meridian on that ship and now it's gone, which means someone else has it."

Fiddler, Flack, and Frost went over to Friend's desk. She was running a rapid series of entries and readouts. "I'm bringing up the ship's history now, but I don't have video feed on what anybody did with it once it crashed.

"What about the ship's movements?" Fiddler asked. "Did any other ships go over there after it crashed."

"Sure. Plenty. There was plenty of scavenger activity around the wreck, too. A few groups went over to try to strip it for parts."

"Can you see which scavenger groups?" Fiddler asked.

Friend tapped on her computers for a while. Then she switched to long-range scans from the high-powered astronomical telescope at Macron Calypso, the next closest Confederate outpost.

"This is the best I can find."

"Holy shit!" Frost whispered. Look!"

She pointed at the screen and a whisper of tension went through the group.

"What's going on?" Lyons came up behind them still licking cherry pie filling off her fork.

"Mount Refractory," Fiddler murmured. "They rifled the *Blood Calliope* for the third component."

"They wouldn't come out this far if the payoff wasn't pretty steep," Fizzle added.

"How do we get it back from them when we don't even know what the component is?" Lyons asked. "We can't exactly go knocking on their doors and ask them."

"They might have already handed it over to the Reserve Wing," Flack countered. "If Typhon Elexor is working for the Reserve Wing, who's to say that Mount Refractory isn't doing the same thing?"

"Can you find out what the third component is, Friend?" Fiddler asked.

She shrugged. "As far as I can tell, we only know the third component exists because Ekol Thaine told Davenport about it. We don't even know if it *does* exist. He might have made it up."

"What about the radioactivity readings inside the *Blood Calliope*?"

"Those could have come from anything. The *Blood Calliope* could have been carrying something totally unrelated to the Ithium. We're banking a lot on Ekol's word. I don't think I'm ready to do that."

"What do you suggest?" Fizzle asked.

"Can you find out what it is?" Fiddler asked. "You know everything."

Friend made a face. "Hardly. There are a few things the third component could be. One of them is a circuit-breaking trigger mechanism, which I'm assuming is the chip

Emmett was carrying. I'm guessing the third component isn't another electronic trigger mechanism since we already know about that."

'Yeah?" Fiddler prompted.

"The only other thing I can guess for the third component is Zeprothil."

A tense silence fell over the group.

"Um.... what's Zeprothil?" Lyons asked.

"It's another toxic substance," Fiddler replied. "It's almost as dangerous as Ithium. If someone was to combine the two of them...."

"They would create a disaster twice as big," Frost remarked.

"Not quiet," Friends replied. "The Ithium and the Zeprothil would react with each other. The chip would trigger an explosion to scatter both substances far and wide, but Ithium and Zeprothil would exponentially enhance each other's toxicity and their explosivity. The explosion would be exponentially bigger and exponentially more deadly."

Frost gasped. "Why in the world would someone want to do all that? What can Admiral Joyce and his posse possibly hope to gain with this?"

Friend shrugged. "Maybe, once he has all three components and he has the explosion all rigged to blow, he can blackmail the rest of the Confederacy to do whatever he wants. He would have the whole Confederacy by the balls. He would be the most powerful person alive."

"Unless the explosion goes off," Flack pointed out. "If it blows, either accidentally or deliberately, he'll die along with the rest of us."

"Unless he has some way to protect himself," Fizzle remarked. "He might have some bunker somewhere...."

"Nothing would protect him from this," Friend replied. "He might be able to survive if he traveled to the farthest edge of Sacron Enigma. If he was all the way out there when the explosion went off, he wouldn't be able to communicate with whoever triggered the explosion. He also wouldn't be able to communicate his demands and instructions to the Reserve Wing. He would be so isolated that he would be effectively powerless....so it's all hypothetical."

"Either way," Fiddler replied, "He has to get all three components, and at this point, he doesn't have any of them."

"Let's keep it that way." Lyons stabbed a carrot and put it in her mouth. She groaned in bliss and rolled her eyes again. "This is divine. I could eat this every day."

"Well, you can't," Flack replied. "Enjoy it while it lasts."

"Oh, I am!" Lyons replied.

"We still have a disaster to avert," Fiddler pointed out. "If the third component is Zeprothil, that explains why we found traces of radioactivity on the *Blood Calliope*."

"It also makes it even more critical that we get the Zeprothil away from Mount Refractory." Flack replied. "They could be planning a disaster of their own with something like that."

"Are you sure the third component is Zeprothil, Friend?" Frost asked. "You couldn't have made a mistake?"

"I've been all over my databases ever since we found out about the third component. I've researched Ithium ..."

"What did you find?" Fizzle asked.

"I'm about to tell you. There are plenty of electronic devices like the chip that someone could use to set off the Ithium release. None of them enhances its toxicity or makes it more widely dispersed. Once it's released, it's still just Ithium."

"Just Ithium?" Frost snorted. "Isn't Ithium bad enough?"

"It looks like not," Friend went back to her computer. "We have another problem, too."

"I don't want any more problems," Fiddler remarked. "All problems are banned as of today."

"The same elements in the hills that we use to stop anyone from seeing our movements also stop us from checking whether the Zeprothil is inside Mount Refractory territory. There's only one way to find out if it's really there and that's...."

"Don't say it!" Flack countered. "Do NOT say those words."

"What?" Friend asked. "What was I going to say?"

"You were going to suggest that someone goes inside their territory."

Friend swiveled her chair around. "Listen to me. We just found out that Typhon Elexor is working with the Reserve Wing. Do you think it's an accident that the Reserve wing is making friends with all the criminal elements on this planet? It's only a matter of time before the Reserve Wing finds a way to work with Mount Refractory, too. Hell, Admiral Joyce might be greasing Mount Refractory's palms right now."

"Maybe there's a way to communicate with them and find out if they even have anything they took from the *Blood Calliope*."

"No way, Fiddler!" Flack yelled. "You aren't going near Mount Refractory territory!"

"There isn't," Friend remarked.

"What do you suggest we do, then?" Lyons asked. "If we can't talk to them and we can't go into their territory...."

"We have to find out if they even have the Zeprothil," Frost pointed out. "What's the point of getting our assess shot off if they don't even have it?"

"Which is why I suggested talking to them," Fiddler remarked.

"You can't," Friend repeated.

"Telling us we can't isn't going to get us there," Fiddler replied.

"So what is going to get us there?" Lyons asked.

Fiddler walked over to Friend's desk and pointed to the computers. "Contact Mount Refractory."

Friend crossed her arms and refused to turn away. "No."

"Do it now," Fiddler repeated in an undertone.

"What are you going to do, Fiddler/" Frost asked in a tiny voice.

"That's my business. Do it, Friend."

Friend glared at her. "You're putting all of us in danger with this."

"It's either us or the rest of the Confederacy. We've been doing this to protect the Confederacy. That's all I'm doing now."

"What are you talking about?" Lyons asked.

Fiddler pointed past Friend's shoulder again. "Do it, Friend."

Friend shook her head and swiveled her chair around so she presented her back to Fiddler. "You're going get us all killed."

She started tapping on her computers. She ran through several screens before one of them blipped.

Another alien appeared on the screen. It had a long proboscis, glassy black eyes, and multiple arms coming from each shoulder joint. Fiddler couldn't see the rest of it.

"What do you want?" it husked.

"I want to speak to someone in charge," Fiddler replied. "I want to negotiate a trade. You took something from the crashed ship *Blood Calliope*. The Reserve Wing is after it and we want to trade for it."

"You have nothing we want."

"I bet we do. Tell me you have the item and I'll offer you a fair swap."

"No, Fiddler!" Frost squeaked.

"We took many things from the *Blood Calliope*...." the alien murmured. "Electronic components.... food supplies.... trophies...."

"This was very small, very powerful, and very dangerous. It's a banned substance in the Confederacy...."

"Then we would not have taken it."

"I think you would have. Do we have a deal or not?"

"You have not offered your price yet," the alien countered. "We will not deal unless the offer price is as valuable as the item you seek."

"It is."

"What is it?" the alien asked.

Fiddler threw back her shoulders and looked down into the screen. "Me."

Chapter 11

 Frost screamed, but Fiddler didn't turn away from the computer screen.

She locked eyes on the alien and waited for the answer she knew she would get. "I'm the trade price. Hand over the item and you can have me."

"Very well," he rasped. "We will trade."

"I'll come over with one companion. You'll let us in and my companion will leave with the item. I'll stay behind and you can do what you want with me."

Someone sobbed behind Fiddler's back, but she didn't take her eyes off the alien. She didn't care anymore what Mount Refractory did to her. The Armageddon Core had to get the Zeprothil back at all costs. They had to make sure no one ever combined it with the Ithium.

"We agree to your terms," the alien replied and cut the line without another word.

Fiddler stared into the blank, black screen. Someone was crying openly behind her back and Fiddler let the reality sink. Did she just do that? Did she just agree to trade herself for the Zeprothil?

Just knowing what the third component was made the decision for her. She had to get it back. One person meant nothing weighed against billions of people living throughout the Confederacy.

Even if Joyce never triggered this disaster, he would still hold the whole Confederacy hostage with the threat that he might trigger it. That made the sacrifice worth it.

She finally turned around. Frost covered her face with her hands. Fizzle hugged her around the shoulders. Fizzle shot Fiddler a scared look and steered Frost away. That left Flack. She scowled at Fiddler, but Fiddler couldn't read her friend's expression.

Flack finally compressed her lips and walked away.

"What was that all about?" Lyons asked when they were alone. "Why are they so bent out of shape about this? Why are you so valuable that Mount Refractory would hand over the Zeprothil in exchange for you?"

"It's complicated." Fiddler pushed past her friend. "I'm going to get some sleep. I'll see you later."

Fiddler went down one of the long side passages and entered her own bedroom. She sat down on the bed. This was the first time she'd had a chance to relax in weeks.

The last time she spent any time in this room was before she attacked Davenport in the Ultra Meridian jail to free Emmett. Even the times when she hadn't been in active danger since then had been one long deadly nightmare.

She cringed when she saw a picture of Emmett on her nightstand. She turned it face down so she wouldn't see him looking at her. He would never approve if he knew what she was about to do, but she wasn't a baby anymore. She had to make her own decisions.

She stretched out on the bed, but when she stared up at the ceiling, she couldn't shut her eyes. A thousand worries and concerns plagued her mind. Where was Emmett right now? Was he even alive?

He would know she came back to the Armageddon Core. If he was alive, he would come back here to find her....so why wasn't he here yet?

If he was dead, that only confirmed that she was on her own. She had to take charge of her own life and the Armageddon Core. None of them could hide in this cave any longer, much as she might like to. They'd already been anonymous for too long.

She sat up and put her boots on the floor. The energy and anxiety that kept her going until now still spurred her to keep going and going and going. She couldn't stop now.

She went back out to the main cavern. Friend was back at work on her computers. Lyons was rummaging in the supplies on the Armageddon Core's many shelves. Was she looking for another PureLife Meal.... or something else?

Fiddler went over to her. "Do you want to stick around here for a while or do you want to get going?"

"What do you mean by 'get going'?'"

"I meant we should go to Mount Refractory."

Lyons's eyes popped. "You want *me* to go to Mount Refractory with you?'

"Of course. Didn't you know that?"

"No, I thought you would want to take someone with a lot more training—someone who knows what the hell this is all about."

"No, it has to be you.'

"Why?" Lyons asked.

"I can't tell you. It just does."

Lons frowned at her. "What's going on?"

"You already know that. I have to go over to Mount Refractory. I need someone to come with me, take the Zeprothil, and bring it back to the Armageddon Core."

Lyons frowned even more and then shrugged. "All right. I'll come."

"You have to. You're the only one who can."

Lyons didn't respond again. She didn't act curious anymore. "Okay. When do you want to leave?"

"As soon as possible—now if you're ready. It just depends on how ready you are."

"I'm ready."

"Are you sure? It could turn into another disaster."

Lyons grinned. "I'm certain it will. You don't think something might actually go right, do you?"

Fiddler nodded and turned away. "Let's arm up and get some supplies. I'll go talk to the others and then we can take one of the Skimmers at least as far as the Rungstea Gap."

Lyons raised her eyebrows again, but she didn't raise any objections. Now came the hard part.

Fiddler went back down the hall and found Flack, Frost, and Fizzle in Frost's room. Frost was still bawling her eyes out. Fizzle sat on the bed next to her hugging Frost around the shoulders. Flack stood off to one side with her hands in her pockets. She scowled at everyone as much as before.

"Lyons and I are going out to Mount Refractory now," Fiddler announced. "You three hold the fort here. Keep an eye out for Emmett. He'll be coming back here as soon as he can. I wouldn't mind betting the others come back here, too. See if you can help them."

"You aren't doing this, Fiddler!" Frost moaned. "You can't do this."

"I guess I can," she murmured. "I don't see that I really have a choice. I'm the only thing Mount Refractory wants more than whatever the Zeprothil is worth."

Fizzle shook her head and went back to looking at Frost. "This affects all of us."

"Don't you think I know that?" Fiddler blurted out and then compressed her lips to get herself under control. "Do you think I'm doing this because I want to?"

"As soon as they get you, everyone is going to know where we are. They'll come after us next."

"Do you have another idea?" Fiddler snapped. Her annoyance was getting the better of her now, probably because her nerves wouldn't settle down. She didn't want to do this. She could think of a thousand things she's rather do. She felt like she was on her way to the firing squad.

None of the others would look at her. Fiddler walked out of the room. There was nothing more to say. She wasn't even sure she could be a part of the Armageddon Core anymore or even if there was an Armageddon Core that she could be a part of.

She returned to the main cavern. Friend had her back to the room as usual. She didn't turn around to say goodbye to Fiddler—if Fiddler had said goodbye to the other three at all. She couldn't remember and it didn't matter anymore.

Only Lyons acknowledged that Fiddler was here. Only Lyons cared.

Something happened to Fiddler. Her old life died somewhere along the road. Did it happen when Fiddler decided to join Davenport? Did loyalty to Davenport and his mission replace Fiddler's loyalty to the Armageddon Core?

This wasn't even about Davenport anymore. It was just Fiddler and Lyons. They had become fused on their journey from HTWV-983 back to Ultra Meridian and finally to this cave. Fiddler had no one left to rely on.

She went over to the weapons crates that Lyons was going through. The two women armed themselves with XQs, sidearms, and backpacks full of food.

Lyons had a field day with the Armageddon Core's foot stores, but Fiddler's heart wasn't in it. She packed regular ration packs, ChunkyTenders, and almost nothing else. She just had to survive to get to Mount Refractory. Lyons would have to trek alone back to this cave.

Fiddler should organize the Armageddon Core to pick Lyons up. Fiddler should arrange for the Armageddon Core to get Lyons under cover as soon as possible after she took possession of the Zeprothil. That would be the safest way and the best for Lyons. Then no random attackers would come out to take the Zeprothil from her.

Fiddler couldn't bring herself to go talk to her friends again. They existed on the other side of some invisible barrier that kept her apart from them. She never noticed it until right now, but it had been there all along.

She loaded her gear onto one of the Skimmers. This would be a much quicker way to travel than hiking all the way to Mount Refractory.

Lyons started strapping her backpack to the rear seat.

"Why do the aliens of Mount Refractory look so similar to Typhon Elexor?" Lyons asked

"They're the same species."

"I realize that, genius," Lyons quipped. "Why are they against each other? Everyone knows Mount Refractory and Typhon Elexor hate each other. They've even been at war in the past, haven't they?"

"They both came from the same planet. They escaped a natural disaster of some kind. One ship, *Typhon Elexor*, crashed on that side of the planet. Another ship of the same species landed and set up shop to the south. They started out as friends and then conflicts broke out."

Lyons nodded. "Don't they always."

"Anyway, they've been enemies ever since."

"Maybe we'll get lucky and Mount Refractory won't be in touch with the Reserve wing.'

Fiddler pretended to adjust one of the straps on her pack. "They will be.

"What makes you say that?"

"If they aren't now, they will be as soon as I show up. Mount Refractory will contact the Reserve Wing that they found me…. which means you'll need to take the Zeprothil and make tracks right away. Get out of there and get lost in the wilderness as soon as you can. In fact…."

Fiddler went over to Friend's desk. Friend looked up, but Fiddler didn't speak to her. Fiddler took a small black box off the desk. It had a single large button in the middle.

She took it back to Lyons and handed it to her. "Push this button as soon as you get out of Mount Refractory's fortress. The Armageddon Core will come and get you. They'll bring you to safety. You'll need all the help you can get"

"Okay," Lyons pocketed the device and finished making last-minute adjustments.

Fiddler waited for the next question, but Lyons didn't ask it. Fiddler climbed onto the Skimmer and Lyons wrapped her arms around Fiddler's waist to hang on.

Fiddler cast one last look around the cave that had been her home for years. Friend still didn't turn around. None of the other three came out to see her off.

Did these four women ever mean anything to Fiddler? She couldn't have meant much to them if they let her go to her death without even saying goodbye to her first. Maybe she vastly overestimated their connection. Maybe it had never been anything more than a convenience that was now over.

She pulled on her mask and goggles, hit the throttle, and streaked out of the cave. She hurtled through the canyons chewing up the miles and her heart pounded faster. She was back on the hunt.

Chapter 12

Fiddler pulled the Skimmer into place behind the Rungstea Gap. She parked it in an out of the way place and started unpacking her gear.

Lyons squinted across the desert. "How far is it?"

"Mount Refractory's fortress is about twenty miles that way, but I can't guarantee we won't see them before that. They could send someone out for us."

Lyons nodded, checked her XQs, and put on her backpack. She was turning into a comrade Fiddler was grateful to travel with. Fiddler didn't have to question anything Lyons did. Lyons always put her goggles and mask on right away now. She was becoming a desert rat like the rest of the Armageddon Core.

Not that Lyons would ever be a member of the Armageddon Core, but Fiddler still liked her. Fiddler harbored a secret sense of relief that none of the Armageddon Core was here with her right now.

Fiddler adjusted her goggles and mask and the two women set off. They had a long way to walk and another hurricane of danger to look forward to once they got there.

Fiddler went in front as usual with Lyons behind. Lyons followed in silence and they trekked over miles of rugged terrain for the first half of the day. The sun blistered on the sand and Fiddler sweated under her mask, but she didn't stop.

Lyons drank plenty of water on the march. She even took out food to eat while she walked, but Fiddler didn't feel like it. She wanted to get this over with.

She pulled up at a lonely rock outcropping toward dusk. She found a place sheltered from the wind and took off her mask.

She nodded toward the horizon. "The fortress is over there. We'll climb down this trail to that plane over there. Mount Refractory will come out to confront us somewhere in the middle of it."

Lyons held out a flask of water and Fiddler finally took it. "Are you ever going to tell me what this is all about?"

Fiddler looked away. "I guess someday I might have to, but I don't want to talk about it now."

Lyons didn't say anything else. Fiddler didn't want to talk about anything, much less what Mount Refractory would do with her once they got her. Thinking about it only made her more nervous.

She couldn't sit still any longer and the sun was going down. She wanted to get inside the fortress before night came.

She set off with Lyons at her heels. Fiddler's nerves frayed to the breaking point as she neared the center of the plane. She scanned the way ahead for any sign of movement.

The sun dipped beneath the horizon and the wind kicked up. Sand scoured her goggles...and then she heard it. The whine of engines approached from across the plane.

It started as a dust cloud in the bigger dust cloud covering the whole landscape. She couldn't see anything until a crowd of Skimmers blasted out of the sandstorm.

They howled to a stop in front of the two women and masked aliens aimed their Howitzers at Fiddler and Lyons.

Fiddler raised her arms and Lyons did the same thing. Half the aliens held the pair at gunpoint and the other half rushed the two women. They yanked Fiddler's XQs away and then took her backpack.

The aliens worked fast and silently. They shoved the two women toward the Skimmers, loaded them behind two drivers, and streaked away into the gathering night.

Fiddler held onto her driver. This was it. She was going inside Mount Refractory's fortress. She wished she could stay there, but that would never happen.

The Skimmers whistled across the plane heading for a massive structure carved out of rock. Turrets overlooked the plane and millions of carved windows dotted the fortress's front wall.

The Skimmer drivers gunned their engines as they approached, shot off the ground, and dove through the windows.

Cool, silent darkness surrounded the vehicles and the drivers pulled their Skimmers to a halt in a stone room hardly big enough for the drivers to maneuver.

More aliens dragged the women out of their seats and started yanking them into a hallway leading somewhere else.

They marched Fiddler and Lyons a long way through winding passages ringing with many footsteps, but Fiddler didn't see any other people. All the drivers and guards who picked up the women stayed behind them where Fiddler couldn't see them. She didn't see the alien she negotiated this trade with, either.

The aliens thrust Fiddler and Lyons into another blank, stone room as bare and small as the first. The door slammed and silence fell.

Fiddler and Lyons exchanged glances. They were alone, and when Fiddler tried the door, she discovered as she expected to that they were locked in.

Lyons sat down on the floor and pulled a ChunkyTender from her pocket. "Good thing I foresaw this. Do you want some?"

She tore open the wrapper, broke the bar in half, bit into one piece, and held out the other half to Fiddler. Fiddler stared at the door for a second. What did this mean?

Maybe Mount Refractory had to figure something out before they handed over the Zeprothil.

An eternity of silence followed. No one came. Fiddler couldn't even hear anything beyond that door. She finally turned away, sat down next to Lyons, and sighed. "I guess we just wait."

Lyons handed her the half bar, and this time, Fiddler took it. "Did you ever think maybe Mount Refractory never had the Zeprothil in the first place?"

Fiddler's head snapped around so fast she made herself dizzy. She stared at Lyons in rising horror.

Fiddler never did consider that. She never once thought the alien on Friend's computer might not have been telling the truth about what Mount Refractory took from the *Blood Calliope*.

A sinking feeling of dread and doom plummeted into her stomach. Did she just make the worst mistake of her life?

"Don't worry," Lyons murmured. "Your friends on the outside still know where we are."

"You don't understand," Fiddler croaked. "They won't be able to come for us because we won't be here."

Now it was Lyons's turn to spin around. "What do you mean?"

Fiddler let her head fall into her hand. "I'm such an idiot!"

"What's wrong?"

"The Reserve Wing! They'll come for us—for me! They'll take me back to Helios Sanctus."

"Helios Sanctus!" Lyons hissed. "Are you out of your mind? That's the science station. Why would they take you back there?"

Fiddler shook her head, but she couldn't answer. She couldn't tell Lyons—not now. Why, oh why didn't Fiddler listen to her friends? Why didn't she see this coming? Why did she have to be so pig-headed about turning herself over to Mount Refractory?

"You better tell me everything," Lyons murmured. "I'm in this now, too. Whatever it is, I could be sacrificing my life for this. I have to know."

Fiddler groaned. She didn't want to talk about it, but Lyons was right.

Fiddler gulped to get her voice working. "Do you ever wonder why all five of us look so much alike? We're clones."

Lyons's jaw dropped. "You're......what?"

"At least the other four are. They're clones of me. I'm the original. The names we use.... they're all code names that the science team at Helios Sanctus came up with for us....to tell us apart."

Lyons gaped at her with her mouth open. Fiddler couldn't look at the expression of sheer stunned amazement on Lyons's face.

"My dad.... Emmett...." Fiddler choked down rising despair. "My mother died when I was a baby. He raised me alone. He worked as an engineer at Chiton's Hold and he had to leave me at the Confederate creche during the day while he was at work."

Lyons shut her mouth with a click, gulped, and finally managed to pull herself together. "So what happened?"

Fiddler shrugged. "I'm not exactly sure. Emmett thinks someone stole me from the creche. He thinks the Reserve Wing hired someone—a bounty hunter or a mercenary or something—to snatch some random child from the creche for the science team to experiment on."

Lyons blinked her big black eyes. She was back to staring at Fiddler like Fiddler had just grown another few heads, but Lyons at least managed to keep her mouth shut this time.

"I don't really remember much from the science station. I was too young. My earliest memories are of living in the lab with Frost, Flack, Fizzle, and Friend. We grew up together. We spent every day together and slept in the same room every night."

"How did Emmett find you?" Lyons asked.

"I have no idea. He won't talk about it and.... well, none of us have ever asked. I don't like to think about it. Anyway, he found out where we were—where I was. He broke into the lab to steal me away. His plan was to take me on the run where no one would ever find me. He got inside and realized the other four were there, so he decided to take all of us."

"So he stole you from the Reserve Wing?"

Fiddler nodded.

"Wow," Lyons breathed. "That's one hell of a story."

"The Reserve Wing sent out Daggers to hunt us down. They tracked us as far as Macron Calypso. Emmett realized it was only a matter of time before they caught up with us, so he took an emergency escape capsule on board at our last supply stop. We flew toward Sacron Enigma and deployed in the escape capsule while the ship continued on without us. The Daggers followed it into Sacron Enigma....and we stayed at Ultra Meridian."

Lyons threw the empty ChunkyTender wrapper on the floor, took another one from one of her pocket, tore it open, and split it in half to share with Fiddler. "Wow. I mean—damn."

Fiddler covered her face. "I'm such an idiot, Lyons. Don't ever let me think I'm smart ever again."

Lyons patted her on the shoulder. "We'll find a way out. You'll see."

"The others won't come. It's too risky that they'll get caught, too. You should leave. You should get out of here. You aren't part of this."

Lyons munched her ChunkyTender for a minute. "Let me ask you this. What experiments did the science team do on you?"

"Huh? I don't know. What difference does it make?"

"It must be something pretty important if they went to all this trouble to retake you.... or maybe they just want to stop anyone from finding out that they're snatching children from creches and running experiments on them in high-security Reserve Wing labs."

"Who cares what the experiments were?" Fiddler countered. "They'll take me back to Helios Sanctus. Even if they don't recapture the other four clones, they'll just clone me again and start over."

"That's what I'm saying. I guess I'm up to my eyeballs in this business now. If retaking you helps their plans, then I guess I have no choice but to stop them. I can't just walk away and leave you here. You might be something as dangerous as the Ithium."

Fiddler burst out in hysterical laughter. She couldn't help it. "I doubt that. I think I would know by now if I had any kind of unusual abilities or something. Emmett and my mother are as normal as any humans could be. Shit! You've seen Emmett. Do you honestly think I'm anything special?"

"Maybe you weren't as a baby, but the science team could have turned you into something special. Maybe they decided to make you into some kind of superweapon."

Fiddler snorted. "You're just making shit up."

Lyons chuckled. "You might be right."

The two women chewed their ChunkyTenders in silence for a while. Fiddler felt better, now that she finally spilled her guts to someone beyond her circle of friends. She had never told anyone before.

She started to realize how hungry she was. Two half ChunkyTenders didn't satisfy the hunger she'd been suppressing all day.

She pulled a few Universal Staples packs out of her own pockets and handed one to Lyons. Lyons made a sour face. "Sweet Jesus, not these again!"

"You're spoiled now that you've had a PureLife meal. Trust me. You'll be back on desert fare if you make it out of here alive."

"We ate nothing but these for almost six months on the *Echo Omicron*. I don't think I can look at another one." She passed it back to Fiddler. "Ask me again when I'm starving to death."

Fiddler had to laugh. She felt much lighter and more hopeful now. "I can't guarantee that I won't have eaten it myself by then."

"Go right ahead. I won't fight you for it."

The two women leaned back against the wall. The silence between them settled into a much more comfortable connection than Fiddler had ever experienced before.

She never had to explain anything to her four friends. They already knew everything. Was that the reason they stayed isolated at Ultra Meridian for so long?

Now someone else knew the truth. One person outside their little circle knew that Fiddler was more wanted, more dangerous, and more of a threat to the Reserve Wing than Davenport could ever be.

Fiddler suffered a pang of fear when she thought about Mount Refractory coming back to get her. They would take her away from Lyons—the one person who knew the truth and still wanted to sit next to her and share food with her. Fiddler would always be grateful to Lyons for that and she dreaded the moment when she and Lyons parted.

Chapter 13

F iddler elbowed Lyons awake. "Someone's coming."

Lyons sniffed, coughed, and shook her hair out of her eyes. Something rattled the door from outside, but neither woman moved from their place on the floor.

Fiddler already knew what to expect. This could only end one way.

The door swung open and a bunch of the Mount Refractory aliens aimed their XQs into the room. "Get up! You're coming with us."

Fiddler couldn't imagine what the aliens were expecting. They must have been waiting for Fiddler and Lyons to resist. The aliens didn't seem to understand how to cope with the women cooperating, standing up, and leaving the room without a struggle.

Fiddler checked their route for any chance at escape, but of course she didn't see one. She resigned herself to go back to Helios Sanctus.

She only regretted that she could no longer hide that her four friends were also at Ultra Meridian. Now the Reserve Wing would come back here to look for them, too. In time, the Reserve Wing would retake all five of them.

Emmett was still out there somewhere—assuming he was still alive. He would know where the Reserve Wing took her and now Lyons knew, too—assuming the Reserve Wing let Lyons walk away with her life.

Fiddler couldn't hope that Emmett or Lyons would come after her again. Fiddler wouldn't wish that kind of danger on anyone she cared about. Even trying to escape from Mount Refractory would only put Lyons in more danger.

Better for Fiddler to cooperate and go along with this. Better for Fiddler to leave the planet and hope that Mount Refractory and the Reserve Wing let Lyons go.

Fiddler didn't know what she would do if they didn't let Lyons go. What if they tried to kill Lyons—or succeeded in killing Lyons? What would Fiddler do then?

Her head spun in confusion. If the Reserve Wing killed Lyons, then Fiddler had no reason to cooperate. What if Lyons was right and the experiment the Reserve Wing did on Fiddler was as dangerous as the Ithium? Then Fiddler would be responsible for stopping that, wouldn't she? She would have to stay free.

She'd done so much and gone so far to help Davenport. She never thought at the time that staying free and keeping herself and her friends hidden might turn out to be even more important.

Admiral Joyce stole the Ithium from Helios Sanctus. Fiddler and her friends had been held at Helios Sanctus. That suggested this experiment was pretty important. Why did it take Lyons pointing it out before Fiddler made that connection?

The Mount Refractory aliens towed the two women into a room full of electronic equipment. They parked Fiddler in front of a control desk.

A middle-aged woman in a pristine Reserve Wing uniform looked back at Fiddler from the other end of the communications link. "Hello, Fiddler."

"Hello, Colonel," Fiddler murmured.

"Who is that?" Lyons asked.

One of the aliens shoved between Fiddler and the screen. "You've seen her. Now pay up."

"We'll pay when we take her on board. I'm sending out the *Nexus Terigon* to pick Fiddler up." The colonel's eyes sliced sideways toward Lyons. "What do you want to do with that one?"

"We'll get rid of her," the alien snarled. "She knows your secret now."

"No, we'll take her. I want to find out how much she knows."

"Are you going to pay for her, too?"

"Nice try, Krex," the colonel returned. "We're doing you a favor by taking her off your hands."

Krex snorted and started to turn away.

"What did you find out about the other four?" the colonel asked.

"Nothing," Krex returned. "The message was encrypted. We tracked it to Macron Calypso and then to Pandora's Needle. Its origin was masked."

"Never mind. We'll find them. We'll be there shortly."

The colonel cut the link and the aliens grabbed the two women again. Fiddler waited until they were back in the same room. "There you go," she told Lyons. "They're taking you to Helios Sanctus, too."

"That's good. Escaping from a Reserve Wing Stalwart will be easier than escaping from here."

"How do you figure?" Fiddler asked. "We'll be surrounded by armed soldiers and the Stalwarts usually travel with an escort of Daggers."

"Exactly," Lyons replied. "That means Daggers will be coming and going from the Stalwart all the time. Besides, the Stalwart will have to land to take us on board."

"I don't understand you."

"You need to think outside the box, girl. We can't let the Reserve Wing retake you and that means we have to escape."

Fiddler sighed and sat down on the ground. "I don't seem to be able to think about anything right now."

"Who was that colonel?"

"Colonel Lillian Casey. She ran the experiment that kidnapped me and cloned the others."

"Charming," Lyons sneered and started to sit down next to Fiddler again.

Lyons stuck her fingers into a different pocket. Fiddler watched to see what secret snack Lyons pulled out this time, but Lyons stopped when the door slammed open again.

"Let's go!" Krex barked. "The Stalwart is here."

"That was fast," Lyons remarked.

Fiddler didn't answer. Her chest tightened. This was it. If she was going to find a way out of here, she should do it now, but the aliens didn't give her a chance.

They headed down the same corridor as before, except that this time, they went in the opposite direction. The party passed several rooms and finally entered one stacked to the rafters with random junk.

Krex turned around to face Fiddler. "Well? Which item did you want from the *Blood Calliope*?"

Fiddler blinked. "Uh...what?"

"We made a deal—you in exchange for the item." He waved to the stuff. "We took all this from the *Blood Calliope*. Which is the item you wanted to trade for?"

"This?" Lyons surveyed the pile. "This is *everything* you took from the ship?"

"Of course."

"But I thought...." Fiddler began. "I thought you planned to hand me over to the Reserve Wing."

"We will. You traded yourself for the item. You're ours to do whatever we want. If we hand you over, you have nothing to complain about."

He walked over to the stack and kicked a crumpled metal bowl. A few empty ammunition cylinders rattled on the floor.

"We thought you were going to hand us over without giving us the item," Fiddler corrected.

"Mount Refractory has a reputation. Our word is still worth something. Take what you want and your friend will take the item.... wherever you want to go. She will have our safe passage and you will go the Reserve Wing.... unless *you* wish to break your word."

"We didn't understand when you put us in that room and you said you would hand her over to the Reserve Wing, too."

"We said we would get rid of her," Krex corrected.

"What will you tell Colonel Casey when she gets here and finds out that Lyons is gone?"

Krex shrugged. "We'll tell her your friend met with an unfortunate accident. The officer doesn't need to know what that accident was."

Lyons strolled around the pile studying everything in detail. "We're looking for.... something special......something with a radioactivity signature."

"Radioactivity! We never took anything like that."

"So you never took Zeprothil from the *Blood Calliope*?" Fiddler asked.

Krex glared at her and then curled his lip at the pile. "We would not take something like that even if we had found it."

"Then it's true." Fiddler meandered over to the pile. "The Zeprothil isn't here."

"No," Krex growled.

Fiddler didn't have to ask any more questions. He was doing this to fulfill his word of honor. If Mount Refractory had the Zeprothil—if the third component *was* Zeprothil—Krex would have said so. He would have traded it for Fiddler exactly the way he promised. He wouldn't go back on his word.

Lyons grabbed Fiddler's elbow and towed her across the room. They huddled in a corner and Lyons whispered low in her ear. "Listen to me. You have to go with the Reserve Wing."

"What happened to escaping?" Fiddler asked.

"Think about it. If you asked Krex to let you go, the Reserve Wing will know you're at Ultra Meridian. They'll follow you and they'll probably find out the other four are here, too. Going with them is the only way you can protect your friends."

Fiddler gulped. She didn't like this at all. Now she had no choice but to go with the Reserve Wing. She had handed herself over for nothing.

She rubbed her hands together. Her nerves were getting the better of her, now that she no longer had a choice but to go. She couldn't escape even if she could find a way.

Lyons walked back over to the pile and picked up what looked like the charred remains of four circuitry boards. A melted plastic junction plate connected them together. Some of the boards had melted across the space between the leaves. "I'll take these in exchange for Fiddler."

Krex snorted and waved Lyons away. "You may go. Our men will escort you back to the plane where we picked you up."

Lyons turned to Fiddler and their eyes met, maybe for the last time. Lyons didn't speak and Fiddler didn't think she could if she tried. Her throat hurt, now that she was losing her last remaining friend.

Lyons put her arms around Fiddler and hugged her. Fiddler felt herself starting to break down. She crushed Lyons close and buried her face in Lyons's hair. They'd only been alone together for a few days, but they seemed to have crossed several lifetimes since they left HTWV-983.

Lyons pushed Fiddler back and Fiddler's vision blurred. She almost couldn't stand it when Lyons kissed her on the cheek, murmured, "I'll see you soon," and walked out of the room without a backward glance.

Fiddler stared at the floor. She couldn't stand to face Krex knowing what was coming.

One of the other aliens nudged her. She turned to leave the room. They guided her somewhere, but she didn't keep track of where. What difference did it make now?

She was going back to the Reserve Wing, back to Helios Sanctus, back to the lab. She wouldn't have her friends when she got there. She would be alone.

A gust of stinging wind hit her in the face and she squinted into sunshine. She was outside and a giant Reserve Wing Stalwart descended outside the Mount Refractory fortress. She didn't need to see its identity signature to know it was the *Nexus Terigon*, Colonel Lillian Casey's ship.

Fiddler drew in a shaky breath and hardened her resolve to do what had to be done. At least Lyons was getting away.

Fiddler couldn't even be certain that doing this would protect her four friends. Colonel Casey would assume they were at Ultra Meridian. Even if she wondered if the four clones got away to some other planet, Colonel Casey would search here first.

Pelting dust and sand blocked Fiddler's view of the Stalwart. The aliens shoved her forward. She shielded her face against the weather and let them guide her. She didn't need to see where she was going.

Two aliens took hold of her arms to steer her toward the big ship's rear hatch ramp. Body shapes moved around in the dust cloud. They were coming from the Stalwart, so they must be Reserve Wing soldiers. Was one of them Colonel Casey?

The Reserve Wing would be a lot more careful about keeping Fiddler under lock and key. They wouldn't let their guard down even for a second. They would make it impossible for anyone to rescue Fiddler a second time.

She got to the foot of the ramp and opened her eyes to look inside. A howl of engine noise overhead startled her. She looked up and saw half a dozen Daggers revolving over the Stalwart to guard it. The Reserve Wing was really taking this mission seriously.

More Reserve Wing personnel appeared from the cargo hold where Colonel Casey stood with another officer with captain's bars on his collar.

He nodded and a bunch of armed Reserve Wing soldiers swarmed to the ground. They surrounded Fiddler in guns as though she really planned to fight her way out of here.

The aliens from Mount Refractory backed off and retreated into the sandstorm. It was over. They fulfilled their side of the bargain. No one could accuse them of breaking their word.

The soldiers tugged Fiddler up the ramp. A self-satisfied smile spread over Colonel Casey's lips. Fiddler just could not wait for the moment when Colonel Casey got to crow over her prize.

Fiddler started up the ramp with a heavy heart when an ear-splitting explosion went off somewhere. Fiddler ignored it at first and then another two blasts echoed across the landscape.

The soldiers reacted first. They shouldered their XQs and pivoted backward to aim at the fortress, but the aliens were already out of sight in the driving wind.

Another crack burst directly over Fiddler's head and everyone looked up to see two Daggers blowing into fireballs. Only one remained....no, two remained.

A single Dagger streaked across the landscape to avoid the second ship's defensive fire. The first craft whipped around the *Nexus Terigon* and came screaming in for another pass.

Both Daggers opened fire on each other. The soldiers, Fiddler, the captain, and Colonel Casey all stared at a Reserve Wing Dagger turning on one of its own.

They traded shots, but the second vessel held its ground as the attacker throttled in a death rush. It hurtled straight in to collide with its adversary.

The second Dagger tried to dodge and veered straight into the attacker's guns. The ship detonated and the captain jumped. "Return fire! Arm all guns! Get that...."

A ground-shaking barrage of Howitzer fire spat from the one remaining Dagger as the ship spun around to target the *Nexus Terigon*. The shots gnawed through the sand getting closer to the ramp.

Colonel Casey darted to the ground and tried to grab Fiddler, but a vicious blast cut her off. Howitzer fire pounded down the ramp and flattened a dozen soldiers in one pass.

Fiddler tried to charge up the ramp to get under cover, but another strike knocked her back. She stumbled and lost her balance.

She somersaulted to the ground and a stinging bite of sand blinded her for a second. Shots pounded the Stalwart with deafening booms and one of the engines exploded.

More Daggers zoomed all over the place. They whizzed close to the ground and threw up so much dust and sand that Fiddler couldn't see a thing.

Explosions and gunfire surrounded her in so much confusion that she didn't even know where she was anymore. She turned right and left trying to find somewhere to get away when someone grabbed her.

A man's voice yelled in her ear, but she couldn't hear it very well over the noise. Strong hands dragged her forward. She had to keep her eyes shut to protect them from the sand.

Her foot touched solid metal and a hatch slammed behind her. She blinked the sand out of her eyes and froze when she saw the person in front of her. "Dad!"

Chapter 14

E mmett smiled at Fiddler once and then spun away. "You might want to strap in, sweetheart. We got a situation on our hands."

He dashed to the Dagger's cockpit, jumped into the pilot's seat, and seized the helm. Fiddler sat next to him and blinked in amazement at the crowd of Daggers sprinting back and forth above the *Nexus Terigon*.

The Stalwart's port engine had completely burned out. A large black scorch mark darkened the sand on that side, but the wind and sand were rapidly erasing it.

At least ten more Daggers rocketed back and forth all over the place. They spat shots at each other, turned somersaults around each other, and ganged up to destroy each other.

"What's going on?" Fiddler yelled over the noise.

"Man the guns!" Emmett hollered back. "I got enough to do flying this thing!"

"What did you do, Emmett?" Fiddler roared. "Did you attack a Reserve Wing Stalwart? Do you have a death wish?"

"I didn't! Are you crazy? It was Davenport!"

She actually forgot about the battle for a second. She turned and stared at her father in numb, mute shock. Davenport? He did this?

A brutal smash plastered the ship right next to her head. She turned back to the battle and all thought of Davenport went out of her mind.

She couldn't tell at first which Daggers she should be targeting, but it quickly became obvious that Emmett and two others were laying into the other seven.

The other two attackers flew in much more confused patterns that distracted and confounded those pilots that obviously belonged to the Reserve Wing. The attackers destroyed two more Reserve Wing ships. That carved the enemy down to five.

"Who the hell is that?" Fiddler asked.

"Beauty and Davenport! Shoot, girl!"

Emmett ripped the ship into the air and plowed into the mayhem. Fiddler brought her cradle around and coordinated with…. someone. She didn't know who was who, but it didn't really matter as long as she hit the right Dagger.

Emmett veered hard from port and Fiddler opened fire on a Reserve Wing Dagger. The pilot rounded on Emmett and another attacker struck from behind. The enemy exploded and Emmett flew straight through the fire to target someone else.

The battle became so frenzied that Fiddler had trouble acquiring a target. She took a second to look around when an even more crushing shot streaked from the ground. The *Nexus Terigon* was firing on her and Emmett.

She clenched her teeth and turned her guns on the Stalwart. She blew out the other engine and then targeted the bridge. She lost sight of the ship when Emmett wheeled to confront another enemy Dagger.

Both of the other attackers plunged in at the same time. Their victim couldn't target all three Daggers pounding the hapless ship in unison. There were three Reserve Wing Daggers left. It was three against three.

Emmett cut a tight curve through the middle of the battle. He and the other two pilots didn't have to communicate. They were all thinking the same thing.

They turned outward, each one targeting a different enemy. The three attackers blasted outward from the center driving the Reserve Wing pilots away from the *Nexus Terigon*.

Fiddler vented all her anger on this one Dagger. It represented everything the Reserve Wing ever took from her and she smashed it to pieces with all her firepower.

"Die, you cocksuckers!" a familiar voice yelled through the communications link.

Fiddler froze. "Davenport?"

"You okay, girl?" he asked.

"I am now. Where did you get these Daggers?"

"We stole them. Help me out, Emmett!"

"I'm coming, buddy." Emmett turned the ship back to the center. Beauty was just finishing off his victim, but Davenport got pinned down.

Two Nitrols descended from the atmosphere and both flanked Davenport's Dagger. His would-be victim joined in to blast him to kingdom come.

"No, you don't!" Emmett snarled. He put on speed and Beauty came over to help.

The three defenders plunged back into a wild shooting spree. Fiddler and Beauty stalked the Nitrols from behind. The enemy tried to turn around and a random shot from Davenport struck the first Nitrol.

It hovered there hesitating and Emmett swerved for the last remaining enemy Dagger. Fiddler read his mind a split second later and laid into the ship while it was still hammering Davenport.

The Dagger burst and Davenport's guns smashed the first Nitrol to smithereens. It exploded and then all three friends unloaded on the last remaining Nitrol.

"Whooo!" Davenport hooted. "You can take that to the bank!"

"The *Nexus Terigon* is powering up again!" Emmett told him. "Let's get out of here."

"Where's Lyons?" Davenport asked.

"You know about Lyons?" Fiddler asked.

"We stopped by the Armageddon Core and they told us you were here."

Fiddler didn't ask any of the many questions crowding her brain. How did these three steal Reserve Wing Daggers to come after her? Lyons couldn't have gotten away that quickly. It would take her hours to walk across the plane to where Fiddler left their Skimmer.

Davenport pulled away from the fortress and Emmett and Beauty fell in behind him. They covered the miles much more quickly until they spotted Lyons in the distance.

Davenport descended to pick her up while Emmett, Fiddler, and Beauty stood guard overhead. "Do I get to find out what's going on now?" Fiddler asked Emmett.

"It would take too long. We'll talk when we get back to the cave, but even then, we might not have time. We need to...."

"I got her on board!" Davenport reported. "Let's beat it, folks."

The three Daggers streaked to the Rungstea Gap and started to descend. "What are you doing?" Fiddler asked. "We can get there a lot faster if we fly."

"The Reserve Wing will just look out for three stolen Daggers. We have to take the Skimmers."

"Skimmers—plural?"

Emmett only grinned at her. That was another question she would just have to wait to get answered.

The three Daggers landed outside the gap. Three more Skimmers waited there and Fiddler recognized them now. They belonged to the Armageddon Core.

Emmett handed Fiddler a mask and a pair of goggles. They abandoned the three Daggers and Davenport climbed onto the first Skimmer. "It isn't the Beast, but who cares?"

Emmett took the second one and Beauty climbed on behind Davenport. "Am I going with you, Dad?" Fiddler asked.

"Don't you dare!" Lyons countered. "I am NOT riding with him."

"You better take that one, sweetie. You don't want to explain to Flack why you didn't bring her Skimmer back." Emmett revved the engine. Davenport was already pulling his Skimmer away with Beauty hanging on around his waist.

That left Fiddler with not many options. She sure as hell didn't want to explain why she didn't bring the Skimmer back. She was already expecting the third degree from her friends on why she thought it would be a good idea to turn herself over to the Reserve Wing.

Davenport rocketed away with Emmett right behind him. Lyons climbed onto the seat and glued her body to Fiddler's back. A streak of wild excitement took hold of Fiddler. She was free! She was going back to the Armageddon Core. They would work out the details later.

The five of them and Emmett had stayed free for almost fifteen years. They could keep doing it. They could always move to another hiding place if Ultra Meridian got too busy with the Reserve Wing hunting for them.

She covered the distance in no time. Beauty was already squatting next to a crate of cocoa-bears and tearing into the wrappers by the time Fiddler and Lyons returned to the cave.

Lyons nearly fell over leaping off the Skimmer. "Holy shit! Dice!"

She staggered over to a stretcher in the corner. Dice tried to sit up when she fell on her knees next to him, but he collapsed with a groan. "I told Davenport not to bring me back." He gulped, shut his eyes, and turned his face away from her. "I'm no good to you like this."

"What's wrong with him?" Fiddler peered over Lyons's shoulder. Dice looked perfectly normal except that he was flat on his back and couldn't even sit up.

"He's been poisoned with truth serum," Davenport replied.

"Truth serum is toxic to Adiks," Friend called from her desk. She hadn't turned around since Fiddler arrived.

"Can you find any antidote?" Davenport asked.

"I'm working on it now."

"Admiral Joyce must not have known," Emmett remarked.

Fiddler gasped. "Joyce did this?"

"Oh, he knew all about it," Friend told him. "Reserve Wing records show he looked up the effects when he had Dice in the Rambler's prison hold the first time Joyce captured him. Joyce was considering using the truth serum to neutralize Dice, but Dice went ballistic before the Reserve Wing could get to him. They were trying to administer the serum when he flipped out."

"That son of a bitch!" Davenport hissed. "We have to find an antidote. We have to bring Dice back."

"Just end it," Dice quavered. "I can't stand this."

Lyons stretched out her hand to touch him, but he had enough strength to jolt away from her hand. He kept his head turned to the wall so no one could see his face.

Fiddler's heart twisted. She ached to do something for Dice, but if Friend couldn't find an antidote, maybe none existed.

Fiddler rested her hand on Lyons's shoulder instead. Fiddler didn't understand the complicated relationship between those two. She didn't need to.

Dice's condition sure hit Lyons hard and that was nothing compared to the way he was acting.

Davenport came over, squatted down next to Dice's feet, and squeezed Dice's ankle. "No one is ending anything, pal. We went to a lot of trouble to bring you back here and we'll find a way to get your strength back, too. Don't you worry about that."

Dice didn't answer. He didn't pull away from Davenport, either. "I don't deserve to be here," Dice growled. "I told. I told Joyce where the Ithium was."

"You didn't," Davenport insisted. "I keep telling you that. The Ithium wasn't there. Someone else must have moved it."

Lyons stiffened under Fiddler's hand. Lyons glanced up at the same moment that Fiddler glanced down at Lyons.

Without warning, Lyons tore away from Fiddler's hand. Lyons shot to her feet and bolted out of the cave.

Fiddler watched her go. She wanted to go after Lyons, but Beauty's voice stopped her. "Leave her alone. She'll be back in a second."

Davenport went over to Friend. "What can you find?"

"It's complicated. There's plenty of records of people using truth serum to subdue Adiks and stop them from going berserk. There aren't as many reports of…. Hold it. Here it is. I found it."

"Let me guess," Dice muttered. "It's somewhere far away and really dangerous to get to. Of course it is. It sure as hell isn't here."

Davenport laughed. It didn't sound right in this miserable situation. Fiddler glanced around the cave. "Where are the others?"

"They went out to check some of our video feeds," Friend replied. "We need to keep a closer eye on things in case the Reserve Wing comes after us."

Fiddler cringed. Of course the Reserve Wing would come after the Armageddon Core. They could blame her for that.

"Mount Refractory didn't have the Zeprothil," she told Friend. "They ransacked the *Blood Calliope*, but the Zeprothil was already gone by then."

"The what?" Davenport asked.

"Zeprothil," Fiddler replied. "It's a toxic...."

"I know what it is. Why are you looking for that? Don't we have enough on our plates with the Reserve Wing hunting for the Ithium?"

"Friend thinks the third component is Zeprothil. She thinks Joyce wants to combine it with the Ithium to make it.... well, even worse than the Ithium alone."

Davenport's hand flew to his head. "Jesus! It can't be!"

"I found the antidote," Friend announced.

Chapter 15

Davenport and Fiddler went over to Friend's desk. "You found the antidote? What is it?"

Friend pointed to a chart of a planet on one of her screens. "It's called *Shulliochet Hublyx.*"

Dice groaned at the word.

"What is it?" Emmett asked.

"If you let me finish, I might be able to tell you. It's an organic extract found on Theitania. That's the planet the Adiks are native to."

"Just forget it!" Dice growled. "You aren't going back there. It's halfway across the Zuzuk Kanz Stream. Just put me out of my misery now."

"The extract is an unstable combination of certain minerals found only on that planet. They get distilled in plant saps—also of plants found only on that planet."

"How the hell are we supposed to get that?" Fiddler asked.

"Don't," Dice grumbled. "Just forget it."

"Will you shut up with that shit!" Davenport snapped. "You aren't helping at all."

Dice turned to the wall again.

"Pollinators spread the extract to other plants and native animals feed on the plant," Friend went on. "The extract makes its way into virtually every other plant and animal on the planet. Adiks eat these plants and animals. It's what gives them their strength....and it's also the substance that causes them to grow when they go berserk."

"That doesn't help us get it," Davenport pointed out. "Dice is right. If we cross the Zuzuk Kanz Stream, we might as well never come back."

"You don't have to. There's a supply of the extract right here in the Confederacy. The only problem is...." Friend turned away from her computers for the first time. "It's probably even harder to get than going back to the planet."

"Where is it?" Emmett asked. "How can it be harder than crossing the Zuzuk Kanz Stream and going down on a planet populated by Adiks?"

"Just give it to us straight, Friend," Davenport added. "Where is this supply?"

Friend studied him for a second and then turned to look straight at Fiddler. "It's at Helios Sanctus."

Fiddler froze and Emmett gasped. Those words sent a chill up Fiddler's spine. Helios Sanctus. She didn't want to go there—ever.

She still hadn't let herself fully believe she was going there, not even when she stood at the base of the *Nexus Terigon's* hatch ramp about to board the Stalwart to fly there.

"There has to be another way," Davenport murmured.

Friend shrugged. "I'm running a few crawlers trying to find another supply of the extract, but I don't hold out much hope. The Reserve Wing has been experimenting on Adiks for years. The science station is the nearest supply, and even if there was another supply, it would be just as hard to access."

Fiddler cast a desperate look around. If going back to Helios Sanctus was the only way to heal Dice......, would she really go through with that? Was helping Dice really worth sacrificing herself and maybe putting the whole Confederacy in danger?

Her gaze inevitably drifted to Davenport. He stared at her hard and she gulped again. What would he say? Would she be able to say no if he insisted?

She almost collapsed in relief when he murmured. "You are NOT going back there. I don't care what it takes."

"No way," Dice growled from his corner. "No way in hell."

A rustling of plastic interrupted their conversation. Beauty upended the carton he'd been rifling through. A pile of empty, crumpled wrappers fell onto the floor along with a shower of crumbs.

He shook out the crate, and when nothing else came out, he tossed it aside and started tearing into the next one. No one paid any attention when he carried the crate to Dice's stretcher, set it down, and started pulling things out.

Davenport paced around the cave studying everyone in that flinty way of his. "First of all, we have to think about moving you girls to a safer location."

Fiddler gasped again. "You know about that?"

"Your friends told me when they explained why you handed yourself over to Mount Refractory."

"What about you, Davenport?" Emmett asked. "You're in danger, too."

"Well, if we're all going on the run, we might as well all go together."

"That means we need some kind of spacecraft to get off the planet."

"What about using ourselves as bait to get a spacecraft to land here?" All eyes turned to Dice. This was the most he'd said since Fiddler and Lyons returned to the cave. "The Reserve Wing is already after all of us. They're bound to land here looking for us. I say we mount a strike, steal their ship, and away we go."

Fiddler turned around. Dice had propped himself up on his elbow and was facing them all now.

Beauty had been holding out something to Dice and, in full view of everyone, Dice tipped up the package, dumped something into his mouth, and started chewing.

He tossed the empty wrapper onto the growing stack of Beauty's discarded trash. Dice ran his wrist across his mouth, sat up, and finally pushed himself to his feet. Beauty had to scoot out of his way.

Dice straightened up, dusted his hands on his pants, and looked around. He blinked and then held out his hand to Beauty. "Got any more of those?"

Beauty gave him a beaming smile and handed him three more packages. Dice downed them all, sighed, and headed over to the supply shelves. He pulled back the cover on a different crate and looked inside. "We'll need weapons for that."

"Dice?" Davenport asked. "Are you okay?"

"I feel fine. What's the big deal?"

Davenport, Emmett, and Fiddler looked back and forth between Dice and Beauty. Beauty smiled at everyone like he had just opened an enormous pile of birthday presents. Then he dove head and shoulders into the crate, rustled around inside, and came out holding an untouched, unopened box of GoGo Yogurt Bombs.

"What did you give him, Beauty?" Fiddler choked. "He's fine now."

"Sure" Beauty rotated the Yogurt Bombs box in front of him and smirked when he located the seal. "I gave him some Maltese Chipmunks. They're known to trigger Adik rampages. I figured it couldn't hurt."

"It can't be as simple as that," Emmett muttered.

"So the question is how we capture this ship." Dice turned to Friend. "Where do you keep your weapons?"

She eyed him suspiciously. "I don't think I want to tell you."

Just then, engines whined outside and two Skimmers whizzed into the cave. Flack, Frost, and Fizzle climbed down and pulled off their masks. "The Reserve Wing is all over the place at Ultra Meridian. They're setting up shop at the jail and it looks like they're getting ready to send out search parties."

"Which ships are they?" Fiddler asked.

Friend turned back to her computers. "The *Nexus Terigon* is still in Mount Refractory territory. Stalwarts *Pioneer, Remorseless....and Rambler....*"

"Great," Davenport snorted.

Lyons strolled into the cave, took a look around, saw Dice, and went over to Beauty's carton before she realized that Dice was back to normal.

Lyons spun around fast and her black hair whipped her face. "Dice!" She launched herself at him, threw her arms around his big chest, and hugged him in front of everyone.

He laughed his normal booming laugh and patted her on the back. "I'm okay. Don't make such a fuss."

She held him at arm's length and beamed up at him while she blinked back tears. "I was so worried about you."

He laughed again. "Well, you can stop. Now we just have to convince these girls to give us some weapons."

Davenport turned back to Friend. "Is there anything on the records about Colonel Casey and Admiral Joyce working together?"

"Nothing yet and none of the Stalwarts has rendezvoused with the *Nexus Terigon* to pick her up, either. It looks like this is Joyce's show."

"Are we going or what?" Dice boomed. "If they're on the ground at Ultra Meridian, we won't get a better chance to ambush them."

"I don't think stealing a Reserve Wing Stalwart is necessarily the best option," Flack observed. "It would only make us easier to track down."

"What's the alternative—wait here for them to find us?" Fiddler asked.

"Of course not, but there has to be some more subtle way of getting off this planet—some way that doesn't alert the Reserve Wing that we have left the planet. It would work better if they kept searching here while we slipped away unnoticed."

"How do we do that without a ship?" Lyons asked.

"Mount Refractory and Typhon Elexor both have ships," Davenport pointed out.

"You want to steal a ship from Mount Refractory or Typhon Elexor?" Emmett snorted. "Now I know you're crazy—not that I ever wondered before."

"I'm not saying we have to steal it. We could trade for it."

"No!" Fiddler snapped. "Don't even think about using me like that again."

"I wasn't about to," Davenport replied. "We have something else they want—something they want a lot more than they ever wanted you."

"What?" everyone asked.

"Me."

Everyone stared at him and Fiddler's guts twisted. Davenport had been Sheriff of Ultra Meridian for seven years. He must have done a lot of things to piss off Mount Refractory and Typhon Elexor in his time.

Then again, he couldn't have survived this long if he didn't know how to keep out of their way. If he ever did anything to piss them off, he would have vanished into the desert a long time ago. They would have made sure of it.

That was one of the main reasons the Sheriff's Service had such a hard time finding sheriffs to man this outpost. It was beyond dangerous even though it was so far out of the way and got so little traffic.

The traffic Ultra Meridian did get was almost entirely criminal. Any sheriff with the balls to man this outpost was probably the only law-abiding person on the entire planet. Every man and his dog was out to slit the sheriff's throat.

"What are you going to do?" Dice growled.

Davenport shrugged. "I know where a few of the bodies are buried. I think I can get Mount Refractory to give me a ship."

"You can't do that, Davenport," Fiddler insisted. "If you crossed Mount Refractory, you would never be able to come back to Ultra Meridian. You would never be able to work here as a sheriff again."

He smiled sadly. "It doesn't look like I'll ever be able to come back to work here as a sheriff anyway. If it means getting you girls off the planet, it will be worth it."

"I don't like this," Flack remarked. "There has to be a better way."

"There is," Lyons added. "Dice, Beauty, and I can steal a ship from Mount Refractory.... or from Typhon Elexor.... or whoever it is. None of us wants to come back to Ultra Meridian when this is all over. Trust me."

"You would do that?" Fizzle breathed. "You'd be earning yourselves a death sentence from whichever syndicate you stole it from."

Lyons shrugged. "That's nothing new to us. We're already wanted by just about everyone."

"Besides," Dice added, "neither Typhon Elexor nor Mount Refractory even know we exist yet. It would take them some time to figure out who stole it."

"I don't like this, either," Davenport rejoined.

"You don't want us stealing your thunder." Lyons turned to Flack. "Where do you keep your weapons?"

"Hold it right there, lady," Davenport cut in. "You said you were going to steal it. No one said anything about blasting your way in with guns blazing."

She grinned and bumped Dice's shoulder. "These chumps don't want us showing them up. They don't want to see three badasses pull off the heist of the century and then come back to rescue them from this backwater planet."

"Now just hold it right there, you foul little...." Flack began.

"That won't work, Lyons," Davenport interrupted. "We're supposed to be doing this by stealth. That's the whole point. If you get Mount Refractory on your ass following you away from their fortress—assuming you make it out alive with the ship intact—you'd alert the Reserve Wing that you're taking us off the planet. Our whole cover would be blown."

Frost finally raised her hand. She hadn't spoken until now. "Um...excuse me, but we already have three Daggers waiting for us at the Rungstea Gap. All we have to do is go back and get them."

Everyone blinked at her and then looked at each other. "Damn it," Dice muttered under his breath. "I was looking forward to shooting something."

"You can shoot all you want once we get away from this planet," Davenport told him. "My guess is we won't have any shortage of things to shoot at."

Chapter 16

Dice hefted a massive XQ85 out of a crate in one of the Armageddon Core's many supply rooms. "Now that's what I'm talking about! It really makes the 65 feel dinky."

"Just make sure you aim it in a safe direction." Fiddler went over to a crate of choke shells and started stashing them in her pockets. "Someone should probably go tell Friend that she has to come with us. I don't think she's gotten the memo that she has to leave her desk to get off the planet."

The other four members of the Armageddon Core exchanged glances. "You go, Fiddler. You tell her."

"Not me. You go, Fizzle. Friend likes you best."

"Who says she likes me best?" Fizzle protested. "You go, Emmett. She'll listen to you."

"Like hell she will," Emmett countered. "She hates me."

"She does not," Frost returned. "You've always been like a father to all of us."

He smiled and put his arm around her shoulder. "It's an honor to hear you say that, darling."

"Don't worry about Friend," Davenport chimed in. "I'll go talk to her."

"Thanks, Davenport," Fiddler replied. "You're a prince."

"Yeah. The Prince of Darkness."

Davenport left the room to chuckles and snorts behind him. He went back into the main cavern. He wasn't looking forward to leaving, either, so he thought he knew what to expect when it came to prying Friend away from her screens.

He got a surprise when he found her poring over a layout of Helios Sanctus. "What are you doing?" he asked.

She didn't turn around or even look up from her work. "Research."

"What are you researching Helios Sanctus for?"

"We were just kids when we were in the lab the last time. We were only about five or six when Emmett stole us from the Reserve Wing. The lab was all we knew. None of us ever left it. We knew nothing about the station's layout, its resources, or anything else. Things are different now."

He studied her on the side. "You aren't going back there, you know. You won't have to escape from there. We'll get you far away from the Reserve Wing, even if it means leaving the Confederacy."

"Anything is possible. You aren't exactly a pillar of the law anymore yourself, Davenport."

He winced. "You might be right about that."

"If I've learned anything in my life, it's that things can always go wrong. You can do everything you can to help us and I'm grateful, but we could still wind up there.... or someone else could. We might need this information someday."

She bent down and removed four interconnected circuitry boards from one of the many component stacks under her desk. A junction plate attached them together so she could remove them as one combined piece.

"What are you doing with that?" he asked.

"I'm copying all this information onto these cards so we can take it with us. I might have to leave my computers, but I won't go emptyhanded." She climbed off her chair, put the boards in her pocket, and faced Davenport. "I'm ready to go now."

This was the first time Davenport had ever dealt with Friend standing up. She barely came up to his chest and he realized as if for the first time that he was looking at an exact copy of Fiddler.

These girls had distinguished themselves as unique personalities in the short time since Davenport met them. He had come to realize just how different they were. He hardly saw their physical similarities anymore.

Friend looked so much sturdier and more resilient, now that she was walking around, arming herself, and doing all the same things the rest of the Armageddon Core was doing. She became a tough survivor like the rest. She was good for more than just sitting at a desk.

The others assembled in the main cave. "We probably shouldn't take Skimmers," Lyons remarked. "That will only make us easier to spot."

"Walking to the Rungstea Gap is going to take time," Flack pointed out.

"It beats getting caught," Fiddler pointed out. "We can hide in the desert."

An alarm went off on one of the Friend's computers. She raced over to her desk. "We got Skimmers incoming! They're heading straight for us!"

"Split up!" Davenport ordered. "*Echo Omicron* crew—you head south. Armageddon Core—you head west and cut south once you know you've lost them." He slung his leg over one of the Skimmers and pointed to the other. "You come with me, Emmett. We'll create a diversion and slow the Skimmers down."

Lyons, Dice, and Beauty marched out of the cave and vanished into the hills. The Armageddon Core pulled on their masks, watched from the entrance to make sure the *Echo Omicron* crew got away, and then the five girls disappeared into the desert, too.

Davenport fired up his Skimmer and blasted out of the cave with Emmett hot on his tail. The two men veered into the canyons around the Armageddon Cores' hideout.

Davenport didn't have to go very far before he found the Reserve Wing Skimmers barreling in at top speed. He turned into a steep defile and nearly collided with three of them coming the other way.

He fired his Howitzers and one of the enemy screamed off to crash into the hillside. That definitely got their attention.

He swerved hard to left and right to avoid smashing into the others. They whipped around to follow him and he gunned the throttle to put separate himself from their guns.

He cut sharp turns into one canyon after another. He didn't care where he went as long as he kept heading east—away from the two crews making their escape. He was prepared to keep this up for days if it meant both crews could escape unnoticed in the stolen Daggers.

The Reserve Wing Skimmers must have been juiced up recently because they gained on him easily. Howitzer fire pinged off his vehicle no matter how much he tried to dodge it.

He skidded around another corner and almost had a heart attack when he spotted Emmett racing straight toward him. They were on a collision course.

Davenport ripped back the handlebars and vaulted over Emmett's head just as Emmett opened fire. His shots pelted the pursuit Skimmers and two more exploded. Emmett vanished around a different corner and Davenport lost sight of him.

Davenport drove on for a while, but he was getting dangerously close to Ultra Meridian. He cut south and then west.

More Skimmers came out of nowhere. They closed on him from side canyons and he couldn't hear them coming with all the engine noise shrieking in his ears.

He fired at a few of them, but he still didn't know where he was going or what he was doing. He couldn't think of anything to do beyond avoiding them.

Four more advanced from his right. They were trying to box him in. He spun backward to make his stand when Emmett dove over a nearby hill, plunged down right on top of the attackers that were trying to finish off Davenport, and opened fire.

Emmett destroyed four Skimmers and Davenport got two more. The last three sprinted away into the desert. Emmett stalled and started to turn back, but Davenport yanked Emmett the other way to follow them. He didn't want to leave anyone alive who might follow him and Emmett back to Rungstea Gap.

They headed for Ultra Meridian and he put on speed to catch up with the enemy. Davenport's Skimmer couldn't keep up. The Reserve Wing must have done something he didn't know about. They would leave him behind and he wouldn't catch up with them before he made it to the Stalwarts.

He did a quick check on the surrounding country and swerved up a nearby hill. He dove over it and prepared to cut them off from the side when Emmett appeared on a ridge to Davenport's right.

The two men took one look at each other before they both banked forward and vanished into more canyons. Emmett flew off in the opposite direction from Davenport, but Davenport saw now what he had to do.

He vaulted three more hills and came up on the Skimmers from the south. He chuckled under his breath when he saw them glancing over their shoulders. They kept checking to see if he was sneaking up on them from behind. They would never see him coming from the side, and with Emmett helping out, he had these cocksuckers in the bag.

He chose his last hill with care, circled it, and nailed the throttle to race up the slope. He caught a flash of Emmett spiraling around another hill farther north and they both sprang their trap at the same time.

Davenport plummeted right in front of the enemy. He whipped around with mind-numbing speed and opened fire. They tried to fight back and then they whirled away to flee. They ran straight into Emmett who materialized out of thin air right behind them.

The three Skimmers detonated in flames. Emmett and Davenport idled their engines watching the wreckage drift to the ground. Davenport still didn't trust to leave.

He pointed up at the nearest hill and Emmett nodded. They rode up there and pulled in side by side to take a look around.

Davenport cast a hard glare toward Ultra Meridian. Before all this shit started, he would have gotten mad if he saw Reserve Wing Stalwarts parked out there. They were blocking him from returning to the jail that he considered his.

Now he knew it wasn't his anymore. He no longer resented them for making him go on the run. He only cared about stopping them and now he had another reason on top of everything else. He had to stop them from recapturing the Armageddon Core.

Davenport didn't understand why the Armageddon Core was so important to the Reserve Wing, but it must be something big. If it was worth them going to all this effort to retake the five women, it was worth Davenport trying to stop them.

That story Friend told him about Fiddler getting kidnapped as a baby and being cloned in a Reserve Wing lab was so much worse than anything Admiral Joyce ever did to Davenport.

It was worse than stealing the Ithium, worse than sending Healey to hunt down Davenport and his friends, worse than dosing Wolf and Dice with truth serum, and worse than threatening both of them with torture and death.

Emmett brought Davenport back to reality by smacking his knuckles again Davenport's shoulder. "What do you want to do?" he yelled over the engine noise. "Are you ready to head back to the....?"

He didn't finish before a dozen Daggers launched from the *Remorseless* and the *Pioneer*. The Daggers swooped southward and gunned their engines to streak across the landscape.

"Bastards!" Emmett muttered.

Davenport's doubts evaporated. "Let's go."

He fired up his Skimmer and dove down the hillside to the canyon bottom. He peeled into the defile heading due east for Ultra Meridian.

Chapter 17

Davenport and Emmett belched out of a valley onto the Ultra Meridian plane. The three huge Stalwarts loomed directly in front of him, but Davenport never slowed down for a second. Time was of the essence. Reserve Wing Daggers were targeting his friends and he had to stop the attack one way or the other.

He was too far away and he couldn't fight Daggers on a Skimmer. He and Emmett were the only people who knew the danger and he didn't have time to pick a safer strategy. There were no more safe strategies anymore.

He chose a target at random and steered on a beeline for the *Remorseless*. One Stalwart was as good as another to him. He spun around the ship's nose and unloaded his Howitzers straight into the bridge. A massive explosion went off behind the window and he turned his venom on the *Pioneer*.

Emmett rocketed into the battle targeting the *Rambler* and another flock of Daggers launched from the ship's hold. They scattered into a fan formation trying to drive the two Skimmers away, but Davenport was all finished playing nice.

Two Skimmers shouldn't stand a chance against three Stalwarts and a dozen Daggers, but none of that mattered.

The *Pioneer* launched off the ground and turned all her guns on Davenport, but he flew too fast and dodged them all. The Stalwart couldn't turn fast enough to keep up with his flight.

The Daggers were quicker, but they had the added problem of trying to avoid hitting the Stalwarts.

The *Remorseless* opened fire, but the ship couldn't launch with the bridge blown out. The Howitzers rotated backward and then stopped when Davenport got directly behind the big ship. They couldn't hit him here.

Davenport lost sight of Emmett in the confusion. The *Pioneer* stalked closer and Davenport couldn't escape with the *Remorseless* in the way. He spun off in the only direction left to him....and spotted the jail sitting right in front of him. The Reserve Wing had been rebuilding it for the second time.

He sprinted for it and the *Pioneer* hounded him across the plane. The ship bombarded him from behind. He tried to wobble, but it didn't work. The ship could spread its fire too wide. He was trapped.

He streaked past the jail with the *Pioneer* right behind him. Hundreds of barren miles of wilderness spread before him. He was too far away from the hills and the ship would only follow him there, too.

He headed due north and the *Pioneer* picked up speed. The guns boomed in his ears. He counted down the seconds and then flung all his weight sideways. He spun his Skimmer backward just as the *Pioneer* flew over the jail roof.

Davenport unloaded on the building and the weapons and ammunition stores hidden in the weapons locker exploded in a towering column of fire. It boomed against the *Pioneer's* underside and the Stalwart detonated with an even more bone-crushing ka-boom.

The explosion enveloped what was left of the jail. So much for that. Ultra Meridian was back to being a desolate moonscape no one would ever want to visit.

Emmett sprinted through the fire and his engine wash scattered the flames. Davenport got a view of the larger battle behind Emmett's Skimmer. Another flock of Daggers whizzed over the landscape coming in at lightning speed. The *Remorseless's* Daggers were coming back from the Runstea Gap. Davenport's distraction worked. Now he and Emmett were facing overwhelming numbers.

Emmett barreled past him making for the hills and Davenport turned to follow. He had no other way to save his own life.

They got into the canyons and defiles again, but the Daggers could track the two Skimmers from the atmosphere. The Daggers could target from far out of range.

Davenport lost sight of Emmett after only a few minutes. Emmett turned a corner, and when Davenport went after him, Emmett wasn't there anymore.

The Daggers hadn't fired yet, so at least Emmett was still alive somewhere in this labyrinth. Davenport could only pray that Emmett got free, but that hope faded when the Daggers split into two groups. One group followed him and the others turned south. They must be tracking Emmett.

Davenport swerved around another corner heading north to draw them away from his friends. He checked over his shoulder and saw at least eight Daggers up there—eight Daggers that weren't going after anyone else.

He put on speed, but his Skimmer was rapidly losing fuel. He couldn't go much far-ther. He tried to steer for the Khuntan Reserve even though he didn't hold out much hope of getting lost in there. The Daggers had numbers and too much technology working in their favor.

He skidded around a corner and spotted the arched entrance ahead. It would lead him into the reserve. He gunned the throttle and the engine choked. The Skimmer stalled, coughed, and restarted. It nearly threw him off when it plunged toward the arch.

He dove under the arch and, at the moment when it was directly over his head, a blast of Howitzer fire punched into it from above. It imploded and tons of rock crashed down all around him.

The impact crushed his Skimmer and pitched him out of the seat. He cartwheeled head over heel and slammed into the stone wall right next to where the arch should have been.

He floundered out of unconsciousness and struggled to lift his head. His goggles had cracked and he couldn't breathe with his mask on. He pulled them off and struggled to see anything around him.

Piles of shattered rock surrounded him. He couldn't see over it until he got onto his knees and finally propped his arms against the wall to stand up.

He didn't see the Skimmer anywhere. The rock mound blocked the entrance to the Khuntan Reserve. He was trapped in one of the reserve's sheer chasms with no way out except to walk the other way. He would have to walk for miles farther north before he could turn south again.

He wouldn't rejoin the others for days. He sure as hell hoped they didn't stick around that long. They should leave without him. At least the Reserve Wing would waste a whole heap of resources recapturing him that they wouldn't send after the Armageddon Core.

He swayed there for a second to catch his breath. He had to harden his resolve to make up his mind to walk north. He had no food, no water, and now he had no goggles, either.

He retrieved his mask and shook the dust out of his hair to pull the mask on when an all-too-familiar whine of engines screamed out of the distance. He froze listening. Could the Reserve Wing be sending Skimmers after him *here*? Why were they coming from the north?

The Daggers no longer patrolled the skies. Did they just give up on finding him in the crash? He half-wished they *would* come after him. If they weren't here, it meant they were going south again.

He drew in a shaky breath bracing himself for another round of mayhem with Admiral Joyce, but when the Skimmers shrieked around the corner, he froze when he saw masked aliens sitting in the drivers' seats.

They were Namialls with long proboscises and several limbs attached at each shoulder and hip joint. They came from the north so they could only belong to one group—Typhon Elexor.

Chapter 18

Fiddler peered out from behind one of Ultra Meridian's tall sand dunes. The Rungstea Gap stood thirty yards away. Sand scoured the Daggers' hulls exactly where the friends left them. "It looks clear."

Fiddler started to stand up, but Flack stopped her. "Do you hear something?"

Fiddler strained her ears. She heard the sand beating on her goggles and the wind moaning through the canyons all around her. She also heard something else. "What is that?"

"It sounds like engines," Fizzle remarked.

The sound got louder with every passing second. "It *is* engines!" Frost shot to her feet. "Come on! We have to get airborne!"

She sprinted into the open as a dozen Reserve Wing Daggers appeared over the horizon. They streaked for the Rungstea Gap, but when they came within range of the parked ships, they didn't fire.

They turned one revolution of the Rungstea Gap. Fiddler checked herself, but Frost and Flack were already diving on board one of the Daggers. That didn't leave Fiddler much choice.

She headed for the second ship and Fizzle took the third. Fiddler lunged for the cockpit and Friend scooted into the seat next to her. "Why aren't they shooting?"

"Does it matter? Frost is away!"

Frost shot into the sky and unloaded on the Daggers. They all rounded on the Armageddon Core and a royal battle broke out even before Fiddler got off the ground.

Frost took dozens of shots and Fizzle rocketed into the mix unloading everywhere. Fiddler tried to match her friends' speed, but it took her a second to tell which Daggers belonged to the Reserve Wing and which ones the Armageddon Core was piloting.

Fiddler was just coming back around for her second pass when Friend took over the Dagger's guns. She pounded five enemy craft and three of them went up in flames.

"Be careful!" Fiddler called. "Don't hit the others!"

"Just fly the ship! Leave the shooting to me."

Those words reminded Fiddler so much of Rodeo that she obeyed instantly. She plunged into the battle flying anywhere and everywhere. She didn't care who were her enemies and who were her friends as long as she kept moving and avoided all the Howitzer fire blasting off all around her.

Readings and statistics streamed across the Dagger's instruments. Friend read them with lightning speed and targeted each enemy ship with brutal accuracy. More Daggers exploded all over the place and the last seven turned tail and broke away.

"What's wrong with them?" Flack asked. "They outnumber us."

Friend checked something on her controls. "There's a battle going on at Ultra Meridian. Two Skimmers are attacking the Stalwarts."

"Davenport," Fiddler growled.

"There's the *Echo Omicron* crew," Frost pointed out. "We should pick them up."

"I'll go. You two stand guard." Fiddler pulled away and followed Friend's directions.

She located Lyons, Dice, and Beauty struggling toward the Rungstea Gap from the west. Fiddler descended in front of them and Friend motioned them on board.

"That went down a lot quicker than I expected," Lyons remarked.

"Hold tight," Fiddler called over her shoulder. "The Daggers are coming back."

"What Daggers?" Dice rumbled.

"Get yourselves strapped into something!" Fiddler hit the throttle and all four of her friends toppled into a pile.

Fiddler didn't have time to help them. The Daggers were already swooping in to attack the Armageddon Core.

"Where are Emmett and Davenport?" she called to her friends.

"There's no sign of either Skimmer," Frost reported.

"I'm going back for them. You three should get away."

"If you're going, we're going with you," Fizzle replied. "Emmett means as much to us as he does to you."

Fiddler didn't argue. She was too glad to have two more Daggers fighting on her side. She throttled to meet the oncoming Daggers, shot through their formation, and sprinted for Ultra Meridian.

She got there just as the jail went up in a giant explosion that enveloped the *Pioneer*. Fiddler caught one glimpse of Emmett shooting through the flames on a dead run for the hills beyond.

Neither Emmett nor Davenport realized that the three new Daggers showing up belonged to Fiddler and her friends. Davenport pulled his Skimmer aside and took off to follow Emmett.

Fiddler tried to catch up with them, but the enemy cut her off. They whizzed past the burning jail and blocked Fiddler from following Emmett and Davenport.

Deafening bangs pounded the hull and Friend fought her way back to the front. She strapped into the seat next to Fiddler and started to return fire. Fiddler heard the *Echo Omicron* crew yelling in the background, but she didn't have time to check what they were doing.

She tried to break through the crowd of Daggers, but a punishing barrage from the *Rambler* jolted her Dagger sideways. She and Friend slammed against their harnesses and Fiddler spun in reverse so Friend could return fire.

Fiddler had to sprint over the Stalwarts to avoid blasts coming from both the *Rambler* and the grounded *Remorseless*. The *Remorseless* could still cause plenty of damage considering that the whole bridge had been destroyed.

Daggers swarmed around Fiddler's craft. She couldn't tell anymore where Frost and Fizzle were. Were they even alive?

A shrill voice stabbed into her brain. "I found Emmett! He's in the canyons to the west."

Fiddler didn't hesitate. She had to find Emmett. "Where is he?"

"He's under heavy fire from the Daggers!" Fizzle replied.

"Where's Davenport?" Friend yelled through the link.

"I don't see him!" Frost replied. "He's gone! No, wait a minute. There's a human life sign over by the Khuntan Reserve."

Fiddler concentrated on Emmett. The Daggers hovering above him whizzed over canyons tracking something down in the bottoms. Her heart pounded and her hands sweated on the helm veering up behind the Daggers. She had to protect Emmett at all costs, but right now, she couldn't even see him.

Friend opened fire and punched three Daggers in the tail, but they didn't break off. Whatever they were following must be moving incredibly fast.

Fiddler wished now that she had foreseen this and equipped Davenport and Emmett with a way to get inside Friend's network of gateways. Then the two men would have been able to escape.

There was no time to correct that mistake now. The Daggers hammered the canyons and most of their shots struck the walls. Friend kept up a steady barrage on the enemy, but they completely ignored her. Not one of them turned around to defend themselves against the Armageddon Core.

The Daggers swerved to follow another canyon and Fiddler spotted Emmett down below. He crouched over his Skimmer cutting around corners at blistering speed.

She caught one glimpse of him before the Daggers opened up. They didn't try to hit him. They couldn't. The walls were too steep and they would have put themselves in danger by getting too close to each other.

They swiveled wide and wove in to cross each other's flight paths. They unloaded on opposite walls and smashed the rock faces to rain blocks and boulders on Emmett's head.

A deluge of debris crashed on top of him and the avalanche enveloped him. "Pull away!" Friend shrieked. "We can't help him now!"

"No!" Fiddler yelled back. "We have to...."

The Daggers broke off instantly and then all of them turned on Fiddler. Dozens of shots struck the hull and pelted Fiddler and Friend from all directions.

"Get us out of here now!" Friend roared.

Fiddler pulled away. She hit the throttle, shot one last hopeless glance toward the Khuntan Reserve, and put on speed to leave the Reserve Wing behind. She still didn't see Frost or Fizzle. Did they make it out of the battle alive or were they already in Reserve Wing custody?

If they were dead, that left only Fiddler and Friend to run from recapture. At least Fiddler had the *Echo Omicron* crew on board, but that was small comfort without the others.

She raised the Dagger's nose to the skies to break orbit when a crushing boom rocked the ship under her. The Dagger wobbled.

"What the hell....?" Friend attacked the controls.

Fiddler tried one more time to fire the engines to leave the planet when another brutal crash punched into the ship.

A screeching alarm went off on the controls in front of her. She and Friend scrambled trying to understand what the problem was. Fiddler almost didn't believe it when she looked through the cockpit window and saw the starboard wing completely gone.

She seized the helm and stabbed down the throttle, but nothing happened. The engines belched once and then the ship tipped dangerously to port.

"Fiddler....!" Friend yelled and then another bone-crunching smash smacked the ship ass over tea kettle. It somersaulted in the air and Fiddler lost all sense of where she was.

Something heavy roared right next to her ear. She saw Dice cartwheeling out of the back. He bellowed once and then his body collided with her chair hard enough to knock her out.

Chapter 19

Fiddler groaned and rubbed her aching head. "What happened? Where are we?"

A familiar female voice murmured in front of her. "You're in Typhon Elexor territory."

Fiddler's eyes snapped open and her blood ran cold when she found herself face to face with Colonel Lillian Casey.

Colonel Casey smiled at her in genuine affection. "It's so wonderful to see you again, Fiddler. You're all grown up and we couldn't be prouder of you."

"What about....?" Fiddler looked around and her heart plummeted into her shoes when she saw Davenport, Emmett, the *Echo Omicron* crew, and the whole Armageddon Core slouching, standing, and sitting near her.

Only Davenport would look at her. The others looked at the floor or at their hands or at some point on the wall away from her.

The whole group was in a room that looked remarkably similar to the one in Mount Refractory's fortress. Even the armed aliens surrounding the party looked like the same species as Mount Refractory.

Only one detail told Fiddler loud and clear that this was not Mount Refractory. This was a much more dangerous situation than anything she'd experienced so far.

A bunch of Reserve Wing officers, soldiers, and security guards surrounded the prisoners and Fiddler gulped when she spotted Admiral Joyce among them. He and Colonel Casey were both in the same place. This was not good. It was beyond bad. It was a disaster.

She started to wonder if anything she might have done led to this catastrophe, but she stopped herself from thinking that. If she did anything wrong, it was over and done now. She did everything in her power to keep herself and her friends free. She also did everything possible to prevent Joyce from retaking the Ithium.

If he was here with the friends in this room, that meant he still hadn't found it and the determined scowl on his face told Fiddler everything she needed to know about his mental state. He was here for the Ithium and he wouldn't leave until he found it.

All the lengths he'd gone to before would be nothing compared to what he did now. Trying to kill Davenport, using truth serum on anyone he pleased—he had crossed some threshold in his mind.

He was no longer thinking rationally about any of this. Colonel Casey's presence must be the one thing stopping him from going around the bend right now.

Colonel Casey straightened up and held out her hand to Fiddler. "You don't have to worry anymore. We'll send out another Stalwart to take you back to Helios Sanctus...."

Davenport shoved between Casey and Fiddler. He knocked Casey's arm aside, put his arm around Fiddler's shoulders, and steered her away from the colonel. "Fiddler isn't going anywhere with you or with any other Reserve Wing officer. These armed men are the only thing stopping me from placing you all under arrest right now."

He pulled Fiddler into a corner and blocked her with his body. "Are you okay?" he murmured into her ear.

She nodded, but she could already see that he wouldn't be able to stop Colonel Casey from taking the whole Armageddon Core wherever she wanted.

"You won't be arresting anyone today, Sheriff," she replied behind his back. "Be grateful I don't strip you of your star right now."

"You might be able to hold me at gunpoint," he snapped over his shoulder, "but I'll find a way to stop you. You're a disgrace to the Confederacy...." He turned to Joyce and spat out the words with bitter venom. "Both of you."

"Enjoy yourself while it lasts, Sheriff," Joyce snarled back.

"What are you going to do to me that you haven't already done?" Davenport turned around with his body still blocking Fiddler from seeing anyone on the Reserve Wing side. "Are you gonna kill me? Go ahead. I don't have the Ithium and I don't know where it is. I've already told you everything I know. We all have."

"Not all." Joyce came forward and strolled down the line of prisoners. He didn't pay much attention to the Armageddon Core. He also pretty much ignored Dice. He paused in front of Lyons and then examined Beauty. "One of you knows where the Ithium is. I'll find out which one and, eventually, you'll tell me whether you want to or not."

A shiver went up Fiddler's spine. She believed him. This man no longer gave one shit about Confederate law. He no longer cared if his actions made him a disgrace to his uniform or anything else he might have once held dear.

He halted in front of Emmett. "Why don't we start with....?"

The door burst open and a bunch of aliens strode in. They looked the same as every other alien in the room, except that one of them was a female.

"The Reserve Wing will have to suspend judgment against these people. Typhon Elexor claims first prerogative in carrying out the sentence against them."

"What sentence?" Joyce countered. "You already captured them for us. You agreed...."

"We agreed to capture them," the tall female replied. "These people were all captured inside Typhon Elexor territory. That makes them subject to a death sentence according to our laws."

Colonel Casey took her place at Joyce's side. They both confronted the aliens and Colonel Casey started protesting, too. "You can't execute these people! Do you have any idea what they're worth?"

"They're criminals. They are worth a death sentence. That is all."

Davenport leaned in close and whispered in Fiddler's ear. "Please tell me you left the Ithium on HTWV-983. Please tell me you moved it somewhere Joyce won't be able to get it."

She didn't get a chance to answer—not that she would have answered even if she could. An argument was threatening to break out between the Typhon Elexor leaders and the two Reserve Wing officers.

The conflict escalated to such a pitch that everyone forgot about the prisoners. Fiddler almost said something else to Davenport when more aliens came in from what looked like a corridor outside. They approached the male and female Typhon Elexor leaders and whispered in the leaders' ears.

Colonel Casey and Admiral Joyce tried to make their point, but the two leaders turned all their attention to their own people. They tried to hold a hasty discussion over the Reserve Wing's objections.

"What's going on?" Lyons asked Davenport.

"I don't know, but anything that delays our execution is my idea of a good time."

"I don't think there is such a thing in this place," Emmett remarked.

The tall female turned around and swiped her finger at the prisoners. "Bring them with us."

The aliens moved in, but Colonel Casey, Admiral Joyce, and the Reserve Wing soldiers tried to intervene. "You can't take these people!" Colonel Casey insisted. "We've been searching for them for decades."

The tall female turned a disgusted sneer at Colonel Casey and all the Reserve Wing staff present. "I do not think you wish to start a war between Typhon Elexor and the Reserve Wing."

Colonel Casey gulped and backed off immediately. Admiral Joyce finally nodded and the soldiers lowered their weapons.

The aliens started forward. Davenport held out his hand to the tall Typhon Elexor female. "Kiriala—Yovis—what's going on?"

The tall female leader paused for the second time. She faced Davenport with a much kinder expression from the one she used with Joyce and Casey. "Mount Refractory has sent a delegation to us for the first time in over three hundred years. They are demanding diplomatic dialogue immediately. They want to negotiate that you be handed over to them instead."

Davenport's jaw dropped and Fiddler's heart stopped right there in her chest. The whole party stared at Kiriala in stupid shock as the words sank in.

Even the Reserve Wing officers gaped at her, speechless. Mount Refractory—demanding diplomatic dialogue? What could Mount Refractory possibly want with Davenport and his crew?

Typhon Elexor didn't give anyone a chance to argue the point further. The aliens moved in, surrounded the prisoners, and marched them out of the room.

The aliens shoved the Reserve Wing personnel aside. The aliens treated the Reserve Wing with such disdain and blatant disrespect that everyone from the Reserve Wing was forced to hang back and exit the room last—including Colonel Casey and Admiral Joyce.

Davenport elbowed his way to the front. The others stayed behind him and he took the lead walking down a long gallery heading somewhere or other. He acted like he knew where he was going.

He strode ahead to walk next to Kiriala and talked to the two leaders like he knew them, too. "Did Mount Refractory say why they want us?"

"They say you violated their laws and broke your bond with them. They claim this breach occurred before we recaptured you. They're claiming first prerogative to carry out your death sentence."

"What breach?" Davenport asked. "What are they saying we did to violate their laws?"

The male walking next to Kiriala spoke up. "They say Reserve Wing Daggers encroached on their territory and fired on a Reserve Wing Stalwart that was trying to take that one as a hostage." He shot a pointed glance behind him toward Fiddler.

"How do you plan to negotiate with them?" Davenport asked. "You don't have diplomatic relations with Mount Refractory."

Kiriala actually smiled at him. "It is true. The negotiations could take quite a long time."

The Typhon Elexor leaders turned off into another doorway and headed downstairs. They emerged in a large courtyard surrounded by tiered galleries rising to the planet's surface. Some kind of galvanic field protected the courtyard from wind and sand.

A crowd of the same species of aliens waited there and the tension spiked off the charts when Fiddler recognized Krex. He stood with three other Mount Refractory people she recognized from the fortress, but Fiddler had never talked to them.

Kiriala, Yovis, and their entourage lined up across the courtyard and faced their ancient enemies. The Typhon Elexor guards held the prisoners off to one side where they wouldn't interfere.

Fiddler couldn't help but notice Typhon Elexor holding the Reserve Wing at bay, too. Was it only an accident that Typhon Elexor positioned themselves to block Admiral Joyce and Colonel Casey from even entering the corridor, let alone getting near the Mount Refractory representatives?

Krex's eyes sliced sideways toward Fiddler and then he boomed out for the whole assembly to hear. "You have heard our conditions. We claim these prisoners as our right. Hand them over now if you want to avoid a war."

The prospect of losing their quarry must have overcome Joyce and Casey's diplomatic scruples. Joyce shoved between the guards and forced his way to the front. "These prisoners hold a special value to the Reserve Wing. The Reserve Wing is prepared to compensate you for your loss in exchange for your prerogative in determining what happens to these people."

"The Reserve Wing has no authority on this planet," Krex snapped. "This is a matter between Mount Refractory and Typhon Elexor. I do not think the Reserve Wing wishes to start a war with either of our peoples—or both of them, for that matter."

Joyce blanched. "Of course not. That's why we would reward you handsomely for turning them over to us. They're much more valuable to the Reserve Wing alive than they will be to you dead."

"I highly doubt that," Kiriala countered. "The Reserve Wing obviously doesn't value its reputation very highly. You come simpering at our doorstep offering to lick our boots in exchange for condemned criminals. Reputation still means more to Typhon Elexor than any reward you could offer us."

"And to Mount Refractory," Krex interjected.

"I'm sure there is something you would value more highly than these prisoners' dead bodies."

Joyce turned to Kiriala and his expression changed to a smile of triumph. He hadn't even stated his offer and he already knew he'd won.

"What about the raw materials to construct another four hundred windmills....and a trade contract with Chiton's Hold to supply the Reserve Wing with all the Scanitine you can mine."

No one moved for a second and Fiddler cringed. A deal like that definitely would be worth more to Typhon Elexor than a bunch of dead prisoners.

Joyce turned to Krex. "I'm sure Mount Refractory would be happy with a hundred brand new Chaser-class fighter craft—fresh off the assembly line."

"How do we know you won't take the prisoners and renege on your bargain?" Krex fired back. "You could take these prisoners off the planet and we would never hear from you again."

"Then you would go to war against the Reserve Wing, wouldn't you?" Joyce turned back and forth between Krex and Kiriala to include both syndicates. "Besides, we don't plan to kill these prisoners. We'll keep them alive—at least until they tell us what they know. If we fail to keep our side of the bargain, you can take them back and kill them all. We won't stand in your way."

Kiriala and Krex exchanged glances. Neither of them consulted with their people about whether to accept the Reserve Wing's terms. Everyone in the room knew both syndicates would take the deal. It was too lucrative and too advantageous to both.

Joyce really knew how to grease their palms. He knew exactly what to offer them so they wouldn't refuse.

Chapter 20

Davenport crowded close with Lyons, Dice, Beauty, and Emmett. He glanced over his shoulder to the opposite side of the courtyard. Admiral Joyce and Colonel Casey talked in low whispers over there. No doubt they were deciding which of them was going to take possession of which prisoners.

"What are they doing?" Emmett whispered. "If they take the Armageddon Core, I swear to Christ I'll tear them limb from limb."

"You wouldn't even get close to them," Dice growled. "These assholes would blow your head off if you looked at them wrong."

He jutted his horns at the combined Typhon Elexor and Reserve Wing soldiers who stood guard around the courtyard. For two groups that hated and wanted to destroy each other, they were sure cooperating well, now that they had a common aim.

"What do you think they're planning to do?" Lyons murmured.

"Joyce already told us," Davenport replied. "He's going to torture us one after the other until he finds out which one of us hid the Ithium and where it is. Once he gets that, he'll probably kill us. He's just telling Casey to wait while he questions Fiddler. He doesn't want Casey to take the Armageddon Core back to Helios Sanctus yet in case Fiddler is the one who took the Ithium."

All eyes turned to the Armageddon Core. The four women stood together in a third corner of the courtyard under Reserve Wing guard. Davenport could see the five of them whispering together, too. Were they planning anything? He didn't see how any of them could do much under the circumstances.

Stalwarts kept migrating back and forth across the courtyard. The Reserve Wing must be in the act of transferring Typhon Elexor's reward right now. Typhon Elexor wouldn't tolerate Reserve Wing ships inside their territory otherwise.

The Reserve Wing must have come through on their promise to supply Mount Re-fractory with ships, too. Krex and his entourage departed shortly after Joyce made his offer.

Davenport cringed when Joyce and Casey parted ways. This was it. Now Joyce would bring out all the psychopathic ways he knew to extract information from his prisoners.

He strolled over to Davenport's group and his cold, hard eyes flicked from one face to the next. He measured each one with precise accuracy.

He halted in front of Davenport and started to say something when Dice lunged for him. Dice snarled in the admiral's face, but Lyons held him back.

Joyce didn't even flinch. "Don't worry, Sir. As soon as I find the Ithium, you'll be on your way to Helios Sanctus with the Armageddon Core. You'll get as much truth serum there as you could possibly want."

The words silenced Dice instantly and Joyce went back to dragging his lazy gaze over the rest of the crew. He barely looked at Davenport. "I know you've already told me everything you can, Sheriff, and so have you two." Joyce nodded toward Dice and Emmett. "That leaves you two." He surveyed Lyons and Beauty.

"We don't know where the Ithium is," Lyons told him. "We left it on the *Artemis Rex.*"

"That's what you'd like me to believe, but we all know it isn't true. Fiddler took it off the ship and hid it in a swamp on HTWV-983, but it didn't stay there. One of you found it and moved it a second time."

Joyce studied Lyons for a moment and then signaled to his guards. They pounced on Beauty and flattened him to the ground. He screeched in surprise and then terror as the soldiers turned their guns toward his face.

Davenport sprang forward, but another ten guards surrounded him, Lyons, and Dice. Dice charged and would have squashed them all, but one of the Typhon Elexor aliens came up behind him and injected something into his neck from behind.

Dice hit the bricks with a ground-shaking thud. Davenport and Lyons both rushed to his side, but it was too late. Dice couldn't move.

Beauty's screeches echoed through the courtyard. He flailed his gangly limbs and struck out. He landed blows, but not for long. More soldiers came forward and the aliens from Typhon Elexor helped out. They really knew which side their bread was buttered on

.

Davenport and Lyons struggled to get to Beauty, but to no avail. Emmett tried to break through the soldiers' ranks to get to the Armageddon Core. The Armageddon Core did their best to rejoin their friends, but the Reserve Wing and Typhon Elexor had the whole courtyard locked up. No one could move.

Joyce strode over and looked down his nose at Beauty writhing under the soldiers' hands. "Shoot him."

"NO!" everyone yelled at the same time.

Joyce glanced over his shoulder toward Davenport. The admiral raised his eyebrows in mock surprise. "No? Are you ready to tell me where the Ithium is?"

"I already told you everything I know!" Davenport yelled back.

Joyce pointed down at Beauty again. "Kill him."

"Stop!" Lyons screamed. "I know where the Ithium is."

"Finally we're getting somewhere," Joyce muttered. "Where is it?"

Lyons cast a desperate look around at her friends and gulped. "I hid it.... under one of the windmills."

All the Typhon Elexor aliens turned around to stare. Joyce raised his eyebrows and he didn't have to pretend anymore to be surprised. "Which one?"

Lyons waved at nothing. "The one on the far northwestern corner. It's under the superstructure between the anchor plate and the bedrock."

Her head sank as the last defeated words escaped her. All the fight went out of her and she looked down at the floor. Davenport put his arm around her, but she didn't respond.

Joyce pointed at one of his men. "Go find it and bring it to me. If you're lying, he'll only be the first to die."

"Don't worry," Davenport whispered in Lyons's ear. "Just let him have the Ithium and we'll deal with whatever happens afterward. It isn't your fault. Don't blame yourself."

The words bounced right off her and she didn't soften at his touch. Davenport's heart twisted. He would have told the admiral where the Ithium was days ago if he'd only known. He didn't blame Lyons, but he could already see the guilt weighing on her. She blamed herself and that could never come to any good.

An ominous silence fell over the courtyard. Only Beauty's squawks and screeches of protest interrupted the tense quiet. Davenport tried to encourage the others with his eyes, but Emmett and Lyons wouldn't even look at him.

Fiddler's terrified stare went straight through Davenport from across the courtyard. He wished he was nearer so he could give the Armageddon Core some assurance, but he couldn't even do that.

The five women were on their way back to Helios Sanctus, and once they got there, he wouldn't be able to do anything for them.

Admiral Joyce would probably shoot Davenport in the head as soon as the admiral got his hot little hands on the Ithium. It was the only smart thing to do with witnesses to Joyce's many crimes.

A door banged and the soldier in question came back. He shoved a frayed cloth bag into Joyce's hands. Joyce tore into it, but he couldn't loosen the strings. He wound up ripping the flimsy cloth and throwing the bag on the floor.

He turned a sturdy waterproof box over and over in his hands before he opened it. The box lid creaked and Joyce gazed inside for what seemed like an eternity.

He shifted the box to his other hand, stuck his fingers inside, and pulled out a tiny computer chip. He held it up for everyone to see. "Does this look like an Ithium cartridge to you?"

Lyons's head shot up and she gaped at the chip in blank, open-mouthed astonishment. "But...it was....it was in there! I swear! We put it in there! We hid it under the windmill! We had to...."

Her eyes darted over to the Armageddon Core and Davenport winced when she and Fiddler exchanged glances. Joyce saw the look and strode over to the Armageddon Core.

Fiddler tore her eyes away from Lyons, but it was too late. Joyce had seen that glance between the two women and all the puzzle pieces fit into place.

Fiddler was the one who hid the Ithium on HTWV-983. She and Lyons must have brought it back to Ultra Meridian and Fiddler must have hidden the Ithium while Lyons wasn't looking. Fiddler must have done it in a way so that Lyons still believed the Ithium was in that box.

"Where's the Ithium, Fiddler?" Joyce murmured.

She shut her mouth with a click and looked down at her hands. She compressed her lips and muttered, "I don't know."

Davenport's chest hurt watching her. She put up a good fight, but she couldn't win. Joyce had everyone she loved and cared about right here in this courtyard.

He watched her struggle with herself. Then he appraised each of the four clones one after another.

Joyce spun away, darted across the courtyard, seized Emmett by the back of the neck, and yanked him toward the Armageddon Core. Joyce snatched a sidearm from one of his men, slammed Emmett down on the floor in front of Fiddler, and crammed the weapon to Emmett's head.

Fiddler screamed and hurled herself at her father. "NO!"

"Where's the Ithium?!" Joyce roared. "You have five seconds before he dies right here! Where is it?"

"I...."

"Four!" Joyce bellowed. "Three.... two...."

"All right!" she shrieked. "I hid it....in a cave....in the canyons....... We were hiding there....and Lyons was asleep.... I hid it in a cave!"

"Go get it—now!" Joyce jammed the gun harder against Emmett's temple and made Emmett cry out in pain. "I'll wait!"

Fiddler stared at Joyce and then at Emmett. She whirled away and had to fight her way out of the courtyard between all the soldiers and aliens standing around.

The silence that followed took a whole hell of a lot longer. The friends spent the first hour on edge watching Joyce's every move. He didn't slacken his posture at all. He kept jamming the gun barrel into Emmett's head and Joyce pushed it in harder every time Emmett breathed.

The first hour passed and Lyons turned away. She went over to Dice, squatted down next to him, and rested her hand on his shoulder. Davenport heard her whispering to him, so Dice must still be at least partially conscious.

At least this time the friends wouldn't have to agonize so much about finding the antidote to the truth serum. Maltese Chipmunks were pretty common in this part of the Confederacy.

Did the Reserve Wing scientists know about Maltese Chipmunks? Had they figured out in all their research on Adiks how easily someone could trigger an Adik into a rage-fueled ballistic fury?

Davenport would pay any amount of money to be there at Helios Sanctus when they found out, especially if the Adik in question was Dice. Seeing that would almost make it worth it to see Dice brought this low.

The soldiers didn't let go of Beauty, either, but they must have softened their hold on him. He kept flopping around on the floor behind the soldiers' shins. Davenport couldn't see him, but at least Beauty wasn't screaming anymore.

The Armageddon Core stayed tense and watchful for far too long, but in the end, they retreated into their whispered conversations, too. They shrank away from Admiral Joyce, but they didn't stop casting desperate glances at Emmett.

His gaze darted between them with the same heartfelt emotion with which he usually looked at his daughter. Davenport could only imagine what had been going on between Emmett and the five girls all these years.

By the time the second hour rolled around, Davenport had had enough, too. He went over to Dice and touched Lyons's shoulder. Davenport rested his back against the wall and slid down it to sit on the floor. God only knew how far away Fiddler had to go to retrieve the Ithium.

By the third hour, all the Armageddon Core were sitting down and Frost had stretched out on the floor with her head in Fizzle's lap. Some of the soldiers guarding Beauty had let go of him and straightened up. They still stood over him and kept an eye on him while he huddled at their feet, but they didn't hold onto him or push him around.

Lyons sat down on the floor pressing Dice's big hand between both of hers. She didn't look at Admiral Joyce anymore. She kept all her attention on Dice.

Somewhere between the fourth and fifth hour, a door slammed out of sight. The sound startled Davenport out of his stupor and he got to his feet as Fiddler walked in with tears streaming down her cheeks. She walked up to Admiral Joyce and held out her closed fist.

He extended his upturned palm and she put something in it. Her face twisted in agony and her lips spasmed all over the place.

He looked down into his hand and a sick grin split over his face. He lowered the sidearm from Emmett's head and turned to Colonel Casey. "You can take them now."

The soldiers moved in and grabbed everyone at once. They started hauling Fiddler in one direction and Emmett in another. "Dad!" Fiddler screamed and tried to fight her way to Emmett. "DAD!!"

More soldiers gathered and Typhon Elexor rushed in to help get rid of the prisoners. Davenport took one step toward the commotion and one of the guards slammed him in the side of the head with a rifle butt.

Davenport buckled and soldiers piled on top of him in such numbers that he couldn't see anything for a second.

They rolled him onto his stomach and yanked his arms behind his back. They tied his wrists together and he got a full view between their ankles of the scene unfolding in the courtyard.

Four soldiers had to get hold of Fiddler to drag her kicking and screaming out of the courtyard. Emmett went nuts and tried to claw his way to his daughter. He kept roaring like a wounded animal, "Baby! BABY!!"

"DAD!!" she screeched. "DAD!!"

Her screams echoed off the walls and set Davenport's hair on end, but that was nothing compared to what happened when Admiral Joyce signaled the soldiers to take Lyons away from Dice.

They took hold of her arms and she flipped. She clutched at Dice's hand and she hit the roof when they succeeded in tearing her grip away from his hand. "Dice!" she bellowed. "DICE!!"

He turned his head in her direction, but he could barely open his eyes. The soldiers wrestled her farther across the courtyard, and when she didn't settle down, they started beating her into submission, too.

Beauty started screaming again. Davenport struggled, but a few more well-placed kicks to his back and head knocked him down. He huddled under the attack. Sinking dread ate into his guts watching the Reserve Wing haul Fiddler and the Armageddon Core out of sight.

Reserve Wing medics loaded Dice on another stretcher and took him away. Davenport ached almost as much at seeing Dice vanish out of the courtyard as Fiddler and the others. Dice wouldn't be on the same ship as Davenport anymore. Davenport no longer held out any hope that he would be able to rescue any of them.

He had his own problems right now. The soldiers picked him up by his bound arms and legs. They carried him out of the courtyard, out of Typhon Elexor's underground headquarters, and into the driving wind and sand.

A Regiment Stalwart waited twenty feet from the exit. Davenport squinted to protect his eyes from the sand, but not before he caught a glimpse of the ship's identity signature. It was the *Remorseless*. The Reserve Wing must have repaired it quickly after he destroyed the bridge.

A second later, they carried him into the cargo hold, down several decks, and deposited him, Lyons, Emmett, and Beauty in the solid metal cell. This one was nothing like the prison hold on the *Rambler*.

The sheer, smooth walls left no view of the outside. There were no bars, no stone, but this cell somehow proved far more forbidding than the *Rambler* ever was.

No one offered to untie the prisoners. The soldiers dumped the four friends in a corner and the door slammed shut.

Davenport twisted onto his seat and scooted over to Lyons. She looked absolutely awful with blood and bruises covering her face. Tears poured down her cheeks and smeared the blood all over her clothes.

Emmett sat dazed and lifeless to one side. He didn't even seem to be aware of where he was. He kept blinking at the floor, beyond grief, beyond despair, beyond anger.

Beauty didn't seem to be any worse for his ordeal, and for some reason, the soldiers hadn't bothered to tie him up.

That didn't help anybody, though. Beauty hadn't gotten away this time. He wasn't at large on the *Remorseless* where he could help the friends escape. He was trapped in here along with the others.

Davenport shuddered and touched his shoulder to Lyons's. "Are you okay? Do you have any broken bones?"

"He's gone!" she wailed. "He's gone and now I'll never get him back!"

Davenport didn't answer. He didn't tell her that losing the Ithium and the chip was a much bigger disaster than losing Dice.

Davenport didn't blame her for latching onto Dice's loss. Davenport understood only too well how she felt. Losing the Chorion Team—losing Marshall Healey—and now losing Dice and the Armageddon Core tore at his heart and mind much more than losing the Ithium.

Davenport had been preparing himself for days to hand over the Ithium and let Joyce do his worst. Now it finally happened and no doubt remained in Davenport's mind which was the greater loss.

Davenport took one long, last look around at the cell. The full weight of his situation sank in and he allowed himself, for the first time, to realize what just happened to him.

It was all over. His futile effort to keep the Ithium away from Admiral Joyce had come to an end. Davenport had failed to uphold and enforce the law. He was a failure as a sheriff and he didn't even have his hands free to take off his star the way he should have taken it off weeks ago.

People had been telling him all along and he didn't want to believe it. Ekol Thaine told him. The Chorions told him. Even Admiral Joyce told him.

Davenport wasn't a sheriff anymore if he ever had been one. He was a common criminal and now he was on his way to the one place where all common criminals belonged. He was on his way up to the Terminus Anathema.

Chapter 21

Confederate Marshall Lawrence Healey angled the Nitrol *Prometheus Vox* into the stars and hit the throttle. "Follow me, boys! We're making tracks back to Pandora's Needle."

"Daggers on our ass!" Rodeo called from the Drifter *Artemis Rex*.

"Hold tight, boy!" Healey pulled the Nitrol back around and sped up to overtake the *Artemis Rex*. "I'm coming to bail you out."

Healey gunned the engines and overtook the *Artemis Rex* buried under piles of Reserve Wing ships. They swarmed around the Drifter pounding it from all sides.

Howitzer fire ruptured from the *Artemis Rex's* sides as the accessory cradles opened up. Three Daggers exploded, but the *Artemis Rex* couldn't break free.

Healey dove in carving a path to the *Artemis Rex*. "Punch it, boy!" he yelled. "Get through to the Needle. I'll take it from here."

"They'll only follow us," Rodeo countered. "We have to make our stand here."

"Cut them away from the Stalwarts!" Healey ordered. "The Stalwarts are leaving. Drive them deeper into space."

The *Artemis Rex* responded instantly. The engines flared to life and an even more brutal volley of gunfire belched from the Drifter's guns as the *Artemis Rex* put on speed.

The Daggers kept pace all the way and Healey took his chance. He turned somersaults through the Daggers and fired at as many of them as he could hit. He didn't take too much trouble to blow them up, though. He didn't have to.

Three Daggers turned on him and left a gap for the *Artemis Rex* to squeeze through. Bandit hit the throttle for all he was worth and the *Artemis Rex* left the Daggers in the dust.

That left all the Daggers to round on Healey alone. He tried to follow the *Artemis Rex* and saw his mistake. If he caught up with the Drifter, he would lead the enemy straight to the Chorion Team.

Healey pulled hard to port and veered almost in line with an enemy craft. He fired into the ship's nose and blasted the front end off before he rocketed away into space.

The rest of the Daggers tried to keep up, but they broke off as he put more distance between them.

Seven Stalwarts hovered in the distance, but they were heading in the opposite direction. The Daggers split off one after another and streaked into space to overtake the Stalwarts.

Healey chuckled. "And that's what you get for always following orders."

"How do we get down on the Needle, Marshall?" Bandit asked from the *Artemis Rex*. "We don't have clearance."

"Follow me. We'll use my clearance."

"How are you going to justify bringing us back?" Rodeo asked. "We're wanted, you know."

"That's why I'm bringing you back. Consider yourselves in Confederate custody." Laughter broke out on the *Artemis Rex* and Healey had to grin. "Don't make it out to be such a joke."

"Sorry, Sir," Rodeo replied. "Taking us into custody didn't go too well for you last time, did it?"

"Do me a favor and don't blow up the jail again, okay?"

More laughter answered him. "No promises, Marshall," Rodeo replied. "We've been known to blow things up just by looking at them wrong."

"You must be talking about Breeze 'cuz I know you aren't talking about yourself. Don't worry, son. You aren't going to the jail. I have another idea about where you can stay until we figure this out."

"What do you have in mind?" Bandit asked.

"I know somewhere you'll fit right in."

"I can't wait," a low voice added from the accessory cradles. It was Laub.

"There's the transmission tower," Bandit observed. "Transmit your clearance, Marshall."

Healey entered his clearance into the *Prometheus Vox's* controls and approached Pandora's Needle. The giant recreational satellite revolved in orbit over Atlas Arcane, the Confederate Corps' headquarters.

Confederate personnel from Atlas Arcane came to the Needle to indulge, to spend their pay, and to blow off steam when they went on leave. The satellite did a thriving trade in all kinds of entertainment, legal and otherwise.

Healey turned his attention back to the jail. He could just imagine the chaos he would have to deal with when he went back there. He'd been gone on this whole Davenport mission for way too long. His deputies would have a million questions. Heaven only knew how the place had been running since Healey left.

He steered toward the jail when a shriek startled him alert. "We got a massive problem!" Bandit screamed. "A great, big, silver one!"

Healey scrambled to see what he meant. It became all too clear a second later when a giant flock of attack vessels launched from Atlas Arcane. Drifters, Nitrols, and Daggers rocketed into orbit and made a beeline for Pandora's Needle.

"Are you sure that clearance worked?" Rodeo asked.

A smash of gunfire cut off all communication as the Reserve Wing attacked the *Artemis Rex* in a fury. So many ships surrounded the Drifter that Healey couldn't see the *Artemis Rex* anymore.

Healey ripped the *Prometheus Vox* backward and raced to catch up with the boys, but he could already see the Drifter going down under a brutal bombardment.

The Reserve Wing spun in wild loops around the ship and hammered it from all sides. The *Artemis Rex* twisted and twirled in the center with Howitzer fire spitting from the accessory guns.

So many shots blasted from the sides and from the tactical cradle that the *Artemis Rex* held the enemy at bay for a second.... just long enough for Healey to get to the Drifter.

He plunged into the battle shooting as many enemy craft as he could, but the Reserve Wing outnumbered him by the dozen. He was only one man and he could only shoot so fast.

Four Nitrols peeled around the battlefield and charged the *Artemis Rex* in a tight formation. They punched the nose, the starboard wing, and the tail at once and the Drifter wheeled off to one side. The ship skidded dangerously close to Pandora's Needle and the other Reserve Wing vessels attacked without mercy.

Five Daggers banked from port only to run into a crushing barrage from the accessory guns on that side. The five attackers had to swerve hard and they all raced off into space, but only for a second.

They came screaming back and laid into the *Artemis Rex's* tail. The exhaust system exploded and the back end tore off. Metal fragments and torn fuselage somersaulted away into space while the *Artemis Rex* tumbled in free fall toward the Needle.

"Rodeo! Bandit!" Healey yelled. "Talk to me, boys!"

No one answered. The Reserve Wing saw the ship in distress and piled in for the kill. Healey fought the helm trying to get to the *Artemis Rex* first, but a crushing strike across his port side caught him off guard. He had to turn and defend himself while the *Artemis Rex* plunged toward the Needle.

He hauled his helm hard to port and rocketed between three Daggers who all laid into his wings, but Healey pulled a sideways roll and sliced a path between them. He yanked the ship into a reverse slide, unloaded on the Daggers from behind, and sprinted away toward the Needle.

The *Artemis Rex* was already in freefall over the densest part of the city. Healey crawled up behind the Drifter and tried one more time to hail the Chorion Team, but he got no answer.

The *Artemis Rex* still had partial engine power. Both engines fired to slow the ship's fall. Healey got within communications range, and a second later, the port engine exploded in a massive fireball that smacked the Drifter a hundred miles off course.

At least the *Artemis Rex* wasn't diving for the thickest population center anymore, but that only caused an even bigger problem. The starboard engine kept firing and spun the ship in dizzy turns. The Drifter couldn't right itself and one engine spitting off didn't slow the ship's fall at all.

Healey thought fast. He had no way to avert the impending catastrophe. The *Artemis Rex* was still diving headlong toward a part of town where it would kill thousands when it crashed. He had to stop it.

He locked his teeth and hit the throttle. He plummeted at impossible speed heading straight for the Needle's surface. If he messed this up, neither he nor the Chorion Team would live long enough to regret it.

He overtook the *Artemis Rex* and inched past the cockpit. Bandit looked up from his controls and the boy gawked at Healey through the glass. Rodeo's mouth moved in the command cradle behind Bandit's seat, but Healey had already made up his mind. He knew what he had to do.

Skyscrapers and hotels whizzed past Healey's eyes. He yanked his stick sideways and veered into the Drifter's path

He released his rear hatch and it smashed open. Pounding wind thundered into the Nitrol and the helm rocked something awful. Healey had to use all his strength to keep the ship on course.

He slowed just the slightest bit and crouched low in his seat bracing for impact. The *Artemis Rex* smashed nose first into the *Prometheus Vox's* rear compartment and the force slammed both ships downward even faster.

The *Artemis Rex* struck the *Prometheus Vox* with brutal force, but the Drifter must have hit at a slight angle. The crash jolted the *Prometheus Vox* sideways and the Nitrol jerked out of Healey's control.

The ship swiveled all the way over on its side and the wind and gravity ripped the *Artemis Rex* out of the hatch. The ship tumbled into space and crashed down hard in a street several blocks away.

Healey gritted his teeth and dragged the nose up just enough for the *Prometheus Vox* to smash belly downward on the pavement. The impact clashed Healey's jaws together and he saw stars for a second.

He hauled his eyes open. The whole front of the cockpit had smashed in, but he didn't care about that. He released his safety harness and charged out the hatch into the open.

He had to look around before he figured out where the *Artemis Rex* was. A bunch of alien locals was already gathering around the crashed Drifter.

Healey charged over there and shouldered his way through the onlookers. He approached the rear loading hatch and found it completely smashed in.

He yanked at it and finally kicked it several times before he got it open. More locals gathered in droves watching the local sheriff break into the crashed ship.

Healey coughed smoke and fumes out of his throat when he staggered inside the *Artemis Rex*. He didn't see anyone alive at first, but he knew better. The Chorion Team was way too tough to go down in a crash like this.

He raced over to the accessory cradles and tore open the first one. "Come on!" he yelled. "You have to get out now!"

He grabbed Breeze and dragged the boy out onto the gangway. Breeze blinked at him and then shook himself out of Healey's grasp. "Marshall! What are you......?"

"Get out, Breeze! Get your boys and get out of the ship now!"

Breeze stood there staring at Healey, but Healey didn't have time for this. He sprang to the next cradle and pulled out Coon. "Get your boys out of the ship now, Coon! It's a matter of life and death."

Coon responded instantly and started going from cradle to cradle. He helped Wolf, Alla, and Axel out while Healey got Laub. Blood poured from a gash in Laub's scalp, but he seemed to be all right other than that.

Healey found Breeze and Alla breaking into the many weapons stores the boys had taken on board at Nyx Anonyma. "No weapons!" Healey ordered. "Get out on the street. Hurry!"

He pushed the boys toward the hatch. Some of the locals were peering inside to see what all the fuss was about. Healey turned back and almost collided with Rodeo supporting Bandit on his shoulder.

Bandit covered one eye with his hand and half his head was saturated with blood. Bandit's knees buckled with every step.

Healey caught Bandit on the other side and he and Rodeo half-carried Bandit outside. "Follow me!" Healey ordered. "We don't have much time!"

The other boys took off after him. The rubberneckers parted to let Healey through. The farther the party moved from the wreck site, the less people noticed them.

The Chorion Team surrounded Healey in front, on both sides, and behind. They kept scanning their surroundings with hard, piercing glares and no one dared to come near them.

Healey kept going for several blocks before he let himself slow down. He steered Bandit and Rodeo into a rundown gambling hall. Healey didn't see anywhere else to put Bandit, so he lowered the boy into a chair at one of the empty tables.

A few patrons looked up when the Chorion Team entered and then everyone went back to what they were doing.

Rodeo sat down in the chair next to Bandit and took hold of the boy's wrist. "Let me see, boy. We need to see how bad the damage is."

Bandit took his hand down and started wailing. "My ship! It's ruined! Do you have any idea how much work I put into that ship?"

"Not as much as I did," Coon added.

"Your head is caved in and you're worried about your ship?" Healey looked around the gambling den. "We need to get some supplies. I'll go talk to the madam and see about...."

Coon laid his hand on Healey's arm. "You stay here, Marshall. I'll go."

Healey started to argue back and then noticed the determined gleam in the boy's eye. The whole Chorion Team surrounded Healey, Bandit, and Rodeo in a guarding posture.

Coon and Axel slipped away through the door and vanished outside. Healey turned his attention back to Bandit, who was still holding forth to Rodeo about the *Artemis Rex*. "Did you see those Kreikals in the crowd? They'll strip the whole ship down and there won't be anything left to salvage."

"There wasn't much left when we crashed," Alla pointed out.

"Don't worry about the ship," Rodeo told Bandit. "You remember what Davenport said? He's gonna buy us each a Drifter as good as the *Artemis Rex* when we got back to Nyx Anonyma."

"Davenport!" Bandit snorted and looked away. "That guy is never going back to Nyx Anonyma—not ever!"

No one answered and Rodeo cocked his ear to listen to the gamblers around him. "What's the plan, Marshall?"

"You saw the Reserve Wing come out from Atlas Arcane," Healey replied. "They came out for you, not me. I need to get you boys under cover. They know you crashed here, so it's only a matter of time before they come down on the Needle to look for you."

Coon and Axel came back and laid armloads of medical supplies on the table in front of Bandit. They edged Healey out of the way and both boys started working on their friend's head. They did it with as much care and precision as they used when repairing their ship.

Healey wandered over to the door and peered out. He squinted up at the sky. "They're still up there patrolling. We need to move."

"Give us a minute." Coon bent over Bandit's head and fired up what looked like a welding torch.

Bandit sniffed and moaned a few times while he kept complaining about losing the *Artemis Rex*. He never even mentioned the pain in his head.

The procedure resembled no medical treatment Healey had ever seen before, but by the time he went back over to the table to see what they were doing, it was all over.

Coon wrapped bandages around Bandit's head, covered his injured eye with a patch, and taped everything in place. "You're good to go, boy."

Laub clapped Bandit on the back. "Keep going this way and you'll be as much of a badass as Rodeo."

The others laughed and Coon turned to Laub. "Let's take a look at your head, boy."

"What for? It's fine."

Coon peered closely at Laub's scalp, but the cut had completely closed. "You better clean yourself up, then. You look like the walking dead."

"We don't have time for that," Healey interjected, "and he'll blend in better like this. Let's go."

Healey ducked his head out of the building, stole a peek at the skies, and hustled the boys back onto the street. They made much better progress now that Bandit was on his feet.

Healey still didn't see how Coon fixed Bandit so quickly. Whatever he did with his welding torch had not only fixed Bandit's head but had also restored him to full consciousness. Bandit moved as fast and sure as the rest of his friends, though he still kept making side remarks about losing the *Artemis Rex*.

Healey picked up the pace as he entered the center of town. "Where are we going, Marshall?" Rodeo asked.

"There's only one place on the Needle you'll be safe from the Reserve Wing. If any Confederate personnel recognized you as Chorions, they would rat you out in seconds. You boys are the only Chorions on the Needle. Take my word for it."

Chapter 22

Healey didn't speak to the Chorion Team until he got to the seedier part of town. The boys kept surrounding him like he was the one who needed protection, but he didn't argue with that. They were the only Chorions on Pandora's Needle and that made them some of the toughest aliens in town.

He entered a crappy store full of customers and trashy goods no one wanted to buy. The proprietor stood in front of the counter with two Xids on leashes. He called to his customers to place bets while the two creatures fought and bit each other on the floor.

Healey skirted the commotion and guided the boys to the very rear. He opened a door and motioned the boys inside. "Get downstairs. You can hide down there until I find a way to get you off the Needle."

"What's down there?" Bandit asked.

"Nothing you can't handle. I gotta go. I'll find you as soon as I can."

The boys filed into the dark stairs beyond the door. Rodeo waited until last. He cocked one ear toward Healey and the boy's sightless eyes made Healey squirm.

The other boys vanished, but Rodeo didn't turn to follow them. He stared at a spot six inches to the left of Healey's face. "You've got a problem, Marshall."

"I know that, son. I gotta get out of here. I can't stick around any longer. You boys will be fine down there. I know you will."

Rodeo inclined his ear the other way. "You should come with us. It isn't safe for you out there."

"And you think it's safe for me down there?" Healey pretended to snort, but his heart wasn't in it. "I'm a dead man down there."

"It's safer for you down there than it is up here. Come on, Marshall. You can't go out there. You're as wanted as we are."

"Then I can slow them down and stop them from tracking you."

Rodeo shook his head. Healey didn't want to argue…. or maybe he just didn't want to go back downstairs. His recent experience down there still haunted him.

He pushed Rodeo toward the door. "Go on, boy. You and your friends are more important than me. I'll take care of things up here. Just make sure you're down here when I come back."

Rodeo tried to resist, but Healey didn't give him a chance. He pushed Rodeo onto the stairs and shut the door.

He stood there watching the Xids fight while he decided what to do. The Reserve Wing was after the Chorion Team, and if Rodeo was right, they were after Healey, too.

Healey already knew Rodeo was right. The Reserve Wing came after Healey, too. Admiral Joyce must have sent word that Healey and the Chorion Team were making for the Needle. Now they were here and everyone in the whole Reserve Wing knew it.

Healey had been playing both sides of the fence for far too long. He actually felt relieved that he could stop pretending to work for Joyce and the Reserve Wing. At least everyone knew now which side he was really on.

He finally sauntered toward the store exit and stopped on the sidewalk. Prostitutes, drug dealers, and a few slave traders greeted him or just nodded. They all knew him and he knew them, but he wasn't here to bust anybody today.

He considered walking the rest of the way to the jail, but Bandit's words came back to him. No ship would be safe in the neighborhood where he left the *Prometheus Vox*.

He went back to the Nitrol and already found several aliens sawing into the hull. He chased them off and fired the engines. The Reserve Wing Daggers had retreated back to Atlas Arcane, but the whole episode didn't bode well for anyone sympathetic to Davenport's cause.

Healey lifted off and floated over to the jail. He landed in his usual place on the roof and powered down the ship. His gut told him not to go inside. Going inside was dangerous. He still had a chance to get away if he went downstairs with the boys—not that that would be any less dangerous and probably more so.

He didn't like running away, not without good reason, and he had every reason to stay and take the fall in the boys' place. He strode downstairs and went to the main office.

Deputies stopped what they were doing to stare at him as he passed. No one greeted him. They looked at him like they didn't even recognize him.

His nerves stretched to the breaking when he approached his own office and heard voices inside.

The first one belonged to Jason Phelps, Healey's chief deputy and the man Healey left in charge when he went out to help Davenport.

He didn't know the other voices coming from inside. They rose and fell in a steadily rising tide of tension and conflict. Healey had rarely heard that tone in the Pandora's Needle jail. Whoever they were, they were arguing with Phelps.

Healey halted at the threshold and looked inside. Six Reserve Wing officers stood around the desk facing off against Phelps on the other side of it. They bombarded him with questions, demands, and accusations while he did his best to defend himself.

"I told you a thousand times," he snapped. "I don't know where he is. He took the *Prometheus Vox* and tracked a freighter to Sacron Enigma. That's all I know."

"You could have tracked him down," one of the officers returned.

Phelps snorted. "Do I look like I have time to hunt for random freighters all over known space and beyond? He told me to handle things here while *he* tracked it down, so that's what I've been doing. You have access to more records than I do. Why don't *you* track him down if you want him so bad?"

"How do we know you aren't hiding him?"

"Are you out of your minds? I never even knew he was wanted until you idiots showed up here today. Even then, I wouldn't have believed it. We're talking about Lawrence Healey. He's the greatest sheriff this satellite has ever had. No way could he betray the Confederacy. I'll never believe that."

The words triggered something in Healey's chest. He couldn't stand aside and let Phelps defend him like this, not without doing something about it.

Healey stepped across the threshold. "Do you boys want something from me?"

The Reserve Wing officers spun around and Phelps gasped. "Marshall! Thank God you're back."

He started to hustle around the desk, but Healey held up his hand. "Stay where you are, Jason. This town needs a sheriff, and unless I'm mistaken, you already got the job." Healey turned to the officers. "Am I right, boys?"

The officers stiffened. One of them glanced down at Healey's star. He'd been promoted to Marshall so recently that he was still wearing his sheriff's star instead of a marshall's star. Another looked down at Healey's sidearms and a third looked over his shoulder toward Phelps.

More than one fidgeted. Their fingers flexed in that subtle way that Healey knew only too well. They were all preparing to grab their sidearms and start shooting. Six against one. Those were pretty long odds.

Healey shot one last look at Phelps. Phelps's fingers twitched, too. He was bracing himself to open fire on the Reserve Wing from behind.

Healey gave him a barely perceptible shake of the head. Phelps shouldn't destroy his career defending Healey. That would be stupid especially since Admiral Joyce would only install his own man at Pandora's Needle in Phelps's place. That would be terrible.

Healey dragged his eyes back to the officers in front of him. "If you boys have something you want to say to me, I'm all ears. What's this about me being wanted?"

"You're under arrest by authority of the Confederate Corps Reserve Wing," the first one told him. The guy's nametag read, *Lucas.*

Healey raised his eyebrows. "That's interesting. The last time I checked, the Reserve Wing doesn't have the jurisdiction to arrest anyone. You need to contact the Sheriff's Service for that." Healey looked past Lucas's shoulder. "Am I under arrest by authority of the Sheriff's Service, Jason?"

"Hell no, Marshall," Jason growled. "These assholes don't even have a warrant."

"You crossed illegally into Sacron Enigma," Lucas pointed out. "Then you crossed back illegally without the necessary stamp from an authorized...."

"You got it all wrong. I already cleared this up with Sheriff Pritchard of the Wide Patrol." Healey waited for the words to sink in. These dopes might not know anything else about Confederate law, but every last one of them sure as hell knew who Deacon Pritchard was.

"Sheriff Pritchard took me into custody and cleared up the matter of me crossing in and out of Sacron Enigma, so that's all taken care of," Healey chirped. "What else do you have against me?"

The other officers exchanged glances. Phelps started to walk around the desk again. The poor guy was going to be draining Healey's supply of Zombie XX before too long.

"There you go," Phelps announced. "If you boys don't have anything else to add, we all have work to do here and Marshall Healey will just...."

The first two officers stepped toward Healey and they both moved their hands to their sidearms. "You're under arrest and ordered to cooperate while we take you into custody on Atlas Arcane. You're wanted for crimes against the Confederacy...."

Phelps pulled his sidearm so fast that Healey didn't see him until it was too late. He leveled his gun at Lucas and snapped it ready to fire. "Get your hands away from your weapons, raise your hands where I can see them, and back away! Move out of this office and ...."

Healey started to warn Phelps not to do this when a different officer at the end of the line yanked his weapon spun around to confront Phelps.

Phelps jerked his sidearm that way and fired even before the officer cleared his weapon from its holster.

The guy buckled at the knees and the whole office exploded at once. All the Reserve Wing guys pulled their sidearms in both directions. Two of them targeted Phelps and the other three rounded on Healey. He dove sideways drawing his weapon and fired into the nearest sucker's head.

The guy toppled. That left four.

Phelps dodged behind the desk and took cover trading shots with the other two. Healey landed hard on his shoulder and dropped a third. That left one more.

He heard yelling in the background and more gunshots coming from outside the office, but he didn't have time to see what was going on.

A fourth officer stormed over to him shooting straight down at Healey.

He rotated onto his back and the two of them blasted away at each other within inches of each other. Healey felt impacts slamming him into the ground. He knew he was getting hit, but he didn't feel any pain.

He jerked his gun up and fired straight into his enemy's head. The guy whipped backward and crashed into his friends who were stalking Phelps's hiding place.

They turned around to see who was bumping into them and the guy's body hit the floor. The last two turned their backs on Phelps to face Healey and he plugged them both in the backs of their head.

A dangerous silence fell over the office—the office that used to be Healey's. Today ended that. He felt his strength and lifeblood draining out onto the floor. He continued aiming his gun straight up at the ceiling, but he couldn't move. He didn't seem to be able to lower his gun.

Phelps came over to him and very gingerly pushed Healey's gun hand aside so Healey wasn't pointing the weapon at Phelps's head.

Phelps went down on one knee next to Healey. Phelps's eyes ranged over Healey's body and Healey saw reflected in that glance that it was bad. It couldn't be worse.

Phelps gulped. "Marshall...."

"Jason..." Healey choked. "Take.... over.... here...."

"Sure, Marshall. No problem."

Healey felt his arm hit the floor and that was the last thing he felt before the whole world blacked out.

Chapter 23

Coon bumped into someone in the dark. Whoever it was tripped over him and grunted. Coon caught hold of one of his companions and tried to push them off. Another body collided with the first and both of them crashed to the floor at Coon's feet.

"Damn you, Breeze!" Axel muttered in the dark. "Now is not the time!"

"I meant to do that." Breeze straightened up. That left one more body at Coon's feet.

Rodeo's voice barked out of the dark from farther up the stairs. "Knock it off, Breeze! We don't have time to mess around."

Coon patted whoever it was and felt a large, squishy body twice the size of anyone else on the Chorion Team. Coon dragged Alla to his feet and dusted off his friend. "You okay, boy?"

"Yeah," Alla panted. "Thanks."

"Is everyone here?" Rodeo asked. "Let me hear you sound off."

"I'm here," Breeze began.

"We know that, asshole!" Axel growled. "We wish you weren't."

"I can't help it!" Breeze replied. "I was just..."

"Shut up, Breeze," Rodeo barked. "I know you and Axel are here, Coon. Where's Wolf?"

A low growl came from farther down the stairs behind Coon's back. "I'm here, too," Bandit added from behind Rodeo.

"I'm here," Laub replied from off to the right.

"Where do you suppose we're going, Rodeo?" Coon asked.

He couldn't see his friend, but Coon could imagine Rodeo cocking his head from one side to the other. Rodeo could hear as much in the dark as any of the boys could see in daylight.

"We're heading for some kind of market underground. It's full of aliens—illegal ones. Marshall Healey must want to hide us down there."

"If it's illegal, it will be dangerous," Bandit remarked.

"Of course it's dangerous, dope," Axel countered. "Healey wouldn't send us there if it wasn't. That's why we're safer there. The Reserve Wing won't look for us there and none of the aliens will tell any Confederate personnel that we're there."

"What's going on down there?" Alla asked. "Don't leave us in the dark."

A slap echoed in the stairway. "We are in the dark, dumbass!" Laub pointed out.

"I only meant...."

"Cork it, all of you," Rodeo ordered. "They're fighting down there which means we'll have to fight."

"We can handle fighting," Laub replied.

"Just stay alert," Rodeo continued. "Don't let your guard down. Imagine we're back home."

Axel chuckled low. "Perfect."

"Let's go." Rodeo pushed between Coon and Breeze and started down the stairs. Coon turned right behind Rodeo and followed his footsteps. Rodeo would never steer the others wrong. Coon made up his mind to keep close to Rodeo no matter what.

The others fell in line behind Coon and he heard them muttering and talking back there. Axel took the place right behind Coon.

Another scuffle broke out when Breeze tried to get in line between Laub and Alla. Laub shoved Breeze hard enough to knock the boy into the wall. "You bring up the rear, chump. You'll do the least damage there."

Breeze complained, but no one listened, and a few minutes later, Wolf snarled at him. Breeze must have run afoul of Wolf which was never a good idea.

Coon almost collided with Rodeo when Rodeo halted in the middle of the stairwell. "Hold up here, boys," Rodeo hissed. "We're right outside the door. We're going in, so stay on your toes."

The others crowded around. "Holy shit! Listen to that!" Bandit murmured. "What the hell is going on in there?"

"It sounds like a fight," Axel remarked.

"That's because it is one," Rodeo replied. "This is it. Be ready for anything. Is everyone here?"

"Yes," Breeze replied and Wolf growled again.

"Okay. Here we go."

Rodeo threw open the door and light streamed into the stairwell from beyond. The place the boys entered was a vast underground cavern packed the walls and ceiling with hundreds of aliens. They came from countless species from all over the Confederacy and some Coon didn't recognize at all.

Almost all of them crowded around one spot on the floor. Empty stalls and piles of goods stood unattended. The stallholders cheered and hooted around some kind of disturbance, but Coon couldn't see what it was through the mob.

Rodeo inclined his head one way and then another listening to the din. Bandit tried to yell in Rodeo's ear, but Rodeo held up his hand to silence him.

Coon surveyed the market while he waited for Rodeo to make some decision. Healey was right about one thing. The boys were the only Chorions in the whole place.

All at once, a deafening roar split the noise. The whole Chorion Team whirled around ready to defend themselves.

They had to stagger out of the way as a huge giant reared out of the crowd. It swelled to a colossal size until its massive back and shoulders smashed into the stone ceiling high above.

Curved horns jutted from its knobbed skull and tusks hooked from its mouth. It looked so much like Dice that Coon instantly recognized that this must be another Adik.

This one was also a male, but he was unlike any Adik Coon had ever seen before. The monster kept swelling getting bigger and bigger by the minute. He smashed his horns into the ceiling and then doubled over to punch his enormous fists into the floor.

A loud electric crackle broke the chaos and sparks erupted from metal collars around the Adik's neck, arms, and thighs. Half a dozen aliens perched on a high shelf fixed to the wall.

They laughed while they pressed buttons on some kind of device. They must be the ones shocking the Adik to drive him berserk.

The shock enraged the Adik into a fresh explosion of rage. He charged the crowd and scattered everyone before him. He stomped on several people before they could get away from him.

Dozens of onlookers stumbled and scrambled to get out of his path before he swiped a huge fist sideways. He sent a dozen people flying and rotated the other way to stab his horns into another group that got caught in the stampede.

His victims couldn't get away and he impaled four, two on each horn. He tossed his head with their bodies flopping and flailing in their death throes.

He threw them off and they wheeled across the cavern where they struck the walls and got trampled underfoot. Other aliens who got away from him turned back to cheer, pump their fists, and continue yelling encouragement and delight.

Coon braced himself for a fight to the death when the Adik turned his ferocious eyes on the Chorion Team. Axel stepped in front of Coon and straight-armed him, Rodeo, and Bandit behind him. Laub and Wolf both moved forward and planted themselves next to Axel.

The Adik narrowed his eyes to deadly slits. He bared his fangs and roared at the Chorions in murderous fury. This must be what Rodeo meant by needing to fight the minute the Chorions showed up at this market.

The Adik hunched his shoulders to charge when another scream tore through the crowd. A wave of bodies peeled aside and a giant horned beast charged from somewhere.

The thing galloped on tree-trunk legs and pounded its iron hooves on the stone floor. A huge boned frill surrounded its neck and three stout horns stuck straight out of its armored forehead.

The thing ran full tilt into the Adik from behind and impaled him in the back. The creature's horns stabbed through the Adik's chest and he writhed there with blood pouring from all three punctures.

He reared backward thrashing, contorting, and roaring in pain, but he couldn't turn around as long as the creature held him there.

The crowd burst into even louder cheers. People slapped each other on the backs, traded money, and pointed at the Adik seething in agony before them.

The creature tossed its head, but it couldn't lift the Adik's weight. The creature yanked its neck back and forth trying to free itself from its burden. The Adik thundered to the skies in pain and fury.

He gave a terrific lunge and tore himself off the creature's horns. Blood gushed from the three wounds and saturated his clothes, but he didn't notice.

He turned around and attacked the creature with all his strength. He seized the thing off the ground, raised it on high, and smashed the creature down across his knee. The Adik cracked its mighty spine and then slammed the creature to the floor.

The Adik pounced on the creature, jumped on top of it to straddle it, and started punching into its armored head.

The creature gave a deafening bellow when the Adik broke it across his knee, but its sounds stopped the second he started punching it. He smashed its head to a sodden pulp on the floor and still he hammered it with ground-shaking blows.

The crowd cheered even more loudly if that was possible. People jumped up and down in ecstasy and money changed hands all over the place.

Bandit said something to Rodeo, but Coon couldn't hear him over the noise. Yells, shouts, and laughter rang off the walls and throbbed with energy.

A scream ripped through the crowd when the Adik finished flattening the creature's skull to a puddle. The Adik sprang to his feet, spun around to face the crowd, and let out a punishing roar.

The onlookers bolted to get away from him. They huddled behind their goods and the aliens on the shelf shocked him again, but he didn't charge.

He towered before them with black blood flowing down his torso and running into his torn pants. He glared out at the crowd baring his teeth....and then he swayed. He snarled at his tormentors, but he didn't take a single step.

Silence fell over the market as everyone held their breath watching him. He teetered on his heels for a second while he eyed them with small, furious black eyes.

The aliens on the shelf shocked him one last time. He threw back his head and let out a broken, anguished bellow before he collapsed. His giant body thumped the floor hard enough to send vibrations through Coon's legs....and then the Adik lay still.

No one breathed for a second and then a collective murmur of relief ran around the market. People sighed, got to their feet, and came forward to surround the two dead aliens.

The merchants started talking fast, gesticulating, and discussing every detail of the fight. Money changed hands and then everyone started migrating back to their business.

"Whoa!" Bandit breathed. "Is that what we have to look forward to?"

"We'll handle it, boy." Rodeo started forward. "Let's see if we can find a place in here. Look. There's an empty spot over there. We can set up over there."

Chapter 24

Rodeo set off to cross the market floor and the other boys fell in behind him. No one paid any attention to the Chorion Team at first. The stallholders were still too preoccupied with the fight that just ended.

Rodeo headed for an empty spot across the cavern, but he hadn't gone more than twenty yards before the merchants noticed who exactly was crossing their market.

A few people watched the Chorion Team pass and then three others started following the boys. The merchants flanked the boys at a distance, but they matched Rodeo's pace and kept a safe gap between themselves and the Chorions.

Rodeo cocked his head to one side and listened while he walked. Coon's hair stood on end. Wolf came up behind him and Coon heard Wolf growling.

Coon laid his hand on Wolf's arm to steady him. The Chorion Team didn't need Wolf attacking before the right time inevitably came.

Wolf raised his hackles and bared his teeth at the onlookers, but that only aroused more curiosity from everyone. People gathered to watch the boys cross the market.

By the time Rodeo got near the empty place, two thick masses of people lined their route. The merchants and stallholders whispered to each other and pointed.

Rodeo kept tilting his ears in all directions listening, but he didn't stop walking. Coon didn't dare to ask what these people wanted. He didn't want to find out even though he thought he already knew.

Rodeo pulled up in the empty place, turned around, and motioned the other boys to join him. "We'll stay here until...."

A short, stout alien with arms and legs far too short for the rest of his body waddled out of the crowd to approach the Chorion Team's position. A tiny head perched on broad, overstuffed shoulders with no neck connecting the two.

"You're Chorions, aren't you?" he squeaked to Rodeo.

"What if we are?"

"Are you here to hire out your services?"

Rodeo inclined his ear the other way. "We might be for the right price. What's your budget?"

The alien surveyed the other boys and nodded at Wolf. "How much for the regressive?"

Wolf lunged for the guy spitting and snarling. It took Coon and Axel working together to drag Wolf back.

"None of us is for sale" Rodeo told the alien. "If you have a legitimate business proposition to make, let's hear it. Otherwise, move along and make way for the real customers."

The guy laughed a high, twittering laugh. "You really must be a Chorion if you talk like that."

"You can see that we are. Are you here to talk business or are you just going to waste my time?"

The guy laughed again and grinned at the other merchants standing around listening. He grinned like a fool when he faced Rodeo for the second time. "You won't get any work until you prove yourselves."

"Here it comes," Axel muttered.

"What do you have in mind?" Rodeo asked.

The alien waved one of his stumpy arms toward the crowd. "We're always looking for new friends to give us some entertainment."

"What's the payoff?" Rodeo asked.

The guy's cheery smile twisted in a grim smirk. "The payoff is that you get to live and do business down here instead of winding up in the plasma stream where all the half-assed wannabes end up. Prove yourselves and you can do all the business you want down here. If you don't...." He waved toward the dead Adik and its equally massive dead opponent.

"Fine," Rodeo replied. "We'll do it. Who's the opponent?"

"That depends on which of you is going to fight." The guy studied each of the boys in turn. "Which one of you will go first—you?" He made a disgusted face at Rodeo.

"Which one of us goes first depends on what species you pit us against. Let us see the opponent and then we'll decide which one to send out."

The alien held up a fat finger. "Only one of you can go out at a time. Those are the rules."

"Agreed."

"What about that?" The guy motioned toward the dead creature that just impaled the Adik. "Could you handle that?"

Rodeo nodded. "All right. Give us a minute to confer and we'll send out our boy."

The guy laughed. "You're crazy! None of you could handle that thing."

Rodeo scowled and his countenance went black and dangerous. "Do you want to bet on that?"

The guy exploded in giggles and a rush of murmurs and whispers went through the crowd. "You want to bet? All right. How much do you want to bet?"

Rodeo bent over and whispered to Coon. "How much do we have between us?"

Coon rummaged in his pockets. "I have forty-five Confederate talents."

"That isn't enough." Rodeo turned to the other boys. "Cough up your money, Alla."

"Aw, man!" Alla complained.

"Do you want to get out of here alive? Hand it over."

Alla started rummaging in his pockets and brought out a hundred more talents. He dumped them into Coon's palms and then turned away to hide his glum expression from the others.

"I have eighty Sritcha tokens." Breeze drew the tokens from somewhere and held them out.

"Where the hell did you get those, you little shit?" Axel countered. "Don't tell me you stole them from Ekol Thaine."

Breeze turned bright red. "I didn't steal them."

"Let me guess," Bandit fired back. "You accidentally tripped and fell, knocked over a priceless vase, loosened a stone in the floor, and the tokens just sort of fell into your pocket. Is that something like how it went?"

Breeze opened his mouth to defend himself, but Rodeo cut him off. "Quiet! How he got them doesn't matter now. If he stole them from Ekol, Ekol will cut his nuts off the minute he gets back to Nyx Anonyma and we can all sleep better at night."

Breeze shut his mouth flushing even more, but Rodeo ignored him.

"Alla, you'll go out against the creature."

"Why me?" Alla yelled. "Why does it always have to be me?"

"Because you're the best." Coon squeezed Alla's neck affectionately. "You're gonna put the fear of God into all these idiots."

"Wonderful," Alla grumbled. "I can't wait."

"Are you hungry, Alla?" Rodeo asked. "This is your chance to impress everyone and get yourself a free meal into the bargain."

Alla perked up. "You're right. Great idea."

Rodeo turned back to Coon. "I'll bet your forty-five talents on the fight. As soon as Alla goes out on the floor, you get into the crowd and wager everything we have on Alla to win. Take the longest odds you can get. None of these shitheads will be expecting him to win."

"If I get skewered by that thing, I want a proper burial," Alla added from behind. "Promise you won't leave me down here to get roasted on a spit."

"I promise." Rodeo turned back to Coon. "Do you understand what you have to do?"

Coon nodded. "You bet."

"Just keep Breeze away from the fight. We don't want any of these people accusing us of sabotaging the betting."

"Hey!" Breeze yelled. "I can hear every word you say."

Rodeo pointed at him. "You stay well out of the way, boy. Don't go anywhere near the fight. That's an order."

Breeze retreated to sulk and Rodeo faced their new friend. "Forty-five Confederate talents on our boy to win."

The guy held up both stumpy hands. "I can't accept that bet until I see which one of you is going out."

Rodeo steered Alla forward. "This one."

The guy burst into more hysterical laughter. "Forty-five on *him*? You got yourself a bet, son! I'll give you odds of five hundred to one."

"You're on." Rodeo handed over Coon's money. "Bring out the creature."

The crowd scattered and didn't even try to whisper anymore. Excited talk rippled through the cavern with everyone gathering around. They talked and bet like crazy.

Coon didn't have to go anywhere. The merchants came up to him. They thrust their money at him offering incredible odds against Alla surviving the next few minutes.

The guy who had been dealing with Rodeo raced away and vanished into the crowd. Coon got distracted by all the people who wanted to take out bets with him. He counted and calculated as fast as he could. He handed money back and forth and scribbled notes as fast as he could write.

A deafening boom jolted him to high alert and all the surrounding aliens spun away looking in the same direction.

All eyes turned to a spot beyond the crowd and the same clomping footsteps trembled the floor. A dozen burly aliens came into view pushing a giant cage containing another one of the horned creatures.

The aliens jabbed barbed prods through the bars and the thing crashed and thrashed to get free. They parked the cage to one side and all the onlookers pushed back to clear a broad section of floor around the cage. That must be where they wanted Alla to fight the thing.

Rodeo eased up behind Alla and murmured in his ear. "Can you take it?"

"Yep. No problem." Alla eyed the creature across the market, but he didn't cringe or complain or moan. He stood up straighter and a hard, determined look came over his flabby face.

Rodeo prodded him forward. "Go on, then. Let everyone get a good look at you before the fight starts."

Alla shambled out on the floor. He swayed slightly when he walked. His fat stomach, arms, and ass wobbled for all the surrounding aliens to see. Many of them pointed at him and laughed.

The light coming from above reflected on his glasses and he shuffled to a halt a dozen yards from the creature's cage. He looked like the absolute last person in creation who would be able to defeat this thing in open battle.

Everyone had just seen this creature kill a fully expanded and enraged Adik. No way could Alla match the Adik in strength and ferocity. The thing would flatten Alla in seconds.

Aliens mobbed Coon yelling at him and waved their money in his face. The betting got so frantic that Axel and Rodeo had to come over and help him out.

Even then, too many people wanted to bet against Alla. The dumpy alien who first approached the Chorion Team had to intervene. He shoved into the mob and waved them away so he could start the fight.

The crowd gathered around Alla and the creature. More betting continued amongst the spectators, but Coon's job was done. He clutched a stack of notes in one hand and a pile of money in the other.

Alla stood still in the center of the floor. He faced the creature's cage without looking around at anyone else.

Coon was just trying to figure out what to do with all the crap in his hands when a big alien guarding the creature unlatched the cage. The barred door swung back with a clang.

The creature didn't react right away. One of the aliens prodded it again. It roared and lunged sideways to crash into the bars, but it didn't run forward.

Three more aliens distracted it while another went behind the cage. The guy prodded the creature extra hard from behind and it rocketed out of the cage with an ear-splitting bellow.

It charged straight for Alla and the crowd exploded in cheers. Everyone started yelling and pumping their fists at Alla and the creature, but he didn't move. He never took his eyes off the thing as it thundered nearer to gore him.

Coon stiffened. Axel flinched and started to look away. Alla waited until the last possible second before the creature plunged its horns through his body. Without warning, he threw back his head, cracked his mouth to a gargantuan size, and he lunged for the creature.

His mouth stretched to a gaping black hole and he dove his head on top of the charging creature. Alla's enormous, oversized mouth engulfed the creature in one gulp and he swallowed it.

The crowd fell into a stunned silence as he straightened up, chewed a few times, and gulped. His mouth returned to its normal size and he stood before them, as whole and undisturbed as before.

The surrounding onlookers blinked at him, at the empty cage, the empty floor—the whole unearthly scene. The creature was gone and Alla remained in the center of the floor, the undisputed champion.

Laub let out a whoop and the boys charged onto the floor. They mobbed Alla laughing, thumping him on the back, and rumpling his hair. Coon fought back emotion hugging Alla and laughing while he and the other boys congratulated their friend.

Alla blushed and tried to bat their affections away. "Cut it out!"

"Do you feel better?" Rodeo yelled over the noise. "Not so hungry now, are you?'

Alla laughed and the others joined in the joke, but only for a second. Rodeo straightened up and turned to face the crowd. He rotated in a circle until he faced the little alien who bet five hundred to one that Alla would lose.

Another tense silence fell over the cavern. The notes burned a hole in Coon's hands. Now came the day of reckoning. The boys tightened into a cluster in case anyone gave them any trouble about paying their debts.

The little alien waddled forward and he wasn't grinning now. He halted in front of Rodeo and eyed the boy with a harsh glare. Rodeo trained his blind eyes to a spot to one side and listened. "A bet is a bet."

"You're right, son. You won that one fair and square." The guy scooted forward and slapped a fat sack of jingling coins into Coon's hand. "I'm Kuvan. I can represent you from now on if you want. I can arrange more fights so you can start building your reputations and earn some more money."

"That would be great." Rodeo extended his hand. "Good to meet you."

They shook hands and the rest of the crowd reacted instantly. They streamed onto the floor and all the people who bet against Alla came toward Coon to settle up.

He spent the next few hours counting and settling until his head swam. Axel and Laub both helped him, but it still took forever.

By the time they finished, they had too much money to carry. They spent some of it to buy a strongbox to store it all. Then they took their winnings back to the spot on the market floor that would become their territory.

Chapter 25

Coon sat on the strongbox counting the latest winnings from Alla's fight against the horned beast.

"When are you going to stop counting that money?" Bandit asked from across the circle. "We've been here for two days. You should know how much is in that box."

"I *would* know how much is in it if Alla didn't keep getting hungry and wanting to spend the money on food. Now stop distracting me. I'm trying to count, and if you keep interrupting, I'll have to start all over."

"Can't you just subtract what he spends from the total?" Bandit asked.

Coon sighed and gave it up. He couldn't concentrate with everyone talking. "I might be able to if he told me how much he keeps taking. Soon we won't have anything left."

"One thing is for certain," Rodeo added. "We have less now than we had right after the fight. We need to buy a ship to get off the Needle which means we need to earn some more. Oh, good. Here comes Kuvan."

The little alien waddled out of the crowd and grinned at the boys sitting around. "Are you boys ready to make some more money?"

"We were just going to come find you," Rodeo replied. "Are you ready to set up another fight for us?"

Kuvan swayed faster on his dumpy legs and squirmed with excitement. "Yes! Which one of you is it this time?"

"Which opponent do you have for us?" Laub asked.

Kuvan giggled. "I'll bring him over and show him to you. Then you can decide who wants to die."

Kuvan scampered off into the crowd. "Great," Bandit grumbled. "He'll probably bring out another Adik. That would be just wonderful."

"Don't worry, boy," Rodeo told him. "You're a hotshot pilot, but you won't be fighting anybody as long as we're down here."

Bandit sniffed and looked away. "It doesn't matter how much money we make. We'll never get another ship as good as the *Artemis Rex*."

"Rodeo," Coon muttered.

"What's up?"

Coon sat rooted to his strongbox, but he wasn't counting anymore. "Look."

"I can't see, you dimwit!" Rodeo started to turn back to Bandit.

Coon grabbed Rodeo's hand, yanked him across the circle, and dragged him down on the box next to him. "Directly across the market...." Coon murmured in his ear. "Talking to the Storrik.... remember?"

Rodeo froze and furrowed his brow. He cocked his head one way and then the other. "I can't hear. There's too much noise."

"There's a Storrik...talking to a Ghrukeds.... talking to a Slotiezt...."

Bandit and Axel wandered over to see what they were looking at. "Son of a bitch!" Axel growled. "Mexia's people are here!"

"Of course they're here!" Rodeo fired back. "Marshall Healey sent them after us and they launched from here. What did you expect?"

"What he means is.... they're back," Coon pointed out. "They're back from HTWV-983."

"Holy shit!" Bandit whispered. "They're looking at us! They recognize us!"

"Everybody keep calm." Rodeo stood up and walked back to his former place. "We'll deal with this."

"How do we deal with it?" Laub asked. "If Mexia's people are here...."

"I think we can assume she'll send her people after us."

"Why would they do that?" Alla asked. "We never did anything to them on HTWV-983. It was always them trying to kill and capture us, not the other way around."

"Grow a brain for once in your life, Alla," Laub returned. "Mexia betrayed Calyx Elkanon by putting Davenport in danger. Marshall Healey only went to her because Calyx owes Davenport. You can bet your boots she'll want to stop us from telling anyone what she did."

"Just try to act normally," Rodeo ordered. "Coon, you go back to counting. We need...."

Kuvan came back and Rodeo stopped talking. Kuvan led a massive Yozain by a leash connected to a collar on the creature's neck.

The Yozain wore black armor covering his soft body. A flared helmet covered most of the alien's face with two blazing red eyes glaring out of the eye slits. An open section at the front left just enough room for the boys to see a fanged mouth. It peeled back in layers to reveal all the spikes hidden in there.

Several tentacles rotated around the creature's body. They sprouted from the alien's sides in place of arms and each sinuous limb held a long sword. More tentacles flowed between his body and the floor. They carried him along in a smooth, seamless flow.

Kuvan yanked the creature's leash to make the Yozain stop in front of the boys. Kuvan retreated to a safe distance and the creature started whirling his swords around with blinding speed.

The many weapons whistled through the air in a windmill blur. When he stopped, all the boys stared up at him, too stunned to speak.

Kuvan giggled again. "Well? Which one of you wants to lose his life today?"

Axel stood up. "I'll take him."

"Excellent." Rodeo gripped his shoulder. "That's my boy."

"What odds do you think you can get for me today?" Axel asked.

"You?" Kuvan laughed out loud. "I'll give you eight hundred to one."

"You're on," Axel replied. "Who else wants to try their luck?"

The boys scanned the market floor. Quite a few of the surrounding merchants had already been watching Kuvan bring the Yozain over to the Chorion Team.

As soon as Kuvan started leading the Yozain away, merchants swarmed the boys from all over. The same commotion of betting followed, but this time, Laub helped Coon tally all the bets and count out all the money.

The pool rose to more than double what the crowd bet on Alla. Axel watched the mayhem rising to a fevered pitch. Coon would have liked to talk to Axel before the fight, but he didn't get a chance.

Axel went over to Rodeo and started pulling off his shirt. "There has to be a faster way to make money than this."

"I'm working on it. It's like Kuvan says. We need to build a reputation for ourselves."

"You'll make an impression on them, Axel," Bandit called from across the circle.

"It's all very well until, one of these days, someone decides not to pay their bets."

"That's why we need reputation," Rodeo replied. "We need to let everyone understand that they don't want to do that."

Axel handed Rodeo his shirt and unbuttoned his pants. He stripped them off and handed them over so that he stood there in his shorts.

"What are you gonna do—make out with him?" Alla called out and Bandit and Breeze burst out laughing.

"Shut your ass," Axel growled. "Just remember I'm protecting you chickenshits by facing this cocksucker in your place."

That shut them up and Axel strode over to the space of floor the crowd was already clearing for him. He swung his arms back and forth a few times waiting for the fight to start.

The crowd seemed to have the same idea as Alla. They laughed, pointed, and jeered at Axel standing there in his underwear, but he pretended not to notice.

The Yozain started whirling his swords around even faster than before. The crowd burst into even more excited cheers and the aliens around Coon dispersed to watch the fight.

Coon happened to be facing in the same direction he had been sitting on the strongbox. His blood ran cold when he saw the same Storrik, the Ghruked, and the Slotiezt across the market.

They weren't looking at Axel and the Yozain. None of the three aliens were paying any attention to the fight at all.

They stared extra hard at Coon, Rodeo, and the other boys standing off to one side. The three aliens' intense scrutiny set Coon's nerves on end, but he didn't have time to warn Rodeo before the Yozain rushed Axel.

The Yozain could move a lot faster on his tentacles than anyone Coon had ever seen. The creature crossed the floor in a heartbeat and attacked Axel with all those swords flying.

Axel didn't move. He stood his ground and the Yozain's swords swirled around him in a blur. A surge of noise exploded out of the crowd as the first sword struck Axel across the neck and cleaved downward toward his bare chest.

The blade didn't even scratch him. It glanced off him and sparks flew from the spot as the weapon glanced off with a ringing clang.

The next instant, all the Yozain's blades hit Axel all over. They pinged and banged bouncing off his skin without touching him or harming him in any way.

He stood still and didn't move under the hail of blows. Sparks and chips of broken metal flew from every strike. Axel squinted to protect his eyes. Other than that, he made absolutely no move to defend himself.

"Yeah!" Alla yelled and pumped his fists with the rest of the crowd. "Give it to him, you son of a bitch!"

The Yozain noticed that his assault had no effect. He doubled down and laid into Axel even harder. The creature chopped and hacked at Axel with dozens of strikes—maybe even hundreds of strikes.

The Yozain became more and more agitated. He rotated around Axel and attacked Axel's back. Axel bowed his head taking the barrage on his head, neck, and shoulders. Nothing penetrated his iron skin.

The Yozain went into a frenzy pivoting here and there. He shifted back and forth, from Axel's front to back. The creature tried everything to find some vulnerability.

His swords struck harder and one of them cracked across the blade. The broken shard clattered to Axel's feet followed by three more split blades. The Yozain roared behind his helmet beating Axel all over.

The Yozain tried to target Axel's face. Axel raised his arm and held it in front of his eyes. That was the first time he'd moved through the whole fight.

Bandit, Breeze, Alla, and Rodeo advanced to the edge of the crowd. They all pumped their fists at Axel cheering him on and Coon couldn't help but join in. His heart soared watching the Yozain ruin his own weapons trying to hack Axel to pieces.

The Yozain shifted back around to Axel's front. The creature raised what was left of his weapons to strike, but Axel leveled him with such a firm, steady stare that the Yozain froze with all his swords raised to attack.

A strange silence fell between them for a second as they sized each other up. Without warning, the Yozain struck Axel a vicious blow right across the cheek. Axel's head whipped sideways from the force of it. Then he straightened up to look straight into the Yozain's eyes. Axel's face was totally undamaged.

The Yozain panted and snarled behind his mask, but he didn't strike again. The two warriors sank into another breathless silence while the crowd watched and waited for the outcome.

When it came, Axel struck back with blinding speed. He dropped on his side, snatched one of the Yozain's broken-off blades, and slashed out with a vengeance. He sliced off five tentacles and swiped back the other way to sever six more.

The Yozain wobbled trying to catch his balance and Axel sprang to his feet. He straightened up and, with no warning at all, he plunged his blade point first into the Yozain's face. Axel stabbed right between the eyes and the creature dropped with a bang.

All the splintered weapons hit the floor and the boys swarmed Axel in a pack. They hefted him off the ground slapping him and jostling him. The crowd responded much more quickly this time. They surrounded the boys congratulating Axel and shoving money at Coon.

Coon got swept up in another torrent of counting and settling. He lost sight of everyone except Laub in the confusion.

Laub took the money while Coon scribbled notes and passed them out to everyone who came near him. The crowd started to thin out and he was just about to relax when a splitting blow struck him across the side of the head.

He toppled, and a second later, he found himself flat on his back looking up at the giant Ghruked he'd seen earlier—the one who'd been talking to Mexia's people.

The Ghruked pounced on him swinging some kind of club. Coon got one good look at his attacker before he snapped. He retaliated on pure adrenaline and instinct.

He caught the club the next time his enemy swung, but the Ghruked's strength overcame Coon's best efforts. The club kept sailing at Coon's face and he guided it past his head.

It smashed into the floor and Coon laid into his attacker in a blind frenzy. He punched the Ghruked square across the head and tumbled on top of the guy. They rolled over and over scrapping, punching, and clawing to gain the upper hand.

Coon downed his opponent for a second and clambered on top of the Ghruked. Coon straddled him swinging for the fences. Coon caught glimpses of the other Chorions surrounded by the crowd. Fists flew and Laub heaved out of the throng.

He raised the big Storrik in his mighty arms, spun around, and hurled the alien into a pile of goods at a nearby stall. The Storrik impaled on a cluster of lances sticking out of a weapons display and Laub whipped around searching for his next victim.

Alla stood off to one side gulping down everyone who dared to come near him. A black blur spun in a streak over by the dead Yozain. Bodies toppled clutching slashed throats and destroyed eyes torn apart by Wolf's fangs.

Seeing his friends throwing down gave Coon new energy and he punched his fallen enemy again. The Storrik grabbed his club and held it up to protect himself from Coon's assault.

Coon was swinging too hard to pull his punch now. He adjusted his trajectory by a fraction of an inch and missed the club. He landed the blow against the Storrik's neck and kept on going.

He punched straight through the man's windpipe and felt the all-too-familiar pull of iron in the big alien's blood.

A roar made Coon glance up. Four more Storriks charged him out of the crowd. None of the other Chorions were close enough to get to him in time. Coon was on his own.

He reacted without thinking, grabbed his dead enemy, and dropped to one knee on the floor. He hauled the Storrik upright and spun the body around so the Storrik faced outward to his oncoming comrades.

The new arrivals saw their friend dead and barreled at Coon bellowing in murderous fury. Coon ducked behind the body and punched into its back with all his might.

He plunged his arm past the wrist in the Storrik's rib cage and all the elements in the alien's body swamped Coon's mind with a drunken sense of power.

He thrust the body toward his new attackers and he seized control of all the iron, copper, magnesium, and zinc in the Storrik's body.

The attackers saw him cowering behind a dead body and put on speed to flatten him. With a single thought, Coon harnessed all that metal and thrust it out through the Storrik's chest.

It formed into a dozen twisted, gnarled metal spikes that grew and formed and twined through the air. They stabbed into the enemy and impaled them all in several places.

The body, the skewers, and the four dead attackers fell out of Coon's hands and he folded to the floor, utterly exhausted by his own efforts. He wavered between drunken intoxication and unconsciousness.

His eyes wavered in and out of focus just long enough to see Rodeo, Axel, and Wolf appear out of the crowd. They stood over him guarding him from anyone else who might come near him. Rodeo had a gash above his eyebrow and Wolf was bleeding, but he still snarled at unseen enemies with his hair standing up across his back.

Breeze and Bandit crouched over Coon. They were both bleeding, too. "You okay, boy?" Bandit asked.

Coon couldn't summon the energy to speak. He hadn't expended his power that much in a long, long time.

Bandit picked him up and carried him across the floor. Coon thought once that he should at least stick around long enough to collect Axel's winnings. He didn't get a chance to before he drifted off and passed out.

Chapter 26

Healey woke up and looked around him to see where he was. He groaned when he found himself in a hospital bed with one wrist cuffed to the bed rail.

Jason Phelps sat in the chair next to his bed. The young deputy rested one ankle on his knee and scrolled distractedly on his device. He didn't look up when Healey raised his head. "Don't even think about trying to escape. The Reserve Wing has the whole building surrounded."

Healey ran the fingers of his other hand through his hair. He felt like shit. "Congratulations, Jason. You'll be made Sheriff of Pandora's Needle now."

Phelps flipped a page and scanned down the screen. "Oh, I already have been. Admiral Killian Joyce sent word for me to be promoted, now that you're going up to the Terminus Anathema."

"Great," Healey growled. "Just what I want to hear."

Phelps uncrossed his legs, tossed his device on the bedside table, and leaned forward to prop his elbows on his knees. He lowered his voice to a barely audible whisper.

"Is it true what they're saying about Mace Davenport? Is it true he confiscated an Ithium cartridge from smugglers—and that Joyce stole it from Helios Sanctus so he could release it somewhere inside the Confederacy?"

Healey had to gulp to get his throat to work. "Who told you that?"

"I went to high school with John Treese. You mentioned that the Wide Patrol was involved with this mess somehow. I contacted Pritchard and he told me everything."

"Then I don't have to explain it to you." Healey looked away. "Anyway, it's all over. Davenport is gone and I can't help him. I'm under arrest and I'm going up to the Terminus Anathema. I did all I could and now...." He swallowed again. "I just wish I could get word to the boys that I won't be coming back for them."

"What boys?"

"Never mind. It doesn't matter. Besides, they can take care of themselves. They're a hell of a lot tougher than I am."

Phelps stood up and paced across the room. He glanced through the door and came back. He stood over Healey's bed and jutted his chin at Healey's body stretched out on the bed. "How are you feeling, Marshall?"

"I feel okay….and you don't have to twist the knife by calling me that. I'm not a marshall or even a sheriff anymore."

"You might want to rethink that." Phelps pulled his keys out of this pocket and started unlocking the cuffs on Healey's wrist.

"What the hell are you doing?"

"Getting you out of here. Why do you think I volunteered to stand guard over you?" The cuffs fell away. "Get up, Marshall. You're leaving."

"You said the building was surrounded."

"It is—which is why we won't be going out that way."

Healey didn't ask any more questions. He threw back the covers and discovered that he was still wearing his uniform under the flimsy hospital pajama top. He was even still wearing his star.

Phelps pulled the curtain around Healey's bed and then pulled a gun belt from under the mattress. He passed it to Healey. "You're probably going to need this."

"Thank you, Jason."

"Shut up. I'm doing my job." Phelps went over to the window and looked out. "Any second now…."

He pushed the window open. This hospital room was at least forty stories above the street. Healey didn't see how he was going to go anywhere that way, but he didn't see any other way out.

He took a step toward the window and a blast of wind hit him from outside as another ship floated up from directly beneath where they stood.

It wasn't any standard Confederate make of vessel, which meant it must be illegal. It swiveled its rear hatch toward the window and the hatch opened.

Four more of Healey's former deputies stood inside. They all aimed their XQs at the window…and Phelps. He snatched another XQ from the corner right behind the chair where he'd just been sitting.

He rotated it to his shoulder and opened fire just as the deputies unloaded from the ship's rear. Blasts struck the window and broken glass splintered into the room. Most of it struck Phelps in the face and body, but he kept shooting back no matter what.

Healey yanked his sidearms to return fire when Phelps turned his twisted face Healey's way. "Go, Marshall! Go now! Get out of the building!"

Healey hesitated. He didn't see what Phelps meant until the ship eased closer to the window. It would have butted right up against the hospital if Phelps didn't keep up such a steady barrage of shots.

"Go, Marshall!" he roared again. "Go!"

Healey darted into the path of all that gunfire. He ducked his head to take another few hits in the chest and back, but by some miracle, no one hit him.

He sprinted for the window and was just slinging his leg over the sill when a splitting boom shattered the din. A crushing blast struck the window frame and the shockwave flattened Phelps to the floor. He toppled and his weapon flew out of his hand.

Healey froze half inside the window and half outside it. He looked back to see Phelps crawling across the floor trying to grab his XQ. Blood covered his face and chest, but he still hauled himself through the wreckage trying to get to his weapon. He was still doing his job.

The ship migrated the rest of the way forward and touched the building. The deputies grabbed Healey and started pulling him onto the ship.

Healey cast one last glance into the hospital room. Phelps had his hand on his XQ and was pulling himself upright against the bed. He would be on his feet in a second and then he would start shooting again.

Healey saw the whole plan laid out in plain view. The deputies had to make it look like they overpowered Phelps and stole Healey from Phelps. They had to make it look like Phelps did everything possible to stop them from taking Healey away. Phelps would be on his way up to the Terminus Anathema himself if they did it any other way.

The deputies dragged Healey the rest of the way onto the ship and took off into the city. He lost sight of Phelps inside the destroyed hospital room. Healey didn't even get a chance to say goodbye.

The ship wheeled away between skyscrapers and headed deeper into the city. Healey barely got his head screwed on straight when one of his former deputies came over to him and started shouting in his ear.

"We'll touch down near the Evasion Pier! You'll have to get under cover pretty fast!"

"What about you boys?" Healey asked.

"Don't worry about us. We'll handle things on this end." The wind and engine noise howling from outside changed tone as the ship descended between some more buildings. It lowered to the street so Healey could see people walking around outside. "Get ready, Marshall!"

Healey moved back over to the hatch and thought fast. As soon as his feet touched the pavement, he would have to make tracks. Where in this crazy town could he go to hide from the Reserve Wing—somewhere the Reserve Wing would never find him?

The answer came to him immediately, and when the ship clunked onto the sidewalk, he launched himself off the back. He didn't wait around to thank these deputies, either. He vaulted onto the street and took off running.

Chapter 27

"Are they still there?"

Coon shot a fleeting glance past Rodeo's shoulder. The same Storrik, a few random Ghrukeds, and the same Slotiezt stood across the market.

They were far enough away that they could blend into the crowd, but Coon could plainly see them watching the Chorion Team. The same three aliens had been watching the Chorion Team for days now. They never went away.

"Yeah. They're still there."

Rodeo turned to Bandit on his left. "Are they still there?"

Bandit checked on a different group of aliens on the farther side of the market and he nodded. "Yep. They haven't moved."

Rodeo turned to his right where Axel stood. "What about it?"

"Still there."

"Any sign of Kuvan?"

"Nope," Axel replied.

"No," Coon replied. "I haven't seen him in two days."

"Me, neither," Bandit added.

"All right. Here's the deal. We gotta get rid of this money before prying eyes decide it's worth more to them than the risk of getting hurt. We have to find Kuvan and we need to buy a ship."

"It's only a matter of time before Mexia's people attack us again," Coon pointed out. "If we go out on the floor, we better be ready for a fight and I don't mean the kind we could get paid for."

Rodeo motioned Alla, Breeze, Wolf, and Laub forward to join their conversation. The four boys had been standing guard over the Chorion Team's little patch of market floor along with the strongbox that was now overflowing with money.

The surrounding stallholders no longer paid the boys much attention. Everyone was too busy with their own transactions and the boys had become a fixture in the market. Coon now recognized nearly everyone around the Chorion Team's spot.

A few nearby merchants had even contracted the boys to do jobs for them and paid handsomely for the Chorion Team's services. They hired the boys to intimidate other merchants, collect late payments from reluctant debtors, and even beat up a few people. The Chorion Team's reputation was spreading just like Kuvan said.

Unfortunately, that reputation wasn't as favorable as the boys might hope. Everyone knew now that Mexia's people were out to kill the Chorion Team. Mexia had sent her lackeys out into the market at least four times since that first battle when Mexia made attempts on the boys' lives.

The boys' skill, attention, and unique abilities had saved them each time, but it wouldn't last, especially since the boys couldn't leave the market. This was Mexia's territory. She could wait and stalk the boys until, one of these days, she succeeded in getting rid of them.

Rodeo pointed to Wolf. "You come with us. The rest of you stand guard and don't take your eye off the ball. The harpies will be circling looking for an opportunity when we're weak. They'll see the four of you alone and they might think it's a good time to strike."

"We'll handle it," Laub replied. "Don't worry about us. Just find that bastard and get us a ship."

Rodeo nodded and signaled Coon, Axel, and Wolf to follow him. Bandit, Laub, Breeze, and Alla returned to their positions surrounding their position and the strongbox. The four boys faced outward and paced around keeping the whole market under surveillance.

Coon cast one last glance over the cavern. The four clusters of Mexia's people still observed the boys from a safe distance. Coon wished they would just go ahead and attack so he could stop constantly looking over his shoulder.

The boys had set up a schedule of sleeping and eating in shifts to keep an eye on things while their friends rested and tried to relax. Coon had found it nearly impossible to sleep these last few days even when he should. He didn't seem to be able to close his eyes or turn off his senses.

He had startled awake more than once to find Wolf sitting up, watchful and alert, sniffing and bristling at random people when he should have been asleep, too. At least Coon wasn't the only one.

He recognized the unmistakable signs of stress and fatigue in the others, too. Even Rodeo was showing the strain although he hid it better than the rest.

He walked out into the market, paused, and turned his head right and left. "I can't hear him. You boys will have to find him for me." Wolf growled and Rodeo pushed him forward. "Good boy. Hunt him down for me."

Wolf went in front and started sniffing everywhere. A few people yelled at him and one merchant kicked him away, but Wolf just moved on somewhere else.

He bent low and sniffed the floor. He nosed into people's merchandise and finally crossed the market to the very far back corner. None of the Chorions had been this far away from their patch before.

Wolf started walking faster. He must be getting close. He stuck his face into a pile of clothes and got another cuff around the head from the proprietor. He started to straighten up and his head whipped around fast.

He flared his nostrils in one direction, bared his fangs in a vicious growl, and raised his hackles even higher. He stiffened and started forward when Rodeo caught his arm. "Hold up, boy. I hear him now. We'll handle this. Come on, Coon."

Coon, Axel, and Rodeo approached a stall surrounded by prostitutes. Some had multiple orifices down their arms and legs and covering their torsos. Others had entire faces spiked with fangs around their gigantic yawning mouths.

Coon tried not to look at them, especially when they called out to the boys and started making suggestive remarks.

The prostitutes sprawled on a mound of cushions and a few wore iron collars anchored by chains to the walls or stone blocks. Dark-colored curtains shielded a large square booth behind where these females sat. Guttural grunting noises issued from behind the curtains.

Rodeo took a few more steps toward the prostitutes. He didn't seem to hear all the rude things they were talking about doing to him and letting him do to them.

Their remarks were really starting to get under Coon's skin, but they didn't bother Rodeo. He yanked back the curtains to reveal a plush bed inside the booth.... but no one was in there besides Kuvan.

The rooting noises came from some kind of device he had rigged up next to the bed. The noises came from a speaker that fell over when the curtains brushed it.

Kuvan jumped a foot in the air and screamed out loud when he saw Rodeo, Coon, Axel, and Wolf peering in at him.

"What the hell are you doing in here, Kuvan?" Rodeo demanded. "We've been looking for you for three days."

Kuvan trembled and then started laughing nervously. "Boys! So good to see you! Where have you been? I've been trying to find you."

"Don't lie, you cringing sack of shit," Axel fired back. "You were hiding from us."

"No, no, no!" Kuvan babbled. "I would never hide from you! You guys are my ace in the hole, the fountain of my success." He giggled again. He wobbled back and forth on the bed trying to look at all four of them and none of them at the same time. "I love you guys. You know that. I can't live without you."

"You're afraid of Mexia's people," Coon countered. "You think she's going to kill us."

"Well...." Kuvan shrugged and opened his mouth to make some lame excuse.

"We want to buy a ship, Kuvan," Rodeo blurted out. "What do you have?"

"A ship!" Kuvan widened his eyes in feigned surprise and then started blustering. "I don't deal in ships. No ships. Can't help you. Sorry, boys." He giggled again and took hold of the curtains. "See ya."

Rodeo grabbed the curtains and slammed them all the way open. "You're going to get us a ship, Kuvan, and it better be a good one. If you don't have one yourself, you can take us to someone who deals in them."

"No, no! I couldn't do that. I have a business to run here. See?" Kuvan waved at the prostitutes who watched the exchange with interest.

"Do we look like we're asking?" Axel stuck his hand into the booth, grabbed Kuvan by his clothes, and hefted the little alien out onto the floor.

Axel jammed the creature down onto his stumpy legs so hard that Kuvan nearly fell over. Axel shook him, straightened him out, and stood him between the four of them.

Coon leaned in close. "You're going to get us a ship and I would suggest you do it quickly. If Mexia's people attack us, you could get caught in the scuffle and you wouldn't want that. The sooner you get us a ship, the sooner we'll be on our way and the sooner you can go back to hiding in corners where you belong. Understand?"

"Uh.... okay." Kuvan nodded fast and cast a desperate look around at the other merchants. "A ship. Okay. I can do that. How much do you want to pay?"

"Five thousand talents," Axel replied.

"I can't do that. Sorry. It isn't enough. You're out of luck, boys. I wish I could, but...."

Rodeo bent over, propped his hands on his knees, and brought his sightless eyes right up next to the little alien's face. Rodeo hissed in an undertone that only the four boys and Kuvan could hear.

"The very next time you say you can't, I'm going to tell Coon here to skin you and we'll sell you for your hide and tallow. You find us a ship for five thousand talents or you won't live long enough to wish you had. Is that clear enough to you?"

Kuvan gulped and looked around once. He blanched and looked again toward his prostitutes. He was acting so shifty that Coon followed his glance and cringed when he saw Mexia's people moving in.

Coon nudged Rodeo, but Mexia's people were still so far away and so buried amongst the crowd that Rodeo couldn't detect them from here.

Axel spotted them and he and Coon exchanged knowing glances. Axel grabbed Kuvan's collar. "Get moving....and make it quick."

Rodeo cocked his ears in both directions, but he didn't sense the danger. Wolf swiveled to one side and flanked the other boys on one side. He positioned himself between Mexia's people and Kuvan. This was going to end badly. Coon could just feel it.

The three of them set off through the market with Kuvan in tow. Rodeo took a second longer and then brought up the rear, but it was already too late. The four clusters of Mexia's watchers closed the gap to box the boys in.

Coon tried to spot Alla, Bandit, Laub, and Breeze somewhere in the crowd, but the merchants on the floor swallowed them up. If they left their spot, they would have to leave the strongbox unguarded and Coon didn't want that. He and these three would just have to handle whatever came.

"Where are you taking us, Kuvan?" Coon muttered. "It better be somewhere we can get a ship."

"It is," Kuvan squeaked. "Turn left here."

Chapter 28

Kuvan guided them through the market and a few people observed the strange party. He halted at another stall. This one had tables covered in weapons, clothes, and a few sets of shoes for different species.

An elderly Yukis manned the stall. He didn't bat an eyelash when Axel yanked Kuvan to a halt in front of him.

Coon checked the surroundings while the two aliens held a hasty conversation in another language. He didn't see Mexia's people anymore, but that only made him more nervous. He wished he could see where they were. Then he would know how close they were.

"He says he has a ship you can buy," Kuvan finally reported.

"Where is it?" Rodeo asked.

"And *what* is it?" Coon asked.

"It's a Gargoyle 1440, very fast and very well armed," Kuvan translated.

Coon nodded. "A Gargoyle, huh? That should make Bandit happy."

"Who cares what make it is?" Axel countered. "What condition is it in?"

"What can you expect for five thousand talents?" Kuvan asked. "Do we have a deal or not....and he wants to know when he can take payment."

"Where's the ship?" Rodeo asked.

"On top of this building—space 479."

"All right. We'll take it." Rodeo nodded to Axel and Axel let go of Kuvan's collar. "Tell him that, after we leave, he can take possession of the strongbox over in our space. All the funds are in there."

"You better not be screwing with us, Kuvan," Coon warned. "If you are, you'll be the first person we come talk to."

"Me? I would never screw with you guys! I'm your agent. You guys are the best thing that's ever happened to me. Are you sure you don't want to do another fight before you go? You'll need funds when you get wherever you're...."

A blast of gunfire cut him off. All four boys spun around to face their attackers. Axel moved out of the way just in time and the shot hit Kuvan. It leveled him to the ground in a widening pool of blood.

Coon had half a second to see Mexia's aliens moving in. They surrounded the four boys with guns before the whole market erupted in chaos.

More aliens launched out of the crowd firing XQs, sidearms, and laser rifles in all directions. Coon lost track of who was shooting at him and who might be shooting at anyone else.

He backed toward Axel and prepared himself to fight his way out of the market. The Storriks advanced from one side and the Grekhuds from the other. They leveled their XQs to mow the four boys down.

Wolf yowled at the enemy and bristled worse than ever. Coon measured the distance and calculated how quickly he could get to one of these attackers without getting his head blown off.

At that moment, Alla charged out of nowhere, dove for the Storrik on the far end, and swallowed three of the aliens in one gulp.

The remaining Storriks rounded on him only to get bowled off their feet by Breeze plowing in just as fast. Wolf launched himself at the Ghrekhuds and slashed four of them.

His enraged shrieks set Coon off and he charged. Laub and Bandit appeared out of the mayhem and the whole battle dissolved in a confused jumble of aliens, gunfire, and body parts.

Coon caught a Grehkud and ripped the laser rifle out of his hands. He turned the weapon on its owner only to get hit by another laser crackling from his right.

Coon swept the gun sideways and the thing merged with his hand. Its metal stock melted into his skin and he got hold of it by some mysterious force pulsing through his veins.

The metal barrel melted outward from his fingers and engulfed the weapon of a Storrik facing him. The metal kept crawling up the alien's arms and started to envelop the guy's chest. The alien shrieked in terror and started to struggle, but Coon was all done playing around.

Ten more of Mexia's soldiers rushed the boys from across the market. Each attacker carried a different weapon. Coon couldn't let them get here or they would run the boys down in no time.

He thought fast and the two combined weapons morphed at his very thought. The liquid metal spat from their combined guns and shot across the market. Twisting, twining, snaking skewers impaled another seven aliens and blasted straight up the barrels of the advancing enemies' weapons.

Their guns exploded in their faces, but the effort of doing that much started to drain Coon's power. He couldn't do it as well here as he used to do it back home on Chorion Osiris. He needed to anchor himself to something and floating in space on a giant satellite left him weak.

He felt himself starting to wilt and he almost fell before Bandit caught him. "Hang on, boy! We'll get you out of here."

Coon barely heard him. He became distantly aware in his dazed state that Bandit and Alla were carrying him away, but he couldn't tell where they were going.

Wolf's screeches echoed in Coon's ears. The boy fought amongst twelve different aliens all trying in vain to tackle him to the ground.

He sent them staggering away nursing bloody gashes or he dropped their lifeless bodies on the floor. The bodies piling around him blocked more attackers from getting near the Chorion Team.

Laub and Axel stood back to back not far away. Lasers flicked out of the crowd and bounced off Axel's chest. Laub backed toward the stairs where the boys first entered the market. Laub caught anyone who dared to stand in his way and tore them apart with his bare hands.

Coon's addled brain took in more detail of the battle than he could possibly act on. He had to concentrate hard to release his hold on his victim's weapon. Even then, he came away still clutching a Frankenstein gun of several weapons melted into one. He didn't even know if he could shoot it, but it was better than nothing.

Rodeo caught Alla by the shirt and towered him backward. Coon stumbled and Bandit picked him up. Breeze was nowhere to be seen, but the chaotic jumble of bodies where Coon last saw him only got bigger by the second. The commotion migrated across the floor collecting people, goods, stalls, and a few alien monsters in its wake.

Laub made it to the stairs. "Go!" Rodeo ordered. "Get out on the street and find a way up to the roof."

Axel started to turn away and Coon spotted a fresh mob of Mexia's people moving in from the market's far side. These belonged to species Coon hadn't seen on the market floor before.

They didn't come close enough for Rodeo to hear them or for any of the other boys to defend themselves. The aliens set up some kind of weapon on the floor and aimed it toward the exit—the only exit the boys knew about.

Coon opened his mouth to call a warning to his friends, but his throat refused to cooperate. He couldn't make a sound and he couldn't move fast enough to stop the assault.

He raised his weapon without thinking and the metal melted without his even trying. It flowed in a seamless, organic slithering beam and blasted across the market. It divided into six glistening tendrils that grew on top of each other and surrounded the aliens' weapons.

The other boys spun around to stare, but the damage had already been done. Coon watched in disconnected fascination as the metal crawled up the barrels of his enemies' weapons and then shot deadly barbs into Mexia's soldiers' chest.

They fell dead, but Coon lacked the strength to let go of the metal structure he'd created. It solidified and the sheath of metal around his hand locked him in place. The whole structure hardened so he couldn't get away.

Alla tugged at him, but he couldn't break Coon free. Rodeo stuck his face in front of Coon's stunned eyes. "Let it go, boy! Break it off now. We can't get you out if you're locked in like this."

Coon already knew what Rodeo meant. Coon already knew he had to break the connection, but the link between his mind and his hand didn't work right. He kept commanding himself to let go of his weapon, but he couldn't make his fingers release.

The glove of metal started to crawl up his arm, but that wasn't the worst part. More of Mexia's people swarmed in from all sides. They would get to the boys any second now.

Without warning, an XQ blast struck Coon inches from his hand. The structure shattered and his arm broke free. The other boys turned to see where the shot came from, and a second later, a mob of aliens surged out of the throng. They overran Breeze carrying everyone before them.

Coon caught one glimpse of Breeze being carried by the stampede and then a grexisite blast ripped the crowd apart. Breeze bowled to Rodeo's feet and bodies toppled in all directions from the explosion.

Rodeo plunged into the mob punching, kicking, and shoving people out of his way. He grabbed someone and got caught in a second wave sweeping in another direction.

Laub dove into the mayhem and fought his way over to Rodeo. Laub flung his powerful arms around someone that Coon couldn't see.

The next wave carried all those people away toward the opposite corner and Laub tumbled out of the swarm. He crashed down at Bandit's feet and the cluster split apart.

Rodeo slammed down on the floor next to Coon and the boys stared at a third figure somersaulting clear. A tall man hit the floor, landed on his back, and swiveled toward the boys aiming two sidearms at everyone.

Marshall Healey's wild eyes darted from one face to the next. He jerked his sidearms from one person to the next and then started looking around for another enemy. "Where are they? Where did they go?'

Axel picked him up. "Easy, Marshall. We were just getting out of here."

Healey surveyed the boys. The light was coming back into his eyes, but he still kept startling and searching in all directions for someone to shoot. "Are you boys okay?"

"We're fine. Are you?" Rodeo nodded at Healey's chest. "You've been shot."

"Forget that. We gotta get out of here. The *Prometheus Vox* is on the jail roof and I don't think I can get to it."

"We have a ship," Axel replied.

Healey suddenly noticed Coon standing there. The marshall's eyes dipped to Coon's hand. "What the hell did you do with that thing, boy?"

Coon looked down at his hand. A metal blob surrounded his hand up past the wrist. He still didn't seem to be able to get rid of it.

"Forget that," Rodeo interrupted. "We gotta get out of here. Do you know a way up to the roof of this building, Marshall?"

Healey nodded. "We just have to......"

A colossal explosion interrupted him. None of the boys saw it coming. It came from somewhere Coon didn't see, but it exploded between the boys. It blew them all outward with a powerful concussion that tore Coon out of Alla's grip.

Coon hit the floor, and before he could move, a whole posse of aliens pounced on top of him. They tied him hand and foot and the rest of the Chorion Team fell under the combined assault from dozens of aliens. The explosion and their surprise attack overwhelmed the boys so none of them stood a chance.

Chapter 29

Someone yanked a cloth bag over Coon's head and rough, strong hands picked him up. "Can you hear me, Marshall?" Rodeo called.

"I can hear you, boy."

"Where are they taking us?"

"Downstairs," Healey growled. "They're taking us to Mexia."

"Oh, Lordy!" Alla moaned. "This is bad!"

"Do you think you could swallow *her*, pal?" Axel asked.

"Not before she swallows him first," Breeze remarked.

Alla whimpered again. "Keep your shirts on, all of you," Healey interrupted. "We still stand a chance to get out of here."

"How do you figure?" Bandit asked. "Last I checked, you're supposed to be the sheriff in this town and you're just as tied up as we are."

"You're also just as dangerous to Mexia as we are," Rodeo added. "If she's trying to kill us, she'll try to kill you, too."

"I hate to break it to you boys," Healey replied, "but I'm no longer a sheriff or marshall of anything."

"You're still wearing your star," Coon pointed out. His brain was starting to reengage and the words spilled out before he thought about them.

"So is Davenport," Laub added.

"Maybe I'm just as stupid and naïve as Davenport," Healey grumbled.

"Don't you say anything against Davenport!" Rodeo countered. "He'll be a sheriff until his dying day. He doesn't need a damn star to be a sheriff and neither do you."

Healey chuckled somewhere in the darkness. "Thanks, boy. I needed that."

A door slammed and the aliens carrying Coon dropped him on a hard stone floor. The bag ripped off his head and he looked around. Healey and the whole Chorion Team lay sprawled in a dim underground room. A bunch of aliens stood off to one side.

The Slotiezt that Coon had seen watching the boys for four days lurked in a corner. Plenty of the others guarded him from the boys—as if the boys posed any threat to anyone like this.

Healey twisted over and struggled to get up on his knees. "Kalvov! What are you doing? We never did anything to you!"

"You did not have to do anything to us, Sheriff," the alien replied in a deep, rumbling undertone. "You know Mexia's secret. We cannot allow word to get back to Calyx Elkanon...but you already knew that when you came down here. Is that why you came—to blackmail Mexia?"

"What about us?" Rodeo called back. "You attacked us first. You can't blame us for defending ourselves."

"Mexia does not blame any of you for doing anything. She must protect her secret and you must die."

"Kalvov!" Healey spluttered, but the aliens were already moving in and hefting their prisoners again.

They picked up Coon and his friends, but Mexia's people didn't bother to cover the prisoners' faces.

Healey went ballistic and struggled. "You can't do this, Kalvov! What do you think Calyx will do when he finds out—and he *will* find out, Kalvov! Calyx knows people in this town. Do you really think you can kill everyone to stop them from telling him? Let us go and we'll tell him to take it easy on you."

"I cannot do that, Sheriff. Goodbye."

The rumbling voice got farther away. The aliens' footsteps echoed on the stairs plunging deeper inside the satellite. Adrenaline woke Coon from his stupor.

"We have to get out of here," Axel called to the other boys.

"No shit!' Rodeo countered. "We just have to find a way to the roof."

"How do we do that when we don't know where it is?" Bandit asked.

"Too bad we didn't send you out to pick up the ship first," Laub remarked. "You could have fired into the building and gotten us out that way."

Another door slammed open and Coon stared in mute horror at the room into which his captors were carrying him.

A giant blob of some boneless body filled half the giant room. The thing had no eyes, no features at all besides its huge, fanged mouth. A long, looping tongue uncoiled from the mouth and looped toward Healey.

"You first, Sheriff," the same deep, rumbling voice intoned.

The aliens carried Healey headfirst toward the alien's mouth and a groaning yawn burbled from the vast body.

"Kalvov.... Mexia!" Healey started thrashing, but he couldn't do much with his wrists and ankles bound. "No! You can't do this!"

Coon glanced around at his friends. None of them could save Healey from this terrible fate. Rodeo. Bandit. Alla. Axel. Breeze. None of their unique powers would do anything for Healey right now.

Coon's eyes blurred out of focus. It all came down to him and he grasped at the only weapons available to him.

The melted steel covering his right hand came to life of its own accord. It extended from him like a part of his own flesh.

He stretched his mind and energy searching for the one scrap of metal he could find—the only piece of metal close enough to Mexia to stop her from swallowing him.

The metal sprouted from his knuckles, arched around Healey, and touched the star pinned to his jacket. Coon felt himself fading in and out of a drunken stupor, but every inch that metal stream covered came from his innermost guts. He could control it with hardly any effort at all.

The stream touched Healey's star and melted it into a puddle. The star joined with Coon's flow and erupted toward Mexia.

A razor blade slashed her tongue off as it snaked toward Healey's face. She shrieked in a deafening siren song of pain and outrage. The aliens watching rushed forward and the other boys reacted in a heartbeat.

Laub yanked his arms and legs apart and the bonds holding him popped off. He landed hard on his side and sprang to his feet.

He seized Breeze's still bound form and hurled the boy across the room at the charging alien enemy. Breeze crashed into them and the whole mob went down.

Laub charged Axel and snapped Axel's restraints with one yank. Axel lunged to his feet just as another group of aliens swamped the two boys in a fury. Mexia's aliens started shooting and slashing with dozens of weapons, but Axel stood guard and took every shot across his face and chest while Laub unfastened Alla next.

Coon drifted in and out of consciousness. Only the slithering, snickering movement of his metallic flow remained real to him. He could control its shape and direction with unnatural clarity. He transformed it into a club, a blade, or a spike. He could move it anywhere stabbing, crushing, and impaling his enemies.

He wound it between dozens of aliens pouring into the room. He freed Wolf and then Healey.

None of the aliens could figure out where the metal vines were coming from. Coon dove his stream into their weapons and melted them to increase his flow. His maze of tendrils expanded until it crisscrossed the whole room.

The aliens tried to fight it. They struck out at it with their weapons only for it to melt into liquid again. It surrounded their heads, crushed their skulls, stabbed through them, and moved on with lightning speed.

The mesmerizing organic river of metal entranced Coon until he couldn't think straight. Everything the flow did and every twist and turn it made weakened him further. He didn't know how much longer he could stay conscious before he passed out completely.

More aliens kept flooding into the room from upstairs. Mexia could call up an infinite number of defenders. Coon had to do something drastic before they overcame him.

Kalvov stood off to the side yelling orders at everyone. He took one step toward the battle and Coon reacted without thinking. His flow streaked at Kalvov and Coon instinctively formed it into a giant blade.

He lopped off Kalvov's head in one swipe, but that flow was moving way too fast for Coon to control it anymore. It took on a life of its own. He hardly realized when the blade turned toward Mexia.

She let out a deep, ground-shaking roar. Her mouth widened to reveal the bloody stump of her living tongue.

The blade broadened into a huge flat arrow. Coon watched from some other dimension as the dart plunged point first into her mouth. It vanished down her throat with the rest of the stream connecting the barb to the rest of Coon's flow.

He felt the arrowhead widen down in the depths of her guts. It flared into a massive disc of sharpened metal that filled her whole body and sliced through her skin from the inside.

A scream broke out among the assembled aliens. It started with the few standing close enough to see what Coon just did. The aliens holding him dropped him on the floor and the shockwave radiated outward to the rest of Mexia's people.

They all turned around to stare at Mexia. Coon couldn't move. He felt Rodeo touching him and trying to shake him awake, but Coon was too far gone.

He lost control of the metallic stream and it dissipated into a million silver droplets. They splashed all over the floor—all except the dart that remained embedded in Mexia's body.

A tense silence fell over the room. Coon couldn't understand it and his eyes swam back into focus. He looked up and had to blink several times to understand what he was seeing.

Healey and the other boys lined up across the room with their backs to Mexia's body. They faced off against dozens of aliens, but Mexia's people didn't seem to be attacking.

Healey had found two XQ65s somewhere. He rotated them from one side to the other holding the aliens at bay, but the boys were all unarmed.

Mexia's people didn't pay nearly as much attention to Healey as they did to the boys. Rodeo, Laub, Axel, and Alla advanced a few steps and all the aliens backed off. The assembled fighters nearest to the door crowded the entrance and started scrapping with each other to get out first. The boys kept pushing until the whole alien force broke and ran for it.

Coon faded out again. He came to hearing voices talking above his head. "Pick him up."

"Damn, he's bad! I've never seen him like this."

"We have to find the roof so we can get out of here."

"I know where it is," Healey told them. "The question is what we do when we get there."

"We have a ship."

"We could probably go back to the market and get our money," Alla suggested. "No one would stop us."

"We bought and paid for that ship," Rodeo countered. "We can get money anytime."

More confused mutterings bubbled in Coon's ears. Laub picked him up and Coon caught glimpses of the stairs on his way up them. Aliens cowered from the boys as the Chorion Team passed through the market. No one bothered them until they got out onto the street.

The light made Coon squint and he didn't seem to be able to fade out anymore. He was starting to recover from his exhaustion. "Rodeo...."

"Easy, boy. We're almost there."

Healey turned to another building that shared a wall with the one on top of the market. "This way."

He opened a door leading to more stairs, but none of the boys moved. A terrible sound of engines drifted down from the atmosphere and all the boys looked up, including Coon.

Dozens of Reserve Wing vessels floated across the sky up there. They blanketed Pandora's Needle and left virtually no part of the sky unguarded. "Shit!" Bandit muttered. "How the hell are we supposed to get through that?"

"You better get your fingers warmed up because it's gonna come down to pure raw talent." Rodeo turned toward the door. "Let's go."

"This ship better be operational," Alla muttered, but no one answered him.

Healey went in front and Rodeo followed right behind him. Laub carried Coon and the other boys trailed out behind with Breeze in the rear as usual.

Coon stayed conscious through the whole climb up to the roof. Healey opened another door to reveal the roof stretched out before them. Three dozen craft of all sizes lined the roof just waiting for someone to get on board and fly away.

"There it is." Bandit's eyes started to gleam. "A Gargoyle 1440! I never thought I'd ever get to fly one of these."

He pushed past Rodeo and stepped onto the roof. Healey held the door while Laub angled Coon's limp body into the open. Coon tried to see the ship, but his eyes kept blurring in and out of focus.

The other boys emerged from the stairs and Laub set off to follow Bandit to the Gargoyle. Bandit picked up the pace. He must be really excited about this ship.

Coon's brain started to fade out again when a crushing boom rocked the roof. Laub stumbled and dropped Coon as three more rockets punched down from the atmosphere.

Rodeo charged to Coon's side. "Get to the ship! Get off the Needle pronto!"

Bandit took off running for the ship and Rodeo scrambled to help Laub pick up Coon. Healey hesitated just long enough to aim his XQs at the sky, but the attacking vessels were too high in the atmosphere.

"How the hell did they find us?!" Alla shrieked.

"You're joking, right?" Healey yelled back. "There are no secrets on the Needle."

"Go!" Rodeo pushed Breeze and Wolf away from Coon. "Get on board. We have to launch now!"

Laub heaved Coon over his shoulder and the whole crew charged the Gargoyle with rockets raining all over the place.

One section of the roof caved nearly underneath Healey. Rodeo turned back to grab him, but a giant crack forked between them and the section under Healey's feet started to sink. Rodeo couldn't get to him in time.

Without warning, Breeze tumbled past Rodeo rolling across the tarmac. Anyone looking at him would think he just fell over and was bowling out of control from the blasts still pounding all around him.

He somersaulted off the broken ledge and slammed down on the tipping section. It teetered the other way under his weight and Healey toppled. He pitched down the slanting roof section and slid straight into Breeze.

Breeze caught him, rotated onto his back, and planted his feet against Healey's chest. Breeze gave him a violent kick and propelled Healey upward toward Rodeo.

Rodeo grabbed him and hauled Healey back to stable ground. That left Breeze still stranded down on the unstable section.

He sprang to his feet, and by some impossible stroke of luck, another rocket smashed into the opposite corner of the section. It slammed down and sent Breeze shooting upward. He turned a somersault in the air and landed on his feet next to Healey and Rodeo.

Alla, Wolf, and Bandit had already vanished inside the Gargoyle with Laub right behind them. Coon lost sight of Rodeo, Healey, and Breeze following and Laub dashed on board.

Laub practically dropped Coon on the floor in his haste to get to the lateral guns. Laub, Alla, Wolf, and Axel all scrambled to get to their positions as the engines cycled up.

Rodeo, Breeze, and Healey dashed inside the ship a second later and Rodeo charged to the cockpit to join Bandit.

Laub's gun placement was near enough to Coon and Laub left the door open. Coon could hear all the communications coming from the cockpit.

"What the hell is the problem?" Rodeo bellowed. "Don't tell me that asshole screwed us over."

"We have a full load of fuel and ammunition!" Bandit called back. "The engines are fine and the...."

"Don't tell me everything that's fine!" Rodeo countered. "Why are we still sitting here?"

"It's the quantum initiation drive. It's too far out of alignment."

"Fix it!" Rodeo fired back. "Get us the hell off this roof before...."

Catastrophic booms echoed through the floor and vibrated into Coon's bones. The ship seemed to be calling him through his very insides.

"I can't fix it!" Bandit screamed. "It would take me weeks. There's only one person who can get us out of here alive."

Coon must have passed out for a second. He came to his senses looking up into Rodeo's milky white eyes.

Rodeo gathered Coon in his arms and murmured in Coon's ears. "You have to wake up, Coon, or we're all dead. Please. You have to wake up......just for a little while longer. Then you can sleep."

Coon tried to tell Rodeo that he was already wake, but no part of his mind or body would work right. Coon was having trouble even understanding the words coming out of Rodeo's mouth.

Coon understood what was wrong with the ship. He could hear and feel and smell and sense every component, every wire, and every circuit. His hair and skin ached to merge with the ship and become one with it.

He had been like this since his earliest memories. He had a hard time learning to keep himself separate from every metal object into which he came in contact. Mechanical and electronic devices exerted an especially powerful pull on him.

He felt Rodeo picking him up and carrying him to the cockpit. Coon heard Healey ask, "What are you doing with him?"

"Stand out of the way, Marshall," Rodeo panted. "This is important."

Rodeo lowered Coon into the command cradle and Rodeo knelt down next to Coon. Coon felt Rodeo's hands touching him and guiding him. "Here, Coon. Do you feel that? Can you feel the quantum initiation drive from here?"

Another brutal smash struck the ship. "Lateral guns—open 'er up!" Bandit screamed into the communications system.

"We can't even see them from here!" Alla yelled back. "They're out of range! We would only waste our ammo."

"Come on, Coon," Rodeo murmured. "Please. You have to wake up. Just for a little while.... just for a minute.... Come on, Coon. You can do it."

Coon's fingertips grazed the console in front of him. He felt Rodeo guiding his hands over the controls. Coon didn't have to open his eyes and he didn't think he could if he tried.

"You can do it, Coon." Rodeo's voice took on just a hint of bite as more blasts pounded the ship. Yells and bellows came from the gun placements.

Coon felt his fingers melt into the controls. He was in, but every passing second cost him his last shred of strength.

"Yes! You're doing it!" Rodeo breathed. "You can do it, Coon. Find the quantum initiation drive."

"He's in!" Bandit called. "Come on, boy! You can make it!"

Coon started to lose consciousness again. He felt himself folding over at the waist. Rodeo propped him up and made him sit up in the chair, but that unbreakable force bound Coon to the ship. He couldn't free himself now if he tried.

He summoned all his concentration and dragged his awareness back to the controls. He found the quantum initiation drive. It was totally fried. The Gargoyle had been sitting unused for too long.

He started to bring it back into alignment when another rocket struck the Gargoyle. The ship bounced on its landing gear and almost knocked Coon out of the seat.

"A hundred more points!" Bandit yelled. "Nearly there and then you can sleep for a week."

Coon struggled to focus on the drive. He couldn't stay conscious any longer.

"Come on, boy!" Rodeo yelled in his ear. "Come on! You can do it! Don't you dare fall over on me now!"

Coon's head lolled on his chest. He felt himself vanishing into the drive and then Bandit gave a wild scream. "He's done it! Pull him out! We're away!"

"Pull out, Coon!" Rodeo ordered. "Pull out now!"

Someone touched Coon's neck. It was Marshall Healey. "He'll kill himself if he keeps this up."

"Lateral guns—fire!"

"Coon!" Rodeo yelled. "Coon!"

Coon couldn't hear anything. He couldn't disentangle himself from the quantum initiation drive. He became one with the ship and whoever he was didn't matter anymore.

He was flying into space and opening fire on the Reserve Wing the way he always dreamed. He never had to come back to this sad, pathetic body ever again.

Chapter 30

Healey helped Rodeo drag Coon's senseless body out of the chair. They didn't have time to carry him into the back so they laid him on the cockpit floor.

"Get in there, Marshall!" Rodeo ordered. "Man your gun and prepare yourself to use it."

"Yes, Sir!"

Healey jumped into the cradle behind Rodeo and the controls powered up. Bandit hit the throttle and gunned it straight into the horde of Reserve Wing vessels.

They had been bombarding the roof from orbit. They couldn't target the Gargoyle, now that the ship was whizzing upward on a collision course for their position.

"Holy hell!" Healey murmured. "He really did a number on the quantum initiation drive."

"He's the man," Bandit replied. "Give that boy a ship and he can do wonders with it. He doesn't care how bad it is. He really worked some miracles with the *Artemis Rex*...."

"Fly the ship, boy!" Rodeo roared. "Lateral guns—target forward to blow a path through them."

"What's our target?" Laub asked.

"Bandit?" Rodeo asked. "What's our target?"

"So many choices....! How about a nice, juicy Stalwart?"

"Yes!" several voices chorused from the back.

"How about it, Marshall?" Rodeo asked. "How would you like a Stalwart for breakfast?"

"I can't think of a better way to end my law enforcement career."

Laughter answered him and Rodeo pulled the Gargoyle into a steep climb. Fourteen Stalwarts stood guard over Pandora's Needle. The Reserve Wing never would have gotten away with this as long as Healey was in charge, but those days were long over.

Bandit drove the engines to the breaking point. "Stand by to fire on my word!"

"Bring it on!" Laub called from the back.

Bandit went into his characteristic crouch over the controls. He crushed his stick in both hands and sprinted almost straight up making for a Stalwart third from the left end of the line.

Daggers, Nitrols, and Drifters whizzed all over the place trying to catch the ship. Word must have gone out on the Needle that fugitives from justice were escaping in this Gargoyle.

Healey didn't have to think too hard to figure out how the Reserve Wing found the boys. These were the only Chorions within a thousand parsecs of Pandora's Needle. The Reserve Wing just had to scan the satellite to know exactly where the boys were.

The market protected the boys these last few days. Now that protection was gone and the Reserve Wing would hunt them down no matter where they went.

The lateral guns swiveled forward and opened fire on the Stalwart directly in front of the Gargoyle. The explosion of gunfire and continuous shots deflecting off the hull triggered Healey's battle instinct.

He hauled his weapon into line with the boys and he and Rodeo both opened fire. The Stalwart loomed huge and deadly directly in Bandit's path. Healey unloaded on the ship's hull and Daggers and Drifters swooped in to finish off the Gargoyle.

Healey searched for any weakness as Bandit cut the ship in tight against the Stalwart's side. He dove in so close that most of the pursuit pulled away first.

He skimmed the ship's circumference and the boys' guns sliced the hull as the Gargoyle passed.

"Coming up on her starboard engines!" Bandit called. "Stand by to slap that bitch into next week!"

"Standing by!" Axel replied.

"Ten seconds!"

Healey held his breath and gripped his firing mechanism tighter. He strained his eyes to see the starboard engine and froze when a disembodied hand appeared out of nowhere.

It slapped down on his controls and then the fingers melted into the console. Healey followed the thin, pale arm and looked down into two blazing, bloodshot eyes looking straight through him.

Coon lay sprawled on the floor shivering with the effort of holding himself up on one arm. His other hand glued to the controls in front of Healey. Cold sweat saturated the boy's gaunt face and lank hair.

"What the......?" Bandit muttered.

"Coon, what are you doing?" Rodeo yelled.

Coon started trembling harder. His whole head and body quaked with the strain. His hand turned to liquid silver and vanished into the controls.

"What is he doing?" Rodeo yelled.

"He's taking over the damn ship!" Bandit yelled. "He's controlling all the guns, the helm—everything!"

Healey couldn't look away from those haunted eyes. They glazed over with madness and registered nothing in front of them.

Coon's features twisted in agony. The engines shrieked to a deafening pitch. The boys in back hollered as all the guns unloaded without them doing anything.

The Gargoyle veered at a spine-breaking angle and plunged straight for the starboard engines, but Coon didn't shoot into them. He banked and skimmed between the engines and the hull. He dodged the support struts by inches and unloaded the lateral guns into a repair conduit buried underneath the engine panel.

Bandit screamed and flung his hands in front of his face. Rodeo kept bellowing for Coon to get the hell out of the controls and a din of yells came from the back.

The next instant, the Gargoyle erupted from under the engines and rocketed into space. All the Reserve Wing attack craft saw it trying to flee and they put on speed to hunt the boys down.

The Reserve Wing vessels made it as far as the Stalwart that Coon just fired on. The next second, a concussion went off underneath the starboard engine. The attack craft drew level with the engine and a catastrophic blast erupted out of the ship's side.

A volcanic geyser of flame and exploding fuel enveloped the pursuers. It consumed them all as the Gargoyle vaulted high into the stars.

The little ship made it five parsecs before the Stalwart went up in a gut-wrenching boom. It blasted outward and flung the Gargoyle so far away from Pandora's Needle that none of the Reserve Wing craft could follow.

Healey kept staring down into those eyes blazing up at him. The impact of the Stalwart's explosion smacked into the ship's tail and knocked Coon's hand away from the controls.

He slammed down on the floor, utterly senseless. "He's out!" Rodeo called. "Take over, Bandit!"

"Get that jackass out of my damn cockpit!" Bandit croaked. "He's ten times the pilot I'll ever be."

Healey scrambled out of his seat, crouched down next to Coon, and checked Coon's pulse. "He's barely alive. We have to...."

"There's nothing to do for him. He knew what he was doing. He just needs to sleep."

Rodeo pushed Healey out of the way and picked up Coon. Coon looked so much smaller and more fragile than Healey ever noticed before. Coon barely looked more than fifteen.

Healey followed Rodeo into the back. He carried Coon to one of the microscopic crew compartments. This Gargoyle was too small to have proper cabins. Each of the two crew compartments had two sets of three bunks each. That was it.

Rodeo laid Coon on one of the lowest bunks, sat down next to him, and pushed the sweaty hair off Coon's forehead. Coon already looked like a corpse.

"What the hell did he do?" Healey murmured. "How did he go into the ship like that?"

Rodeo shrugged. "It's just the way he does it. He's been like this all his life."

"Why does it weaken him so much? He could kill himself if we got into another scrape and he tied to do it again to help us. It's a miracle he survived this long."

"There's nothing we can do about that."

"There must be something."

Rodeo gazed down at Coon's lifeless face. "He was never like this on Chorion Osiris. He could do it a thousand times a day without weakening himself."

"How is that possible? How could being on Chorion Osiris make any difference?"

"Something in the planet gave him power. I don't understand it. You can see none of the rest of us need that connection to Chorion Osiris to use our abilities, but he does. He'll be all right. He just needs to rest."

"Are you sure?"

"He's done this before. He's just tired."

"There must be something we can do for him."

"You're already doing it." Rodeo approached the door and clapped Healey on the shoulder. "I hope you're happy now, Marshall. You're now officially a fugitive like the rest of us."

"I can't think of any higher compliment."

Chapter 31

Alla opened a cabinet in the Gargoyle's tiny galley. "At least that crook supplied us with plenty of food."

"Too bad it's all Qhelqien food." Axel pushed over to Alla's side and took a large carton out of the cabinet. He put it on the table in front of Healey and the other boys. "Let's see what we have here."

Rodeo took a box out of the carton and held it up to his nose. He took a deep sniff and sighed. "Dried Qhelqien taas fruit! Delicious!"

"Don't you even think about eating it all!" Alla tried to grab the box out of Rodeo's hand, but Rodeo yanked it away.

"Since when have I ever eaten it all?" Rodeo asked. "You're the one famous for eating it all, pal. You can wait your turn and take your share after the rest of us get some."

Healey looked into the carton and pulled out a sealed plastic package of compressed pink tentacled sea creatures. "Kaakkans fire squid. Who wants 'em?"

"Me!" Laub's hand shot up. "They're all mine."

"You can have them with my blessing, son." Healey placed the package in Laub's outstretched hands.

Alla went back to the cabinet sulking. A second later, he screamed and startled everyone. "Holy shit! Look at this!"

He took down a square box wrapped in black shiny wrapping paper. A skull and crossbones emblazoned the silver label. Fancy italic lettering read, *Zombie QP 10.*

"No way!" Axel breathed. "Do you have any idea how much that stuff is worth?"

The boys exchanged glances. No one breathed for a second.

"What's the matter?" Healey took the bottle out of Alla's hands and studied the label. "I think this moment calls for a shot each, don't you?"

He started to tear off the label. Alla, Axel, and Bandit backed away from him, especially when he tore open the box to reveal the full bottle with the seal still intact.

Healey got a bunch of glasses from the cupboard and lined them up on the table. "What's wrong with you kids? Don't you want some? I could drink it all myself if you really want me to...."

He meant it as a joke, but he saw instantly that the boys didn't think it was funny at all. "Ekol doesn't let us drink on the job," Rodeo murmured under his breath.

"You aren't on the job for Ekol anymore," Healey pointed out. "You deserve a drink every now and then. Just one shot each. What do you say?"

He cracked the seal and poured one shot—just one. If they were that reluctant, he would at least enjoy one shot to take the edge off his nerves. He needed it after escaping from Mexia for the second time.

The boys watched him pick up the glass. No one said a word when he tossed it back and shuddered. He had to gasp for breath before he could breathe again.

Rodeo rubbed the back of his neck. "All right. Just one."

"No, Rodeo!" Bandit breathed. "You can't!"

"If Ekol wants to sack me for this, let him."

"He won't. He knows a good team when he sees one." Healey twisted off the cap, poured Rodeo a shot, and held up the bottle to the rest of them. "Anybody else?"

Bandit and Alla recoiled from the bottle like it might bite them. "Aw, what the hell!" Axel muttered. "I'll take one."

"Me, too," Laub chimed in.

Wolf growled from the end of the table. "Good man," Healey replied and poured out four more shots.

Rodeo sniffed his. "It doesn't smell too bad."

"It is," Healey told him. "Maybe you shouldn't...."

Rodeo threw down the shot in one gulp and didn't even shudder "It's pretty good."

Laub sipped his like was enjoying an afternoon lemonade at the park. Wolf bolted his and slammed the glass down with no trouble. Axel only raised his eyebrows in mild surprise while he rolled the drink around in his mouth tasting it with elaborate attention.

"That's it!" Healey complained. "I'm never drinking with you boys again."

Laughter broke out around the table. "Don't worry, Marshall," Laub replied. "Chorions react different to alcohol."

"Obviously," Healey muttered.

"You can keep the bottle," Rodeo told him.

"Thanks. I'm gonna need it if I keep flying with you boys."

They laughed at him and then Alla and Rodeo started digging into the rations again. They brought out one treasure after another until each boy had his choice. Then everyone settled down and started eating.

Talk turned to their favorite foods until approaching footsteps made everyone look up. The whole Chorion Team cheered when Coon dragged himself into the galley.

"My boy!" Bandit jumped up, grabbed Coon, and hugged him. Alla and Breeze both mussed up his hair and they made a big deal over him while they guided him to the table.

He still looked like he just recovered from some deadly illness, but his shadowy eyes sparkled when his friends made a place for him. They practically yanked him down on the benches to join them.

"What are you eating, boy?" Rodeo peered into the carton and frowned. "It looks like Alla has already stolen all the good stuff."

"I did not!" Alla howled. "You bastard!"

"Chill out!" Rodeo pulled out a package of Smoky Hotskin Duckwhats. "Hey! Check it out! It's Breeze's favorite treat!"

The whole table erupted in laughter and the boys started chanting, "Breeze! Breeze! Breeze! Breeze!" They pounded the tabletop and their voices rose to a thunderous bellow.

Breeze turned bright red and then split into a grin. He put out his hand for the package and took the Duckwhats. Everyone nudged him and he started laughing.

"What's the deal?" Healey asked. "Don't you know how dangerous those things are?"

"Do you ever wonder why everyone calls him Breeze?" Laub yelled back. "Just make sure you're standing far enough out of the way."

"What do you mean?" Healey asked.

The others were laughing too hard to answer. Everyone got up from the table. The boys backed away and pulled Coon and Healey to the rear wall.

Breeze kept grinning like a fool and carried the package of Duckwhats to the other side of the room. He shot his friends knowing smirks while he tore the package open with his teeth.

He stuck his fingers inside and was just pulling out one of the Duckwhats when Axel yelled out, "Hold it! Look what I got!"

He rushed forward and handed Breeze something. More laughter and rude remarks broke out among the friends and Axel laughed when he retreated to join the rest of the crew.

"What is he going to do?" Healey asked.

"You'll see!" Coon replied.

Healey looked down at the boy. Coon's drawn face still looked like a skeleton, but he was laughing and grinning along with the others.

All eyes turned to Breeze. He pulled out a Duckwhat and ate it with a ridiculous expression on his face. He looked up at the ceiling and frowned like he was pondering the flavor.

The others laughed at his antics while he ate his way through the whole package. Healey didn't see what the big deal was until Breeze finished the very last Duckwhat.

"It's a good thing he has the balloon or we wouldn't be able to breathe in here," Bandit remarked and everyone laughed.

Breeze threw the empty package aside and pulled out the thing Axel had given him. Breeze unfolded it with delicate care. He furrowed his brow in concentration and got a few more laughs from his appreciative audience.

He finally got the thing unfolded and Healey realized that it was an inflatable life raft out of the Gargoyle's emergency supplies. It unfolded into a square fifteen feet wide.

Snickers and giggles broke out among the boys, but they started to go quiet while Breeze unfolded the raft. He made a big show of laying it out on the floor and positioning the inflation aperture in the right direction.

The group went still and quiet. Everyone held their breath and waited for something to happen.

Healey still didn't get the joke until Breeze walked around the raft to where the inflation aperture was. He turned his back to the raft, dropped his pants, bent over, and held the aperture up to his backside. It covered most of his ass.

He let out the biggest, loudest, most disgusting fart that Healey had ever heard. All the boys burst out laughing and Healey found it impossible not to join in.

Breeze kept blasting into the raft again and again. His farts lasted so long that they didn't seem biologically possible. He kept this up until he managed to inflate the whole damn raft.

Healey's ribs ached and tears streamed down his cheeks from laughing so hard at the sight. The boys hugged each other and slapped their thighs with delight, but the show wasn't over yet.

Breeze gave one more stomach-turning fart and the raft started to contort. Faces appeared in the stretched and swollen plastic. They opened their mouths and made burping noises synchronized with the farts still forcing their way into the raft.

The plastic stretched in different places to make animal shapes. The farting noises matched these stretches and twisting shapes to make trumpeting animals, roaring aliens, and even a few human faces.

A bushy-browed older man scowled down at the crew and opened his mouth to scold them for their childish behavior. Then a low, guttural fart belched from his mouth and the crew erupted in laughter.

This went on for so long that Healey started to feel sick from laughing so hard. He really wanted to stop, but Breeze kept making so many ridiculous shapes and sounds that no one could stop.

He finally created one last colossal fart that made the raft take the shape of Admiral Joyce's face. The admiral barked an order with Breeze's last fart and the whole group dissolved in laughter.

Breeze started to stand up and Axel darted forward. He caught the aperture before Breeze could pull it away and Axel pinched the aperture closed so none of the gas escaped. "Hang on, boy! You'll kill us all!"

The others laughed as Axel carried the raft out of the galley. Healey didn't see what Axel did with it and Healey didn't want to know.

The crew headed for the table still laughing and wiping away tears of mirth. The boys went back to eating and Rodeo and Alla started going through the carton again.

"What do you want to eat?" Rodeo asked Coon again. "You need to build up your strength."

"I'm not hungry. I'm okay. Maybe later."

"Do you want a shot of Zombie QP10?" Healey held out the bottle.

"Don't ask him that!" Laub yelled. "Are you trying to kill him?"

"It might make him feel better," Healey replied. "How about it, boy? Rodeo and these three had some."

Coon laughed. He was looking more lifelike now. "I don't think so. Thanks, Marshall."

"All the more for me." Healey put the bottle back in his pocket.

"Are you having Zombie QP10 for dinner, Marshall?" Laub asked. "That stuff will rot your guts if you don't eat something."

"Oh, do I get food, too?" Healey rubbed his hands together. "Great! What do you have?"

"We have Barbequed Alligator Tarts...."

"Forget it," Healey snapped. "I'd rather starve."

Some of the boys laughed and then Rodeo held up another package. "Sorry. All we have left are BoilBuns and Universal Staples."

"Give me the Universal Staples. I won't starve on those."

"What—you don't want to live on booze?" Axel asked.

"Until your guts rot out and we have to dump you in the plasma stream?" Coon added and everyone laughed.

Healey took his Universal Staples and started eating with the rest. This was the closest he'd felt to the Chorion Team since he met them on the Needle. That seemed like a long time ago.

He felt much closer to them, now that he was just as much a fugitive as they were. They were all in the same boat now. He really meant it when he said he didn't want to be anywhere else.

These boys gave him the feeling that he was in the presence of some of the best people that he'd ever met. They might even be the best people alive.

He couldn't think of anyone he'd rather see right now.... except maybe Davenport and his crew. They really were the salt of the galaxy.

They made him feel honored to be near them—even more than the Wide Patrol or any of the other heroes he'd always admired. He didn't need any fancy food to feel happy with them. Universal Staples were more than good enough with company like this.

The talk turned to other subjects and several conversations split off in different directions. Healey started to feel warm and happy from all this food when an alarm went off in the Gargoyle's cockpit.

The whole crew shot out of their seats. The boys fell over each other trying to untangle themselves from their food and get out of the galley.

Healey followed Bandit and Rodeo to the cockpit. He almost asked what the problem was, but he saw right away and didn't say it.

Four giant warships loomed off the Gargoyle's starboard side. These ships dwarfed the Reserve Wing Stalwarts by a mile. The warships' vaulted black hulls didn't gleam with lights and windows that might indicate people inside.

"Koleks!" Bandit whispered. "No wonder we didn't detect them until it was already too late. They can mask their approach."

"Can we get through?" Rodeo asked in an equally hushed undertone. "Do we have the speed to outrun them?"

"It's too late. They already have us."

A thump hit the Gargoyle's outer skin and the little craft started gliding toward one of the warships. A black, lightless opening widened in the warship's side and an invisible force pulled the Gargoyle into the dark. Healey and the Chorion Team were prisoners.... again.

Chapter 32

Davenport turned his back to Lyons. "See if you can loosen these ties."

She fiddled with the ties around his wrists, but she only wound up tightening them. "Ow!" he snarled.

"Sorry. I can't see what I'm doing."

"Can you help us out, Beauty?" Davenport asked. "Can you get us untied?"

Emmett surveyed the cell in which the Reserve Wing imprisoned the four friends. "We have to get out of here. I have to save Fiddler before she gets to Helios Sanctus."

"Don't worry about her," Davenport replied. "They won't hurt her."

"Hurt her! So you're okay with them locking her up in a lab and running scientific experiments on her for years?"

"I didn't mean that. I only meant...."

"Did you know they created more than fifty clones?" Emmett's voice started rising. "What do you think happened to them? They died in the experiments."

Lyons gasped. "Really? Fiddler never told me that part. She said she grew up in the lab with the four clones."

"She didn't know about the others. The Reserve Wing had ten different labs with five clones each. They experimented on all of them, and if one of Fiddler's companions died, they moved one of the clones in so there were always four others with her. She was too young to tell they weren't the same people."

"Are you saying....?" Davenport gulped. "You never told her?"

"Of course I never told her! Would you tell a four-year-old child that the Reserve Wing had been torturing and killing clones of her for years while they kept taking DNA samples for her to make more clones? Are you insane? Of course I never told her."

Davenport fell silent and Lyons and Beauty didn't answer. Davenport had no way to get out of here and no way to help Fiddler. He couldn't even free his own wrists.

"Beauty!" Lyons called out. "Come get these ties off us."

Beauty scooted over to her. He had a way of contracting his butt muscles so he hopped across the floor. He positioned himself behind her, fiddled with her hands, and her wrists popped free.

"How did you do that?" Davenport exclaimed.

"He has very strong fingers." Lyons rubbed her wrists and then started on her own ankles. In a matter of minutes, all four of them sat around free, but that didn't help anyone get out of this room.

Davenport and Lyons leaned against the wall and watched Emmett pace the room. "I don't think I've ever seen him so animated," Lyons remarked.

"I guess I can't blame him," Davenport replied.

"So what's the plan, Sheriff? You always come up with the brilliant ideas."

"Not this time." Davenport looked away. "It looks like we're going up to the Terminus Anathema."

"Look on the bright side," she countered. "You wanted to send *us* up and now you are. Mission accomplished."

He shook his head. He couldn't appreciate the joke. "At least they'll let us out of this cell and we'll be among friends there."

"Do you mean Calyx Elkanon?"

He spun around and stared at her. "How do you know about that?"

"A couple of sources. One—your friend Donovan on Scion of Hubris mentioned that you went up to the Terminus Anathema before you became a sheriff. Two—Marshall Healey told us that you saved Calyx's life while you were inside. Hence the reason he thought Mexia would help you on HTWV-983."

Davenport snorted. "I guess I don't need to hide it anymore."

"Why should you? You're a damn good sheriff—the best I ever had the misfortune to get inspected by. You changed your life. That's saying something. I kinda wish I had."

He couldn't stop gawking at her. "You're blowing smoke! You do NOT wish you had changed your life."

"These last few weeks have been something else, you know? I really regret now that you basically had to force me to change. I wish I had seen the light and done it on my own. Then maybe I could be proud of myself the way you are. I could say I did it because I'm a good person and not some lowlife smuggler who doesn't care about the rest of the Confederate population."

Davenport couldn't stop staring at her. He hardly believed he was hearing this from her of all people.

She refused to meet his eye. "We're in this mess because I took the Ithium. I agreed to transport it knowing what it could do. I knew someone was up to no good with it. It wouldn't be outside of Helios Sanctus otherwise and I took the job anyway. If anything happens, it will be my fault."

Davenport relaxed back against the wall. He never thought about what it must be like to actually carry that burden.

He'd been holding the high ground ever since he left Ekol Thaine's service. He turned over a new leaf and no one could fault his actions since.

It must be terrible for Lyons to blame herself for a disaster that might happen because of her negligence. He held himself responsible for finding the Ithium and keeping it away from Joyce. That was nothing compared to what Lyons must be going through.

Emmett came back over to them, but he didn't sit down. He propped his hands on his knees while he kept studying the cell. "They have to feed us sometime. When they do, we'll find out how they're doing it. There has to be a vulnerability in this...."

A scuffling noise made all four friends look at the wall to their right. Davenport stared in shock as a sizzling sound came from the steel wall next to where he and Lyons were sitting.

His jaw dropped when the wall started to melt. A one-foot section turned to liquid and dripped fizzing onto the floor. Smoke billowed from the stuff as it congealed on the metal floor.

A familiar head poked through the gap and grinned up at him. "Morning, Sir!"

"Bandit!" Davenport scrambled over to the hole and pulled Bandit through followed by Axel and Wolf. "What the hell are you boys doing here?"

"It's a long story, Sir," Bandit replied. "Anyway, we were just trying to find a way out of this mess when Rodeo heard your voice."

"Where the hell have you boys been? I thought I'd lost you."

"Let me put it this way," Axel replied. "Mexia isn't after us anymore."

"But the Reserve Wing is," Bandit added.

Healey stuck his head through the hole and looked around. "Where is everyone? Is it just you four?"

"We got a big, big problem," Emmett began.

"What—you mean bigger than being locked up on a Regiment Stalwart on the way to the Terminus Anathema?" Bandit countered. "Somehow I think that's bigger than whatever you got."

"It isn't," Lyons replied.

"What's the problem, then?" Healey got to his feet and surveyed the four of them more closely. "Who's missing? Dice, Fiddler...."

Davenport gave Healey and the Chorion Team a rundown on everything that had been happening at Ultra Meridian since the crew's escape from the *Rambler*.

He covered the whole story behind the Armageddon Core, the Zeprothil being the third component, and finally, the Reserve Wing using truth serum to weaken Dice and take him and the Armageddon Core back to Helios Sanctus.

"Damn!" Rodeo exclaimed.

"That's what I said," Lyons replied.

"So...what do we do?" Coon asked.

"The first step is to get the hell off this ship," Emmett replied. "Then we can find a way to get Fiddler and the others out of Helios Sanctus."

"We're going to find it a lot easier to escape from the Terminus Anathema than this Stalwart," Davenport countered.

"We can't go up to the Terminus Anathema," Emmett argued. "*You* might have friends there, but the rest of us would be dead for sure."

"Does this have something to do with why you don't like the Wide Patrol?" Davenport asked.

Emmett turned bright red and snapped his mouth shut. "I don't know what you're talking about."

Lyons frowned at the boys. "If you boys melted that wall, you could melt your way out of the cell. How *did* you melt through that wall?"

"The question isn't so much how he melted the wall but what we're going to do once we get out of it," Healey pointed out. "We had a ship, but I guess that's gone now."

"We don't need a ship," Coon replied. "We're already on one."

Everyone turned to face him. "What do you mean?" Rodeo asked.

"We're on a Reserve Wing Stalwart—*Remorseless*, isn't it?"

"So?" Emmett asked. "What good does that do us?"

"I'm going to guess that Fiddler and the others are on another Stalwart.... or at least some other Reserve Wing vessel," Coon went on. "Which means we would need at least a Stalwart to get them back or even to slow them down."

Bandit jumped a foot in the air and started waving his arms in front of Coon's face. "No, no, no, no, no! You are NOT flying the ship. I'm the pilot here."

"I'm sorry, Coon," Rodeo added, "but I can't let you do this. We've been over this before..."

"What are you talking about?" Davenport asked. "Who said anything about flying the ship?"

"He wants to steal the Stalwart," Axel explained. "He wants to hijack this ship while we're still on it."

"Do you have any idea what kind of weaponry we would need to take a ship this big?" Lyons asked. "We might destroy it in the process and ourselves along with it."

"You don't understand," Laub replied. "He could take the Stalwart without ever leaving this cell."

"No," Rodeo snapped. "He couldn't. You can't do this, Coon. I won't let you."

"Why not?" Coon asked. "It's better than getting shot. Isn't it?"

"How exactly would you take the ship from in *here*?" Emmett grimaced at the walls again. "We're locked in."

"It's complicated." Coon turned back to Davenport. "Give me a shot, Sir. I won't let you down."

"I said no, Coon," Rodeo cut in. "You already practically killed yourself escaping from the Needle. If you did this, you could drop dead in the middle of the battle and then where would we be?"

Coon looked away pinching his lips together.

"Can someone please explain to me what the hell is going on?" Davenport called.

No one answered for a minute before Healey broke the silence. "It seems our young friend here has the unique ability to manipulate anything made out of metals. The geology of Chorion Osiris affects his body and gives him an affinity for metals and electronics. He can infiltrate them and change them any way he wants to—which is how he can repair ships so fast—but it drains him. He repaired our Gargoyle and flew it through a Reserve Wing assault, but he almost died doing it."

"And he isn't doing it again now," Rodeo barked. "We'll come up with another way, Coon."

"There is no other way." All eyes turned to Beauty. He had sat off to one side through the whole conversation without saying anything.

He still sat in the corner, but this time, he looked up at the rest of the group with his large, wary eyes.

Davenport ran over the possibilities in his mind—except that there were no other possibilities. The crew had no other options.... except for one.

"I still say we wait until we get to Terminus Anathema. I'm serious. We would have the most powerful allies we could ask for there. Yes, it would be hard, but we could make it work."

No one answered him. Rodeo cocked his head from side to side listening and scowling at everyone. The boys, Healey, and Lyons all started looking more closely at Coon. His plan was starting to look a lot more attractive to them than going up to the Terminus Anathema.

Davenport finally relented. "How would you take the ship from here—not saying that you would—just hypothetically? How would you do it?"

Coon brightened up instantly. "I could get into the bridge controls and...."

"Why don't you take control of life support?" Lyons suggested. "You could suffocate the whole crew and we would have the run of the ship."

"You aren't killing an entire Reserve Wing crew," Healey countered. "That's barbaric."

"Besides, we'd be stepping over dead bodies everywhere we turned," Alla pointed out. "Gross!"

Some of the boys laughed. "I wouldn't have to suffocate them," Coon decided. "I could change the atmospheric concentration of the life support system to something dangerous—methane, say. They would evacuate the ship and then I could change the concentration back to normal."

"You can do that?" Lyons asked.

"Once I get hold of the controls, I can do anything."

"Then what?" Bandit asked. "So we've got a Reserve Wing Stalwart. What do we do with it?"

"Hold the phone," Axel interrupted. "The Reserve Wing wouldn't just abandon this ship just because they evacuated the crew. The crew would be in other vessels...Daggers, maybe. They would still be near enough to us to attack us."

"I can pre-program the Daggers to fly the crew back to Atlas Arcane," Coon suggested. "Then we'd be alone."

"Whoa, there, little buddy," Rodeo interjected. "Excuse me, but if you were hooked up to the system for that long, you'd be dead."

"I don't like it, either," Healey added. "We can't risk something happening to you, Coon. It's too dangerous."

"I don't have to be hooked up to the system for very long," Coon argued. "I can take control of the Stalwart, pre-program the Daggers, and get out. The rest of you can fly the ship once we take over. I would only be inside for a few minutes at the most."

Rodeo shook his head and turned to Davenport. "Will you please stop this madness, Sir? This is a terrible idea."

"What do you suggest we do instead?" Davenport asked.

Dead silence answered him and the other boys went back to looking at Coon like he might be some kind of messiah figure. Even Healey gazed at the boy with a mixture of awe and fear.

"I have a suggestion," Lyons began. "Stalwarts don't move very fast and they aren't very maneuverable in battle. I say, if you're going to evacuate the crew in Daggers, you should keep some of the Daggers on board. We can use them to fight whatever ship Dice and Fiddler are on."

"Good idea," Coon replied. "I can affect the atmospheric concentration on certain Daggers, too. That will make them off limits for the crew. I'll leave only a few operational for them to evacuate. In fact, once I get inside the ship's systems, I can see what other craft the Stalwart has on board. We might be able to evacuate the crew in something else—something that won't do us as much good in a battle attack."

Everyone fell silent again and they all looked at each other.

"It looks like we're doing this," Healey remarked.

Rodeo pointed in Coon's face. "You get in, you do it, you get out. That's it."

"Of course," Coon agreed.

Rodeo looked around at everyone else. "I'm assigning Breeze to stay with you, Coon. If anything goes wrong, he'll pull you out."

"How exactly will I do that?" Breeze asked.

"You'll figure it out," Rodeo replied. "Understand, Coon? If anything goes wrong and you get stuck in there, Breeze is taking you out for good or bad. Do I have your promise on that?"

"You're talking about him getting stuck inside the ship's controls," Lyons pointed out.

No one paid any attention to her. The whole crew watched Rodeo read Coon the riot act. Coon didn't back down, though. "Of course, Rodeo. I understand and I promise. If it goes wrong, I'll pull out. I give you my word."

Rodeo compressed his lips and his nostrils flared. "All right. We'll do it."

Coon started grinning. "I've never taken over a ship as big as this."

"Don't do it at all if you aren't certain you can take it," Rodeo countered.

"Oh, I can take it." Coon moved over to the door.

Davenport stopped him. "Hold it."

"Now what?" Axel asked.

"Okay. So we've got control of a Stalwart and a bunch of Daggers—hopefully. Then what?"

"We're going after Fiddler," Emmett chimed in.

"And Dice," Lyons added.

"How?" Davenport asked. "What if another twenty Stalwarts are escorting whatever ship Dice and Fiddler are on? What if they've already docked at Helios Sanctus? Are we going to assault the station?"

"Yes," Emmett replied.

"No," Healey countered. "No way."

"Why don't we just take the *Remorseless*, fly away, and save our own asses?" Alla suggested.

Everyone else rounded on him and yelled, "No!" at the same time.

He shrank away and said nothing else.

"Why don't we get in control of this Stalwart and see where we are?" Coon replied. "We'll be able to use the *Remorseless's* controls to tell which ship our people are on, how much opposition we can expect, and how close they are to the station."

Davenport couldn't argue with this. "All right. We better do that, then."

Coon nodded toward the door. "Are you ready for me to take the ship now?"

Davenport nodded, but he didn't really want to. This was one of the most outlandish plans he'd hear yet. "How are you going to do this?"

"Stand back and watch. This shouldn't take too long."

Chapter 33

Coon placed his hand flat against the cell's metal door and cocked his head the way Rodeo usually did. He looked up at the ceiling and his eyes lost focus.

"What is he doing?" Lyons whispered.

"Shh!" Laub hissed. "Don't distract him!"

"It doesn't look like he's having any trouble," Alla remarked.

Coon just stood there in silence for a minute. Davenport didn't see him manipulating anything.

"How many Daggers does the Stalwart have on board?" Axel asked.

"Fourteen," Coon replied.

A gasp went through the group. "Fourteen!" Lyons exclaimed. "That's tons!"

"There are also five Nitrols and seven Drifters."

"Keep a Drifter for me," Bandit interjected.

"Not now!" Rodeo snapped. "What is the system looking like, Coon?"

"It's pretty basic. I'm in the bridge controls now. I'm changing the life support gas mixture. Oh, look. The emergency alert is going out now."

"Don't forget to keep these cells at normal," Lyons added.

"I already did that. The order to abandon ship is going out."

Davenport watched Coon's bright face. His eyes darted here and there and everywhere without seeing anything.

The boy changed before Davenport's eyes. He got a haunted, ghostly look like his spirit had taken leave of his body. He didn't look human anymore—not that he ever was.

Coon's expression cleared for a second and he met Davenport's gaze. "Admiral Joyce is on board. Do you want him to evacuate, too?"

Davenport hesitated and Lyons spoke up again. "If he leaves the ship, he'll probably take the Ithium with him."

"Much as I would love to thump his daylights out," Healey added, "there won't be any way you can evacuate everyone else and leave him on board."

"Let him go," Davenport decided. "We can deal with him later. This is more important."

"More important than wiping out the whole Confederacy?" Alla asked.

Coon faded again and his eyes slipped out of focus. "They're loading up in the Daggers. They're leaving. I'm changing the Daggers' navigation programming. They'll fly away to Atlas Arcane as soon as they...."

He removed his hand from the wall and turned to Davenport, Rodeo, and Healey. "It's finished. The ship is deserted. We're the only people left on board."

"Just like that?" Healey asked. "We just walk out there and...."

"Oh, I forgot something." Coon touched the wall one more time and the door clicked open.

Everyone stared at it and then at Coon. "It can't be as simple as that," Lyons muttered.

"Why didn't you use this power before?" Davenport asked. "You could have gotten us out of the Mad Men's custody and out of the Pandora's Needle jail. We could have been using this all along."

"We have been," Laub replied. "We've been using it to repair all these ships."

"Anyway, it's dangerous." Rodeo shouldered past Coon and pushed the door open. "Let's go. We have a rescue mission to carry out."

The crew left the cell and stepped into the corridor outside. Coon was right. The whole ship was empty and silent as the grave.

"I'm going up to the bridge," Davenport announced. "Bandit and Rodeo—you come with me. You better come, too, Coon. Lyons, you take these badasses down to the launch bay and see about manning up our Daggers in case anyone comes around to stop us."

The crew split up. Davenport and the others went up to the bridge and Bandit sat down in the captain's chair. "We're adrift in the Naelkae Cluster."

Rodeo took a different bridge station. His fingers flew over the controls even when his eyes looked at something else. "Coon is right. The *Remorseless* crew is on their way to Atlas Arcane."

"Can you find out which ship Dice and Fiddler are on?" Davenport asked.

Coon stepped forward. "I can...."

"No. You can't," Rodeo snapped. "Go sit down over there. You aren't doing anything unless we get into a life-threatening emergency."

"At least let me do something!" Coon pleaded.

"I'll tell you when I need your help."

Coon slumped into a chair at the communications station. He kept eyeing the controls, but he kept his arms crossed over his chest and didn't touch anything.

"I found them!" Bandit called. "They're on the *Trailblazer*....and they're less than a hundred lightyears from Helios Sanctus. We better move fast."

"Are there any other Reserve Wing vessels nearby to stop us?" Davenport asked.

"Nope." Bandit looked up and grinned at him. "We got a straight run all the way there."

Davenport spun away. "I'm going down to the launch bay. You boys handle things here."

Bandit moved over to the pilot's station. He beamed at the controls as he took the helm. He wriggled with excitement working everything as fast as he could.

Davenport didn't stick around to see any more. He hustled away and went down to the launch bay where he found Lyons, Healey, Emmett, and Beauty. They and all the rest of the boys having a grand time with all the ships the Reserve Wing left behind.

Lyons, Emmett, Beauty, and Healey had all taken Daggers. The boys had distributed themselves amongst a collection of Nitrols and Drifters.

Davenport decided to go big with a Dagger of his own. He sat down in the empty cockpit. A ship this big felt strange to pilot alone, but he would be able to do the most damage with this.

"Is there still at least one Drifter left for Bandit?" Alla asked through the communications system.

"I don't think he wants a Drifter anymore," Davenport replied. "He's lost his heart to this Stalwart. He'll never be happy with anything less."

"He's going to have to," Rodeo interjected from the bridge. "We're closing on the *Trailblazer*. Stand by to kick some ass."

"What's the plan, Captain?" Davenport asked. "We don't want to blow up the ship."

"I have an idea," Coon chimed in from somewhere. "One of you can land me on the *Trailblazer* and I'll neutralize the ship from on board. I'll make sure your Daggers can land and lift off our people."

"Will you stop making suggestions that could get you killed?" Rodeo fired back.

"Land *me* on the *Trailblazer*," Alla suggested. "I can neutralize the ship. I'll make sure there's no one left on board."

Laughter broke out among the rest of the Chorion Team. "There's an idea," Laub replied.

"Fine," Rodeo replied. "Coon and Alla will land on the *Trailblazer*, but it will work better if only one Dagger lands."

"I'll take them," Davenport offered. "The rest of you give us some cover and we'll sneak on board in the confusion."

"I don't like it," Rodeo snarled, "but it's better than sending Coon over there alone."

"Yay!" Coon yelled. Alla climbed down from the Nitrol he had commandeered.

His fat body wobbled when he half-ran, half-rolled across the launch bay to Davenport's Dagger. "He's way too excited about getting to a Reserve Wing buffet," Laub teased.

"We won't have to feed him for a month," Axel agreed and the others laughed.

"What do you mean?" Davenport asked, but Alla came on board the Dagger before anyone could answer.

Coon came down from the bridge and the two boys strapped into the Dagger's rear accessory cradles. "We're ready to roll down here," Davenport told the bridge.

"Keep our attack craft on board until I give the word," Rodeo ordered. "Wait until we get near enough. We don't want to spoil the surprise."

More laughter and jokes fired back and forth between the friends while they waited. Davenport's onboard instruments showed him the *Remorseless* picking up speed on an intercept course for the *Trailblazer*.

Davenport's pulse quickened to match the ship's speed. This would be the first time he went into battle against the Reserve Wing knowing ahead of time exactly what he was getting into.

He was going in much better prepared this time, even if he didn't know what Coon and Alla would do once they got on board.

Davenport's adrenaline started pumping and his fingers itched to launch this Dagger. He wanted to get into battle against the Reserve Wing. He wanted to shoot and kill and destroy.

Too bad he couldn't blow up the *Trailblazer*. That would be fun...but no. He had to focus on the mission. That meant getting Dice, Fiddler, and the Armageddon Core off the *Trailblazer* alive and unharmed.

Coon and Alla whispered together behind his back. They sounded more excited about this than they should, but hey. Who was Davenport to deny them some fun when and where they could get it? They'd had so little recently.

"Coming up on the *Trailblazer* now," Rodeo reported. "We're hailing them and ordering them to a full stop. Stand by the launch."

"Standing by," Healey replied.

Davenport glanced across the launch bay. He was never so glad to see Healey, Lyons, and the Chorion Team all loaded up and ready to roll. Davenport was back with his friends. Life didn't look so bleak now.

Even Beauty sat behind the window of a Dagger, a wild grin plastered across his face. He worked the controls in a frenzy and his ears twitched with anticipation. Davenport could just imagine what Beauty would do once he got outside with the order to neutralize the *Trailblazer*.

A blast of Howitzer fire thudded somewhere in the distance and everyone looked up. "Launch!" Rodeo ordered. "We're under bombardment from the *Trailblazer*. Scramble and be prepared to meet *Trailblazer* Daggers launching from the...."

Davenport didn't hear the rest of the order. He slammed the throttle down and rocketed through the *Remorseless's* galvanic coil. The rest of his friends sprinted out right behind him. Sure enough, they launched straight into a flock of Daggers coming from the *Trailblazer*.

"That's right, assholes!" Axel called. "Clear the launch bay for us!"

"Get around behind the Stalwart, Sir!" Breeze yelled. "We'll distract them for you."

Davenport couldn't even see the *Trailblazer's* rear end in the mayhem. Daggers flew in all directions and he couldn't tell which ships belonged to his friends and which to his enemies.

Beauty, Wolf, Breeze, and Lyons vanished in a cloud of explosions. Healey, Axel, and Laub closed around Davenport trying to protect him from the assault.

The *Remorseless* stood off trading devastating barrages with the *Trailblazer*. The two Stalwarts pounded each other in such a hail of gunfire that no one else could get near either ship.

"How much longer?" Rodeo yelled through the communications link.

No one answered him. Davenport could only fire at every ship in front of him and pray to High Heaven he didn't hit his friends.

He rushed the Reserve Wing vessels and tried to punch his way through. They returned fire and drove him back. He closed position with Axel and Laub only to face another bunch of Nitrols coming from the *Trailblazer*.

He almost suggested breaking out of position to make an end-run on the *Trailblazer* when three Nitrols exploded right in front of him. The smoke cleared and he stared through the gap at a single Dagger planted behind the Reserve Wing line.

The ship sliced back and forth carving up enemy Daggers. They swiveled to confront the threat and the friends pounced. Axel and Laub hammered five more Daggers from their side and drove the others into the newcomer's guns.

"Did you forget about me?" Emmett called. "Break away, Davenport! Get on board and find my daughter."

"You got it!" Davenport pulled back, dodged Healey and Laub, and skimmed around the battle. Four Daggers tried to cut in front of him to block his path, but Emmett and Axel nailed them again and Davenport sprinted for the *Trailblazer's* tail.

No one on the *Trailblazer* noticed one more Dagger slipping out of line. The *Trailblazer* was too busy defending itself against the *Remorseless*.

The *Remorseless* laid down a punishing assault against the *Trailblazer*. Davenport had never seen any Reserve Wing Stalwart fire that fast, but they never had a Chorion at the helm before.

Whatever Lyons might have said about the Stalwarts not being maneuverable, Bandit was outdoing himself at the helm. The *Remorseless* whipped back and forth and danced circles around the *Trailblazer*. The *Trailblazer* had to work overtime just to keep up with his crazy flight patterns that left the *Trailblazer* more vulnerable than ever.

Bandit's antics caused Davenport problems once he finally located the *Trailblazer's* launch bay. The ship kept pivoting to stay facing the *Remorseless*. "Hold your position!" he called. "I can't get on board!"

He heard voices talking to him, but he couldn't understand them above the noise of explosions pounding all over the field. The *Remorseless* stopped twirling and stood still for the first time since the battle started.

The *Trailblazer* must have thought something was wrong with the *Remorseless*. The *Trailblazer* pounced and started hammering the *Remorseless* with crushing fire.

Davenport darted into the launch bay. "I'm in! You're all clear!"

He couldn't be certain if anyone heard him and he had no time to find out. He unclipped his harness and sprang out of his seat to find Alla and Coon already on their feet.

They both looked way too enthusiastic to get on board a Reserve Wing Stalwart, but Davenport didn't have time to lecture them on safety.

He ripped open the weapons locker and started handing out guns to both boys. All three loaded themselves with ammunition and hustled out of the Dagger.

The launch bay was deserted. "We have to find the Armageddon Core."

"I'll find out." Coon extended his hand toward the wall next to the weapons locker.

Davenport grabbed the boy's wrist. "No, Coon. You heard what Rodeo said. If you weakened yourself here, you could throw all our lives away. Save it for when we really need it."

Coon's face fell. "Do I have to?"

"Yes. You have to. Stick to shooting."

Coon giggled and Alla elbowed him.

Davenport turned to Alla. "Well? How do you plan to clear the ship?"

"Just...cover me. I can't do it if they're shooting at me."

Davenport frowned. "What do you mean?"

"You'll see. Come on."

Chapter 34

Coon and Alla set off for the stairs. The Stalwart shuddered and boomed from gunfire pounding the hull. Blasts went off just outside the *Trailblazer's* galvanic coil.

Davenport had no idea what Coon and Alla had in mind for taking this ship. Davenport didn't like going into this operation blind, but he got his answer even before they made it to the stairwell.

Davenport kept his weapon at his shoulder pointing the barrel at the floor. He checked and double-checked the launch bay, but it was deserted....at least until the three got near the stairs.

Two pilots burst through the door into the launch bay. They sprinted for their attack craft.... stopped dead when they came face to face with Davenport and the two boys. Davenport swung up his XQ, but Alla reacted first.

He threw back his head, opened his mouth to a massive gaping hole, lunged for the two pilots, and swallowed them in one gulp. He chewed once, sucked his teeth, and made a face. "They don't shower enough."

Coon laughed and nudged his big friend. "Save room for dessert, boy."

Alla snickered. "Bring it on."

Davenport stared at Alla in shock for a second. He knew these boys had unique abilities. He never dreamed Alla's obsession with food could go this far.

Coon had other ideas. He peeked into the stairwell. "It looks clear." Then he ducked back out. "I say we set up a trap. Davenport and I will stand in one place with our guns. You hide behind a corner, Alla, and we'll lead the crew in front of you. They'll see us and open fire on us. Then you come out and grab them from behind. Understand?"

"Yeah, perfect!" Alla's eyes widened. "That will be great. Then I won't be in danger from their guns."

"But we will be," Davenport remarked.

"We don't have to put ourselves in danger," Coon replied. "We just have to be there…to lure the crew where Alla can get them. See? They'll all come down and we'll clear the ship."

Davenport wasn't so sure about this plan, either, but Coon didn't wait for him to argue. The two boys entered the stairwell and Davenport followed them up about ten decks.

The noise of gunfire faded the farther they got from the launch bay. The signs of battle didn't, though. Crewmen raced back and forth rushing to and from their stations. Many of them were armed and officers kept giving them orders.

Coon snuck to a random corridor and pointed beyond the intersection. "You hide there, Alla. Come on, Sir."

Coon dragged Davenport to a different intersection. Davenport was just about to point out how exposed this was when they got their first test of Coon's plan.

A whole mob of Reserve Wing crewmen came around the corner and they were all armed. They charged into view calling orders and instructions…. until they saw two armed intruders. They stopped dead in their tracks. They were nowhere near enough for Alla to catch them.

Davenport suffered a pang of indecision. Was he really going to allow let people to get eaten…by a boy? Getting eaten by a fearsome monster was one thing.

Alla was turning out to be more terrible than any nightmare Davenport had ever heard of prowling Chorion Osiris.

That planet haunted the nightmares of plenty of people in the Confederacy. Most decent people would never dare to set foot there and now Davenport was starting to understand why.

He always imagined the native dangers there to be huge, gruesome, and hideous—maybe even poisonous. He never imagined big, soft, food-loving Alla to be one of them.

Davenport shuddered when he thought about Alla's love for food, but he didn't have a chance to think twice. The crewmen examined Davenport and Coon and some of them snickered. Then they all came forward to confront the strangers.

A tall officer with lieutenant commander's bars halted in front of Davenport. The man hefted his XQ in a threatening way, but he stopped short of holding Davenport and Coon at gunpoint. He looked like was perfectly capable of shooting them right here. "Who are you and what are you doing on this sip? State your business."

Davenport opened his mouth to answer....and so did Alla. He lunged out of his hiding place and engulfed the whole group, lieutenant commander and all. One minute they were standing there. The next, they were gone and Alla patted his bulging tummy and smiled at Davenport before returning to his position.

"This is working better than I planned," Con murmured. "We'll have the ship cleared in no time at this rate."

"Is he....?" Davenport couldn't say it.

Coon cocked his head and studied Davenport on the side. "You've never been to Chorion Osiris, have you, Sir?"

"God, no! Of course I've never been there."

Coon nodded and returned to looking straight in front of him. "I thought not."

Davenport didn't ask why Coon wanted to know that—not that it mattered very much right now. Another bunch was coming into view, but these people didn't see the strangers at all. They passed down a different corridor and started to pass out of sight.

Coon saw them about to leave and yelled out. It sounded like a broken scream of pain and it caught the crewmen's attention instantly.

They advanced and met their end at the corner where Alla hid. The boy seemed to be getting fatter by the minute. Davenport didn't see how he and Coon would be able to get Alla off the *Trailblazer* when this was all over.

Alla finished off another group of six. Word must have spread that something was going on down here. A bunch of armed security guards showed up next. They got a few intersections away and ducked behind corners to aim their XQs at Coon and Davenport.

"Put your weapons on the ground!" someone shouted. "Put your hands above your heads and get down on the floor! Don't move or we'll open fire!"

Davenport hesitated a second, but Coon didn't. He swept up his weapon and fired down the corridor.

The response came swift and sure. Gunfire erupted from the security guards' position. Coon and Davenport darted for cover on both sides. The security team kept up such a steady torrent of shots that Coon and Davenport didn't get a chance to shoot again.

Davenport glanced around and spotted Alla wobbling away. He vanished into a different corridor. The gunfire kept up for a few seconds and then started to ebb.

All at once, a scream echoed from out of sight and the noise died instantly. Davenport looked down to find Coon crouching on the floor at Davenport's heels.

Coon pressed his hand to the wall and his whole hand had melted up to the wrist. It merged with the wall and his eyes had gone dull and unseeing.

"I found the Armageddon Core," he husked. "I'm letting them out of their cells. ...Dice is in the infirmary.... He's conscious, but very weak. We'll have to carry him back to the Dagger..."

Davenport charged Coon, grabbed the boy's arm, and tried to pull him away. "Stop, Coon! Stop now. You promised Rodeo."

Coon's hand came away covered in a giant blob of melted metal that solidified instantly. His eyes remained glassy, but at least he seemed aware of what was going on. He got to his feet and set off in the opposite direction. "Come on. Let's go find them."

"What about Alla?"

"He's fine. He'll take care of the crew for us. This is more important."

Davenport didn't want to abandon Alla, especially with more gunfire breaking out somewhere up the last corridor. It was far enough away from Coon and Davenport that it didn't threaten them and Coon led him off in the opposite direction.

A second later, that spate of gunfire died, too, but not before a few more screams punctured the silence. What was Alla doing to them? Davenport already knew and he didn't want to think about it.

Coon returned to the stairs, descended four levels, and set off at a fast walk. "The Armageddon Core is this...."

He turned a corner and he and Davenport ran smack dab into the Armageddon Core coming to meet them. The five women had somehow managed to get hold of weapons. Flack and Fiddler nearly blew Coon's head off before they realized who it was.

"What are you doing here?" Fiddler hissed.

"We came to get you out," Davenport replied. "Come on. We need to find Dice and Alla...."

"Alla! What is he doing here?"

"Having lunch," Coon replied.

"You don't want to know." Davenport turned back to Coon. "Where's the medical deck?"

"This way." Coon led the party back down the stairs. They went two levels the way they came. The Armageddon Core kept swiveling their weapons into every room, office, and corner, but everyone must still be too busy defending the Stalwart. At least the party was heading toward the launch bay. That would make getting out of here easier.

Coon led the way into a side room where Dice lay on an exam table. He had his eyes open and sturdy metal cuffs restrained him to the table. He couldn't break them in his weakened state.

Fiddler rushed forward and bent over him. "Are you okay?"

"You came back!" he croaked. "I didn't think I would ever see you alive again."

"Hang on, Dice," Davenport told him. "We're getting you out of here."

"How?" Dice asked.

"Good question," Friend interjected.

Coon came over to the table. "Take your hands off the table, Fiddler."

"Huh?" She frowned at him. "What do you mean?"

"Take...your hands.... off...the table. It's metal."

"So?"

"Just do as he says," Davenport ordered. "We don't have time to explain."

Coon nodded behind him. "Go over there and see if they have any Maltese Chipmunks in this place."

"They had some in the cell where they were keeping us," Frost remarked. "We could go back and get them."

Coon raised his eyebrows. "You could? That would be great."

"I'm sorry..." Dice choked.

The instant Fiddler took her hands off the exam table, Coon touched it. The restraints melted off Dice's arms and legs. He bellowed in pain when the molten steel burned him, but a second later, he was free.

Davenport helped him sit up. "Can you walk?"

"What did you do?" Dice rubbed his arms. "You burned me."

"You'll be fine as soon as you have a few chipmunks," Coon told him. "Come on. We have to get out of here."

Davenport supported Dice toward the exit. The Armageddon Core minus Frost and Fizzle guarded the threshold. Davenport saw this mission spiraling out of his control, but it never had the makings of a textbook rescue operation in the first place.

He stumbled under Dice's weight, but Davenport was the biggest person here by far. None of the others could even think about holding Dice up.

He swiveled Dice toward the stairwell when more gunfire exploded from nearby. Shots ricocheted down the corridor coming from the stairwell.

Davenport tripped under Dice's weight trying to drag the huge Adik back toward the medical room. Davenport had to find a place to put Dice down so he could return fire.

At that moment, another squad of Reserve Wing soldiers charged out of the opposite stairwell. They pinned the friends under two opposing barrages and the whole group scattered for cover.

Davenport dropped Dice and scrambled to an open doorway. Davenport fumbled to get his weapon into position and kicked backward behind the nearest wall.

Fiddler and Coon crawled over to join him. Fiddler swiveled her XQ out into the corridor and returned the soldiers' fire. Davenport caught sight of Flack and Friend across the corridor in another room. They aimed for the second squad shooting from the other direction.

Davenport turned around to yell something to Coon and Fiddler....and stopped. Coon crouched in a corner with his hand buried up to the wrist inside the wall again. His eyes went blank and Davenport's blood ran cold when he saw Coon's expression.

The boy's skin took on a ghastly, waxen color and his eyes sank deeper into his skull. He shrank into a ball not seeing or hearing anything around him.

Davenport didn't want to think about what Coon was doing, but it couldn't be anything good. Davenport should have listened to Rodeo's warning. What if Coon got stuck like this, or worse, died because he couldn't stop doing whatever he was doing?

The pounding concussions of Howitzer fire on the *Trailblazer's* hull stopped suddenly. The soldiers outside cut their fire, too, and a breathless silence fell over the medical deck.

"You're under arrest!" one of the soldiers yelled from far away. "Lay down your weapons and show your hands! You're trapped in here."

Flack screamed and Davenport dared to steal a peek out of his hiding place. He fought the urge to be sick as Alla stormed into the corridor from the stairwell behind the soldiers. He approached one group who were facing down the medical deck and he swallowed them in one gulp. He cleared everyone from that end of the corridor.

He stood amidst broken glass and shattered plaster while he looked around for his next meal. The second squad eyed him over their XQs and then they all opened fire.

Alla dove into the stairwell, but Davenport had seen enough. He grabbed Fiddler. "Get your Core and beat it down to the launch bay. You'll find a Dagger waiting there. Load up, and if we aren't back in five minutes, take off without us."

"No!" she hollered. "We can't...."

"Your dad and the rest of the crew are waiting for you outside. You can get away. Go!"

Davenport turned back to Coon. The boy had shriveled even more in the seconds since Davenport last looked at him. Davenport couldn't stand this.

He attacked Coon and yelled in his ear. "Get out now, Coon! You promised Rodeo! Get out now before you die here!"

Coon didn't hear him. He didn't respond to Davenport shaking him. Davenport gave it up. He couldn't help this boy.

Davenport turned back to Dice, and to his utter horror, Davenport discovered that Dice had passed out on the floor. Davenport shook Dice, too, but nothing budged the big alien.

Davenport looked everywhere. Only Fiddler remained, and the instant he saw her, she sprang out into the open corridor.

She joined Flack and Friend jumping out at the same instant. Davenport jerked his XQ to his shoulder and advanced into the open. He leveled his weapon at the soldiers hunkered by the opposite stairwell.

Davenport stepped out in front of the three women and backed them toward the stairs. Flack and Friend darted away, but Fiddler hesitated a second longer.

"Get out!" Davenport yelled over his shoulder. "Go now!"

She whirled away, and at that moment, Alla materialized out of the opposite stairwell. He materialized behind the soldiers and enveloped them in his colossal mouth. Alla had gotten so fat that Davenport didn't see how he could keep walking at all.

All the shooting stopped in a heartbeat. A few sprinkles of broken glass disturbed the stillness. Davenport took a step toward Alla and Alla advanced. He started to turn into the room where Davenport left Dice and Coon. Maybe Alla and Davenport could save Coon and Dice after all.

Davenport took a single step when something clicked right behind his ear. A woman's voice cracked in the stillness. "Freeze! Don't move or we shoot!"

Davenport froze and started to raise his hands. He was still holding his XQ and someone yanked it out of his grip. More disembodied hands snatched his sidearms and disarmed him in a split second.

"Turn around.... slowly...." The woman ordered.

He rotated to face the stairs. A dozen Reserve Wing officers and more security guards all aimed their XQs straight at his head. They held Fiddler at gunpoint, too. Did they see Alla? They couldn't. He was in that room with Coon and Dice.

The soldiers attacked Davenport and tackled him to the ground. He slammed down hard and went limp in their control. At least he gave the Armageddon Core a chance to get away.... if they got away.

Fiddler yelped when they captured her, too. He didn't give *her* a chance to get away. The Reserve Wing still had their prize—one of the most valuable prizes they ever wanted.

He didn't try to fight. The more time the Reserve Wing spent arresting him, the more time they wouldn't spend searching for the other prisoners. Maybe the Dagger was flying away right now. Davenport could only hope.

Chapter 35

Emmett took another turn around the battle, but the *Trailblazer* wasn't firing on the *Remorseless* anymore. "What the hell is going on? Did you knock out the Stalwart or something?"

"I'm receiving a message from Coon," Rodeo replied. "He's blocking the *Trailblazer* from firing on us. He's locking down the ship and neutralizing the crew, but there are a few holdouts still trying to take it back. He can't neutralize them without suffocating our people into the bargain."

"What do you mean by 'neutralizing' them?" Lyons asked from her Dagger.

"Does it matter?" Laub asked. "We got our work cut out for us here!"

More Reserve Wing attack craft swooped around the battlefield and plunged into the confusion. They fired on the Chorion Team and Emmett pulled his ship back the other way to defend the boys.

He cast a backward glance toward the *Trailblazer*. Fiddler was on board that ship. He should have gone with Davenport and the others. Emmett should have been the one to rescue her. His face should have been the first one she saw when she got free from the Reserve Wing.

He couldn't rest without knowing where she was and if she was all right. She was all he had. He had sacrificed everything for her and he would do it all over again at a moment's notice.

He fired at the Daggers attacking the Chorions, but his heart wasn't in it. He started to retreat back toward the launch bay when the *Trailblazer* suddenly erupted in an even more devastating assault on the *Remorseless*.

"What the hell!" Axel yelled.

"Coon is out! He's no longer in control of the Stalwart."

"What does that mean?" Lyons asked, but no one answered. The friends plunged in shooting anyone and everyone they could hit.

"The Dagger is launching from the *Trailblazer*!" Rodeo called. "Fall back to the *Remorseless*! Everyone get back on board. We're pulling out as soon as we get our people inside."

"Do they have the prisoners?" Emmett tried to keep his voice steady and failed. "Did they get everyone out?"

"Is Dice on board?" Lyons asked.

Rodeo's tone changed. He barely spoke above a murmur. "There are no Adik life signs on board....and only two Chorions and four human female life signs. We lost Dice and Davenport."

"Which females are they?" Emmett asked. "Is one of them Fiddler?"

"I'm sorry, man," Rodeo replied. "All four are showing genetic anomalies characteristic of cloning. Fiddler isn't with them."

Emmett swallowed hard. She had to be there. She had to be. He started to turn back toward the launch bay. He had to get back on board the *Trailblazer* and find her. To hell with Dice and Davenport. Nothing mattered but Fiddler.

He pulled the helm to starboard only to run into another phalanx of Reserve Wing Daggers gunning for him. They cut him off from getting near the *Trailblazer*. He had no choice but to retreat.

He opened up with his Howitzers to drive them off, but more enemy ships assembled from all over the field. They buried him under gunfire and he roared trying to shoot all of them at once.

He felt himself sinking under the barrage when Lyons, Wolf, and Beauty rocketed out of the mayhem. They surrounded Emmett and blasted their way through the enemy line. "Get back to the *Remorseless*, Emmett!" Lyons yelled. "There's nothing more we can do from here."

Emmett fought the urge to argue back. If Lyons and the boys kept up their defense just a little longer, he could break through and get onto the *Trailblazer*. He could find Fiddler and....

He wouldn't find Fiddler. The friends had blown their chance and now Coon and Alla were beating a retreat to the *Remorseless*, too.

"Get out of here, Emmett!" Lyons roared. "Dice is on that ship, too! You aren't standing out here killing yourself because Fiddler is still there. I said GO!"

He couldn't stand the cracked emotion breaking in her voice. He wasn't the only person who lost someone dear to them today.

He pulled away feeling sick. Lyons, Beauty, and Wolf defended him until he pulled into the *Remorseless's* launch bay. A Dagger already sat there with its hatch open. Alla came out carrying Coon's lifeless body slung over his shoulder. Alla headed straight for the stairs leading to the medical deck.

A second later, Lyons and Beauty sailed into the bay. Healey and the Chorion Team stood guard and fired outward to hold the enemy at bay.

The instant everyone got inside, the launch bay slammed shut and the *Remorseless* streaked away at impossible speed. It abandoned the *Trailblazer* with Dice, Davenport, and Fiddler still captive on board.

Emmett didn't want to think. He wanted to die. He hadn't felt this way in years—not since that fateful day—the day he went back to the Chiton's Hold creche to pick up his darling daughter, only to find her gone.

He spent nearly three years searching for her. He burned through every penny of his savings bribing people and paying off criminals before he found out where she was. Then he had to take illegal jobs to earn the money to get onto the station and rescue her.

At least this time he knew where she was. She was old enough now to take care of herself. She was smart and strong and resourceful.

She was probably working out a way to escape right now. She had Dice and Davenport, so that was something. She wasn't alone. She had friends near her who were as strong, smart, and resourceful as she was.

Then Emmett remembered. She didn't have either Dice or Davenport. The Reserve Wing would send Davenport up to the Terminus Anathema. Dice would go to Helios Sanctus, too, but he was piss weak. He could barely stand and might not even be able to do that.

The Reserve Wing would house him far away from Fiddler. They wouldn't risk putting her near him. That would be stupid.

Emmett slumped in his seat. He didn't realize that he was still in the Dagger's cockpit until someone touched his shoulder.

He looked up to find Lyons at his side. He didn't want to see or talk to her, either. He didn't want to see or talk to anyone except for Fiddler.

The pained understanding in Lyons's dark eyes was too much for Emmett to bear. Dice was on the *Trailblazer*, too, and he was in much worse shape than Fiddler was.

The Reserve Wing would never harm Fiddler. Emmett knew that in his bones. That was the problem. She was too valuable to them. They would never let her go, and if he ever found a way to free her a second time, the Reserve Wing would hunt her to the ends of the universe. They would never give up the way they did last time.

Lyons took Emmett's hand. Her touch felt soft and made Emmett's guts ache even more. He didn't want to face any future without his daughter in it. He didn't want to be alive right now and Lyons's touch called him to keep living.

He had to keep living. He had to find a way to get Fiddler back. His life wasn't worth shit without her.

Lyons led him up to the crew quarters. She found a random cabin that must have belonged to some officer. Pictures of strangers lined the shelves and a chess board had been set up on the table.

Lyons parked Emmett in front of the couch and pushed him down to sit on it. Then she sat next to him. She let go of his hand, but she didn't leave the cabin.

She just sat there in silent vigil for the lost ones. She didn't try to make Emmett feel better. She didn't promise that they would get Dice and Fiddler back. That was asking too much under the circumstances.

Emmett sent up a silent prayer of gratitude that Lyons also didn't mention Davenport. Emmett didn't give a shit about Davenport. Emmett didn't give a damn that Davenport was going up to the Terminus Anathema for trying to save the whole Confederacy from Admiral Joyce's madness.

Emmett knew he should care about Davenport. Emmett should care that Davenport got recaptured trying to save Fiddler.

Emmett should care about the Ithium and Joyce and Dice and all the rest, but he couldn't bring himself to care about anything besides Fiddler.

His little girl. The light of his life. His one joy.

He had to find her. He had to get her back. He had to save her and he *would* save her. He would die trying. He had nothing else to do with his life.

Emmett and Lyons sat together in silence for several hours. Lyons watched the stars floating past the cabin windows. She never said anything.

She never betrayed the slightest sign that she was suffering the same agony about Dice. She didn't have to because Emmett already knew she was. Lyons brought Emmett to this cabin because they were both feeling the same thing.

They were the half-dead, the half-living, the zombies left suspended somewhere between life and death. They were the ghosts of the missing.

Exhaustion threatened to drag Emmett into a stupor, but he couldn't shut his eyes. He had to stay awake at all costs. He had to stay constantly on watch in case he found some clue to Fiddler's whereabouts.

It happened like this last time. The moment he discovered her gone, he went into this half-trance, half-madness. He couldn't relax. He spent years on edge and then, after he found her, he spent more years looking over his shoulder for anyone following them.

The door swished open and startled him into turning around. Rodeo, Bandit, Healey, Beauty, the four remaining women of the Armageddon Core, and the rest of the Chorion Team entered the cabin—all except Coon.

Lyons turned away from the window, put her feet on the floor, and stood up to meet them, but Emmett didn't get up. He glared at them all—the people he had come to love and trust as his closest friends. He hated them all. He hated them for not being Fiddler.

Rodeo handed Lyons something. "We tracked the *Trailblazer's* movements. It rendezvoused with Stalwart *Salome* before the *Trailblazer* went on to Helios Sanctus. The *Trailblazer* docked at the station an hour and a half ago. Dice and Fiddler are there for certain."

"The *Salome* left the rendezvous and went straight to the Terminus Anathema," Healey added. "We think the *Salome* took Davenport on board, which means he's at the prison now."

"We're going to get them," Rodeo went on, "but we need to regroup first. We need to rearm and resupply....and we need a plan."

"We also need to go after the Ithium," Flack pointed out. "Admiral Joyce took it back to Atlas Arcane. He'll be up to his ears in his plans by now."

"We also still need to find the Ziprothil," Axel pointed out. "Joyce might have the Ithium and the chip, but he won't release the Ithium without the Ziprothil."

"We know Mount Refractory doesn't have it," Lyons told him. "As far as we know, it never left Ultra Meridian. It could still be there."

"Unless Joyce already has it," Frost suggested.

"He doesn't," Healey countered. "He spent way too much time searching for it."

"How do we find it, then?" Lyons asked. She had recovered way too fast for Emmett's liking. He was starting to hate her for being able to function so well after losing Dice. Maybe she didn't understand how Emmett felt after all. She wouldn't be able to take such an active part in this conversation if she cared about Dice as much as she made out.

"I guess we just have to go back to Ultra Meridian and keep looking for it," Healey replied. "There are only so many people who could have searched the *Blood Calliope* well enough to find it."

"Looking for it could take years," Flack argued. "We could spend years looking and still never find it—and while we're at it, do I need to remind you that we're in a Reserve Wing Stalwart? The minute we land on the planet, the whole Reserve Wing is going to know where we are. They'll be all over us and we'll be right back where we started."

No one said anything for a minute. Emmett still didn't understand why the hell anyone was talking about the Ziprothil when Fiddler was behind locked doors on Helios Sanctus. Didn't these people understand at all what was really important?

That silence drew out longer and longer. Emmett was just about to say that, if they weren't going to go after Fiddler, he would do it himself when Friend spoke up.

"We don't have to search for the Ziprothil. I know where it is."

"You do?" Frost gasped. "How? Where? How did you....?"

"I took it off the *Blood Calliope*. The Ziprothil was stored on Atlas Arcane for exactly the reason Joyce is looking for it now. The Reserve Wing didn't want it at Helios Sanctus in case it accidentally combined with the Ithium. I found out someone stole both substances and I tracked the Ziprothil on the *Blood Calliope* until the ship crashed at Ultra Meridian."

"But scavengers were all over the wreck as soon as it crashed," Flack countered. "We never saw you away from your desk."

"You never saw me, but I was there. I knew it would take the scavengers days to find the Ziprothil so I disguised myself as one of them. I took it first and brought it back to the cave before any of you noticed me gone. I've been hiding it ever since."

"If that's true," Rodeo interjected, "maybe we should leave it hidden. Joyce has already scoured the planet looking for it. The Ziprothil will be safer where it is."

"That won't work," Healey cut in. "We already saw what happened with both Lyons and Fiddler. It only took the right incentive to make each of them tell where the other two components were. We need to get the Ziprothil away from Ultra Meridian and we need to make sure Joyce doesn't get his hands on it."

"How are we going to do that when we're in the middle of trying to stop him?" Bandit asked. "We would be carrying it straight to him."

"He's on Atlas Arcane," Axel pointed out. "We're going in the opposite direction—toward Terminus Anathema and Helios Sanctus." He looked around at everyone. "Aren't we? Tell me we aren't leaving Dice, Davenport, and Fiddler in Reserve Wing custody."

"Hell no!" Emmett shot to his feet. "We're going to get her—I mean, all of them."

"First things first," Rodeo decided. "First, we're going to get the Ziprothil, which means we're going back to Ultra Meridian."

<u>End of Book 3</u>

Keep Reading

Ultra Meridian Series Book 4: Terminus Anathema

Life looks all but hopeless after Admiral Killian Joyce captures Sheriff Mace Davenport, steals back the doomsday weapon Davenport has worked so hard to keep out of Joyce's hands, and throws Davenport in prison for the crime of doing his job to protect the Confederacy.

There's just one problem with Joyce's plan. Davenport has been inside Terminus Anathema before. Everyone here knows him and he knows everyone here.....and not in a good way. A Confederate sheriff is a dead man walking inside these walls, but Davenport isn't like the other prisoners.

Throwing Davenport in jail could be Admiral Joyce's worst mistake yet if it wakes up Davenport's buried past—a past he's worked hard to erase from existence. No one will be prepared for what he's about to become. Nothing will be able to stop him once he breaks the chains and goes on the rampage he's been holding back since this whole disaster started.

You can find it at your favorite book retailer.

Sign Up Once--Get all Theo Mann's free books including brand new releases

Sign Up Once--Get all Theo Mann's free books including brand new releases

Humanity on the brink of annihilation.

A mysterious package, a corrupt officer, and a conspiracy that goes all the way to the top? What could possibly go wrong?

When a routine mission goes horribly wrong, Warrant Officer Ewing Archer and a handful of faithful friends get trapped in a battle to save the last survivors of Earth.

The human race has abandoned the ecological disaster of Earth. Now all that remains is a network of interconnected ships, stations, and satellites surrounding the planet.

But when war breaks out, Archer becomes a firebrand that could destroy it all....or save it.

Sign up at www.theomann.com to read it for free

About Theo Mann

I write 70 books per year—and yes, before you ask, all these books are my original creative work. Nothing written under my name is AI-generated or ghostwritten because I write better than AI and any ghostwriter out there.

People don't read fiction for entertainment or to escape from reality. People read fiction to see their humanity reflected in another person's character and story.

This is my promise to you. When you read my books, you'll see your own humanity reflected in the characters and stories. I take this commitment to my readers very seriously. My books are an intimate form of communication between us. I would never disrespect my readers by turning that over to a machine or another writer. This is my bond between me and you as my reader.

I write 20,000 words per day as my daily work output. If anyone with a public platform would like to challenge me to prove this in a controlled environment, feel free to contact me on this website's contact page.

I worked as a professional ghostwriter for fifteen years. Now I'm on a mission to set a Guinness World Record by writing 700 books over the next ten years and 1400 books over the next twenty years, all originally written by me. See my website for the full book list.

I'm also the author of *Proof for the Existence of God* and the *Crimes Against Fiction* blog. You can find all my nonfiction work at www.crimes-against-fiction.com.

If you have a story idea, or if you would like me to explore a series in more depth, or if you'd like me to explore a character by writing a spinoff series about that character or world, leave me a message on my website's contact page. I answer all reader emails, so ask me anything, tell me what you liked and didn't like, and let me know where you'd like your favorite series to go. I would love to hear your ideas and find out what you'd like to read next.

Find out more at www.theomann.com.

Also by Theo Mann (so far)